Careful Flowers

SCARLET CLOVER PUBLISHING, L.L.C.

This book is a publication of Scarlet Clover Publishers, L.L.C.

Red Clover comes in three varieties: Scarlet - the most intense, crimson and pink

Fields of Scarlet Clover are not bashful!

*For all those who have lived
and those who have died
in the captivity of hatred.*

ALSO WRITTEN BY KIERAN YORK:

Night Without Time

Earthen Trinkets

Appointment With A Smile

Crystal Mountain Veils (A Royce Madison Mystery) 2nd Edition

Timber City Masks (A Royce Madison Mystery) 2nd Edition

Sugar With Spice (Short Fiction)

Blushing Aspen (Poetry)

~~~~~~

Contributor to Award-Winning Sappho's Corner Poetry Series

(edited by Beth Mitchum):

Wet Violets, Volume 2

Roses Read, Volume 3

Delectable Daisies, Volume 4

COMING SOON FROM KIERAN YORK:

Touring Kelly's Poem (Fiction)

Loitering on the Frontier (Fiction)

Shinney Forest Cloaks (Royce Madison Mystery)

www.scarletcloverpublishers.com

Careful Flowers

A SCARLET CLOVER PUBLISHING BOOK

By

Kieran York

This is a work of fiction. All characters, locales and events are either products of the author's imagination or are used fictitiously.

CAREFUL FLOWERS

Copyright © 2013 by Kieran York
First Edition: Published October 2013
Second Edition: Published January, 2015

This is a work of fiction. All characters, locales and events are either products of the author's imagination or are used fictitiously.

Cover design by Ann Phillips
Second Edition Formatting by Karen D. Badger

Published by Scarlet Clover Publishers, L.L.C.
www.kieranyork.com
P.O Box 621002
Littleton, Colorado 80162

And www.scarletcloverpublishers.com

ISBN-13: 978-0692363447
ISBN-10: 0692363440

Printed in the United States of America and in the United Kingdom

Acknowledgements

First Edition: I want to thank the extraordinary women at Blue Feather Books for publishing *Appointment with a Smile*. Publisher Em Reed, Jane Vollbrecht, Editor Chris Paynter, Line Editor Nann Dunne, and Artist Ann Phillips. They became friends, and we were family, and I'll remember with love and gratitude – each one.

I am profoundly appreciative for Blue Feather Books. It took courage to publish a book by, about, and for the Sapphic golden woman. A romance! That romance, by a relatively unknown author became a 2013 Lambda Literary Society Award Finalist in the romance category. I'm also appreciative for the chance they gave the controversial *Careful Flowers*. Many publishers would have rejected it. They didn't. Thank you, Blue Feather Women!

Second Edition: I want to thank the extraordinary women working to make Scarlet Clover Publishers happen. Beth Mitchum – mentor, artistic and technical director, and friend. Karen D. Badger worked her magic to reinstate *Appointment with a Smile* and *Careful Flowers* into print, and onto e-book. I thank my friend Karen, for riding to my rescue. A shout out to my favorite radio host, Shawn Marie Bryan – I thank her for building my website www.scarletcolverpublishers.com. Words can never express my gratitude that these women are all part of my life.

I am so very blessed with the friendships that publishing made possible. We are book-loving women!

I thank all of my friends, and my family. Their encouragement makes it worth the doing.

And I thank the Scarlet Clover CEO and Centerfold, Clover York. Keep on barking, my schnauzer friend.

A voice is not a story but a way of presiding over a story, if one were to happen by.
—Lynn Emanuel *Then Suddenly–Poems.*

Chapter 1

The stark reality of the long-distance telephone conversation hammered Fleur Hamilton's mind. The revelation had jarred her. As if she had not heard correctly, she tilted her head forward. The jolt through her body those words produced transformed into a cacophony of questions. She scrubbed her knuckles against her temple and wrenched her eyes shut for many moments.

At last, she opened them and glanced around the inside of her great aunt's small kitchen. It hurt to be in Aunt Golda's cottage home without Golda there. Though experiencing the stabbing sensation of anger and the agony of her loss, she must concentrate on the absurd conversation she was in the middle of.

How could this be? Her great aunt had raised her from her earliest childhood. Forty years ago, Golda Hamilton had taken Fleur in after the infant's parents and grandparents were killed in an auto accident. That was what Fleur had been raised to believe. Over four decades, everything her beloved great aunt told her became gospel. Golda Reine Legarde Hamilton never strayed from reality's truth. Belief was a commodity she rarely discussed, because knowledge was paramount.

Fleur was confused. "I'm having trouble processing what you're saying about my parents' death," she said. The voice on the other end of the phone line was a stranger's. He had identified himself as Bernie Maylor from San Francisco.

"When I heard of Golda's passing last week, I wanted to call and offer my condolences. I hadn't planned to discuss your parents' death. I believed Golda had intended to tell you when you reached legal age. It was not an automobile accident that killed them."

"Mr. Maylor, I know they were in California at the time. It was before Aunt Golda and I moved here to Denver. We've been here the past forty years. We moved here before my first birthday. I believe you're confused. It was an auto accident that killed my parents in California. Maybe you're mistaken."

1

"Look, I'm sorry I bothered you."

"Wait!" She recognized that his voice held a tone of authenticity. "This is something I should know. You said my parents weren't killed in a car accident. Then how were they killed?"

There was a pause before he said, "I'm not going to lie to you. They were very young. Hippies. We were all together back in the late sixties. They died in 1970. Your parents were terribly messed up kids. Maggie was a wild child, and Shane was an angry Viet Nam vet. I guess Golda didn't want you hurt."

"Hurt by what?" He had verified her parents' first names. That confirmed he at least knew her parents, or knew of them. Her fingers clutched the telephone as if it were a lifeline, as she repeated, "What could hurt me?"

"Your parents didn't die in a car accident. I regret to tell you this. Their deaths were murder and suicide."

Fleur covered her gasp and sucked in a deep breath. She had entered an area of perplexity. Each block of her life had been built on certainty; now each block seemed to be tumbling. "How do you know all this?"

"Back then, I lived in the same apartment building as Golda. My apartment was across from hers. We were friends. The kids, your parents, lived on the first floor."

"Aunt Golda told me about them, and she always said they were killed in an auto accident. My father's parents were also killed."

"That wasn't what happened. Living in the same apartment building, that's how Golda met them. She was your mother's music teacher. Golda befriended many of the hippies."

"What do you mean by 'how Golda met them'? My father was her nephew. I'm her great-niece."

"It gets complicated. I honestly thought she would have told you by now. She said she planned to tell you when the time was right. I'm truly sorry, my call has obviously upset you. And I apologize for where the conversation has led."

"I think it's important that I know what this is all about." Fleur took a deep breath. She blinked several times before shutting her eyes for a moment. "It's difficult to believe a stranger who calls and tells me a version of my life I've never heard before. My Aunt Golda was the most honest person I've ever known."

"Look, I'm terribly sorry about this. I feel like a damned fool, but I promise you, I'm not a liar. I wasn't aware you hadn't been told that your parents weren't related to Golda. But Golda had to take you. She did it to protect you. And, well, to be honest, nobody else wanted you and she did."

Stunned, Fleur attempted to gather in the words he was saying. "You said your name is Bernie Maylor. She never mentioned you."

"You don't believe me. I guess there isn't any reason you should. Like I said, I didn't call to spring secrets from your past on you. And I don't know why Golda didn't mention me before. We've talked numerous times over the years."

"How did you know she'd died? She was only buried yesterday."

"Your mother's best friend talked with Golda more than I did. Gemma Rae called from California to check on you and your aunt on a regular basis. Gemma Rae is believed to have a special power when it comes to clairvoyance. She called last week because she was feeling foreknowing. She'd had a dream. A woman answered the phone and told her about Golda's passing."

"Gemma Rae called because she had a feeling from a dream," Fleur repeated in disbelief.

"Yes, she's known for her unusual dreams. She has a little shop down the street from where I live. When I popped in yesterday, she told me Golda had passed away."

"This best friend of my mother, did she know about my parents' murder and suicide?" Fleur attempted to make her interrogation as conversational as possible. Tremors in her knees made her sway against the kitchen counter. She clutched the edge of it for stability.

"Yes. Like I said, she was around when it happened. She knew the story. She was part of the story. We all were."

"And my aunt was in communication with the two of you?"

"Right. Well, with Gemma Rae mostly."

"How can I contact Gemma Rae? And could I have your telephone number?"

Fleur figured if he refused to provide her with the information, he might possibly be perpetrating a cruel hoax. Or perhaps he was selling bogus information as part of some elaborate con. These people from San Francisco could be attempting a fraud.

"Yes. Yes, of course." He rattled off his phone number, followed by Gemma Rae's. "And her name is Gemma Rae Rawley. She's got a little pottery shop a couple of blocks down, where she sells the pottery she makes. Also, she sells posters, all kinds of new-age trinkets and spiritualism doodads. There's a little tea and coffee bar in one corner of the shop. I usually get my coffee and a pastry there a couple mornings a week. The place is called Gemma Rae's Earth. Funny name, funnier woman. However, she's very dear."

"I hope you aren't offended, but…" Fleur's words dwindled. "Look, it sounds preposterous. My Aunt Golda was a person of sterling truth."

"That's why I was certain she'd have told you of the circumstances of your parents' deaths when you became an adult. I honestly didn't mean to upset you. I only called to offer my condolences and to tell you how much I admired Golda. She was special to us back in the day."

"While I appreciate your sentiment, of course I need to check this out. And I would like to contact you again, if I have additional questions."

"Not at all a problem. Please feel free to call at any time."

Fleur disconnected the call. She would have to look into his claim, no matter how outrageous she believed it to be. She was, above all, a scientist. Her field was botany, and her passion was experimenting with plant life. Her research with genetically modified plants often produced unexpected results. Her life, however, had always gone exactly according to plan.

And now, life suddenly seemed to be forcing an investigation on her that she would really rather not pursue. Aunt Golda had always encouraged her to embrace every opportunity the world offered. During Fleur's youth, her explorations had resulted in an intellectual awakening, as she and Golda experienced life together. Often it would be something as simple as a flurry of crabapple-tree buds, a colorful butterfly, an amazing aria sung by a well-designed bird, or a scampering squirrel.

Days in their backyard and nearby parks were filled with new scenarios to savor, as well as experiments from which to glean information. From the mysteries of growing vegetables, to the intricacies of fractals and DNA, the earth became a gigantic examination table.

No corner of the planet was ever dull. Through star-filled skies, their evenings were opened to the amazing reach of eternity. The stars blinked down new coordinates each night. They would locate the wondrous planets as they swirled above.

During summer vacations, she and her great aunt trekked foreign lands to decipher other cultures. Golda taught her that respect for differing opinions and ways was essential for a peaceful society.

Now there was a mystery concerning her own life. Picking pansies had prepared her for molecular biology, and the wonder of science should have prepared her for the investigation into her parents' deaths.

Pressing the disconnect button on her phone had distanced her from the initial shock, now replaced by overwhelming blocks of doubt. Maybe Bernie Maylor was a prankster, or maybe he'd actually known Aunt Golda. Perhaps he was a poor old soul experiencing dementia or some other disorienting problem. After all, Golda was eighty-one when she'd died. If he actually was her friend, he was undoubtedly of advanced years. Yet, on the phone he sounded younger than either Aunt Golda or her best friend, Sophia Wenzel. Aunt Golda had met Sophia in a concentration camp in Poland during the Second World War. Captives, they had become friends and, finally, survivors together.

"That's it," Fleur said aloud. "I'll drop by to see Sophia Wenzel. Find out if she knows anything about this."

"That's what?" Abigail Vance, her partner of sixteen years, asked distractedly from the dining area where she was packing dishes. "You're going to visit Sophia?"

"Yes. I've just had the strangest call." Fleur twirled a lock of her curly dark hair, a habit she displayed when she was perplexed, nervous, or bored. Blinking rapidly, her pale blue eyes were intense as she moved quickly out of the kitchen and joined Abby at the round oak table in the dining area.

"Your face is paper white," Abby said. "What's going on?" Abby placed a cardboard box on the floor beside her. "What call? What was strange about it?"

"A man named Bernie Maylor called from San Francisco. He claimed to be an old friend of Golda's and said he'd just recently found out from a friend of theirs that Golda had died. This woman was supposedly my mother's best friend. But the strangest part of the call is that he said my parents didn't die in a car accident. According to him, their deaths were murder and suicide."

"That's a shocker!" Abby sat back in her chair and took off her gold-framed spectacles. "A woman called last week. She seemed surprised when I answered the phone. She asked for Golda, and I told her that Golda had passed. The caller didn't leave a name." She wrestled her denim-clad, lanky, athletic body around in the chair. "My God. What a time for some stranger to call with such a bizarre message."

"Maybe he was delusional, I don't know."

"That's why you said you're going to see Sophia. You're going to ask her if she knows anything about it."

Fleur's eyes narrowed. "She was best friends with Golda from the time they were children. They never kept secrets from one another."

"I remember hearing them talk about their younger days and how they met in the concentration camp."

"Yes. Back in the forties, in Poland, when they were little girls. After the camps were liberated, Golda moved to California. She had a distant relative there who took her in."

"But they usually steered clear of talking about Golda's time in California."

"As Golda told it, she got married there, and later, after her husband died, she remained in California. It was sometime later that the auto accident happened, and she took me and relocated to Colorado. Of course, this is where Sophia lived." Fleur mulled over the newfound information. "If there's anything to this man's assertions, Sophia would know. Aunt Golda would never have kept anything like this from Sophia. But then, I also wouldn't have thought she would have kept it from me."

"Look, this old Bernie What's-it, he's probably confused. Let's find out what's what before you indict Aunt Golda."

Fleur was experiencing an indescribable anxiety. It felt as though it might be in the deepest recesses within the very hollow of her heart. She pushed it aside. "I think I'll drop by the retirement home now. Maybe Sophia can clear up some of the mystery."

"And if she refutes this Bernie's rendition?"

"Then I guess I'll have to go find the woman Bernie said was my mother's friend. They're both in San Francisco."

"You've been a scientist for a couple of decades. If anyone knows how to research something, you do."

"When it comes to past events, sorting fact from fiction is a great deal different from locating the RNA in a leaf."

"Both take diligence," Abby said. "But if what he says is true, there must be reports on what happened in San Francisco back then. I'm betting there's a paper trail. If there was a murder-suicide, it would have made the newspapers. I'm not as handy on the computer as you are, but I could begin a little electronic research to get the process started while you visit Sophia."

"You aren't coming with me?"

"Naw. I can begin the Internet search. What facts do you have?"

"Aunt Golda told me my parents and my grandparents all died in an auto accident. Her husband's brother was my paternal grandfather. All their names would have been Hamilton. I've never heard my grandparents' first names. We called them Grandfather and Grandmother Hamilton when Aunt Golda and I talked about them. My father's name was Shane, and my mother's was Maggie, probably short for Margaret."

Abby jotted down the meager details. "Too bad you never met any of the relatives."

"Golda's family was murdered in concentration camps throughout Europe. It made Aunt Golda sad to talk about it. There were times she'd open up about them a little bit, but not in much depth. She did tell me that her father was sent to a different camp, as were her young brothers and a sister. Aunt Golda and her mother were together until her mother died. That would have been in the 1940s. And on the Hamilton side of the family, aside from my dad and his dad, there was Golda's husband. He died before I was born. My father and my grandparents were killed in the accident. At least that's what I was told."

"And Golda never said anything that might have indicated their deaths weren't an accident?"

"I was curious sometimes, but believing that your family was wiped out in an automobile accident is very final. Asking Aunt Golda about it just made her relive the pain of their loss. Maybe children are more sensitive to that. She had lost her blood relations in Europe, and together we'd lost the remainder of ours in a tragic circumstance." Fleur recollected that her great aunt had not wallowed in the tragedies of her life. "Aunt Golda said we mustn't drag our bad memories along behind us."

"Wasn't she pissed off about losing her entire family in death camps?" Abby shrugged. "I'd want to get retaliation."

"She said there was an old saying: Revenge is a meal best served cold. As a child, and an adolescent, I never grasped the idea."

"Do you now?"

"I think I understand the old saying. I'm not certain if I agree with it."

Abby touched Fleur's arm. "Aunt Golda once told me the Second World War was a time of treachery and fear, when people's hearts were feral and ugly. Guess there was no more to be said."

"She and I tried to make each other happy. Even a small child knows when questions are leading to unhappiness. It seemed wisest not to invite hurt."

"Golda was the happiest person I've ever known. I don't know how she could stand the pain of her past." Abby's eyes reflected her empathy for Aunt Golda.

"I suspect she tried to always live in the now. Her years in the camp required that. Our minds are so fragile and yielding in the face of danger," Fleur said. "Sophia's mind is whirling like a dervish. She's completely centered one moment, and the next she's in another era. It's all very puzzling."

"Aunt Golda had such mental strength," Abby said. "Even at the end, she kept a tight rein on her emotions. I wonder what she meant about death coming to her in waves. She said something like that, something she was trying to tell us when she died, remember?"

"Just a guess, but maybe she died a little in the camp."

Abby took off her glasses and rubbed her eyes. "How could any of them not feel that way?" Her eyes lost their sparkle when conversations were difficult, as this one was. "I never really had the opportunity to know more about that time in her life. It was like I was intruding, so I certainly understand why you didn't like to bring it up to her."

"I know she and Sophia talked about those times."

"While you're visiting Sophia, I'll find if there's any information available. An auto accident with four fatalities in San Francisco forty years ago should be easy to confirm or disprove."

"Thanks, Abby." Fleur stood, moved behind her lover, and looped her arms around Abby's neck. "I hope we can get this cleared up, so we can finish getting Aunt Golda's home ready to sell." Tears filled her eyes. "I hate to sell." Fleur thought about the backyard groves of spring blossoms, and how her aunt would warn her that if a plant looked tired, it meant it needed a drink of water. "Such lovely memories."

Abby nodded. "You could rent it out. Maybe we could give it a facelift by painting, redecorating. It would give you time to figure out what you'd like to do with it."

"Maybe. Although hanging on to it might keep the pain of losing Aunt Golda too fresh."

"If the grant you're working on comes through, her house would be a perfect place to set up the studies. It has lots of room and light. And our daily walk over here from our house is an easy stroll."

"If I were to get the grant, it would work out perfectly. Moving the lab into Aunt Golda's would definitely free up space at our house. And," Fleur said, a hint of amusement in her voice, "clearing our upper floor would make space for a recreation room. You'd love to put a pool table where my experiments are. A nice little entertainment cave instead of a growing lab."

"See, *you're* even finding uses for it."

Fleur hugged her lover. "*You're* impossible."

"Now, how about a smile?" Abby said.

"It wouldn't be a legitimate smile."

"Okay, don't smile," Abby teased. "You'd only get my hopes up if you did."

Fleur barely chuckled as she picked up her car keys, stuck a small journal for taking notes into her handbag, and left to visit the assisted-living retirement home where Sophia resided.

She would go in search of secrets she hadn't been aware were part of her life.

Although genetically defined by her parents, she didn't feel as though she knew them. Their dying so young in an auto accident had always seemed very sad, but the idea that they had been murder-suicide victims really grabbed her attention.

Almost equally alarming was the statement about no one wanting her when she was an infant.

Chapter 2

When she turned the hall corner inside the assisted-living building, Fleur could see the facility's community room. Gazing through the wide window, she saw her own reflection. It occurred to her that her appearance had come from her parents, but she'd never considered herself actually resembling them. She'd seen a few photos, but she'd never attributed her features to one parent or the other; she believed herself to be more of a combination.

She was tallish and trim. Her curly dark hair, now streaked with silver, fell in waves to her shoulders. Her features were attractive, but not filled out perfectly enough for her to be deemed beautiful. The pale blue eyes were her face's focal point. In most lighting conditions, her complexion appeared rosy. A few years younger than Abby, she was about to turn forty-one. Both women were aging well. Fleur attributed her fitness and good health to her constant walking and health regimen inspired by her Aunt Golda.

Sophia Wenzel was sitting alone at a small table. She was shuffling the magazines and planting each issue securely on top of another. When she completed the rectangle of periodicals, she would mess them up again and begin anew.

Hoping this didn't indicate Sophia wasn't having a lucid day, Fleur approached her. Sophia's condition varied greatly. Fleur had taken Aunt Golda to visit her friend in the residence nearly every week for the past two years. At times Sophia was completely rational, and she would gab with Golda as they had throughout the years. Their reminiscences would be of their husbands, their families and friends, and their gardens. At times, the conversation would even stray to when they'd been captured and lived in the concentration camp.

Fleur was well aware of the camp years, when Golda and Sophia were in their prepubescent and early teen years. Those years had undoubtedly been terrifying and heartlessly cruel. References to that time in their lives were few. Rarely, they would refer to a humorous event, and they would share a laugh. They would then become serious, and their eyes would dull with the pain they'd endured.

Many of Sophia's days were now lost to an oblivious mental side street, so Fleur was thankful that Sophia's head lifted at her call. The eighty-year-old's eyes looked bright. Sophia had already seemed elderly to Fleur when she was a child. She might well have been born old for her years, but Fleur attributed it to Sophia's time within the captivity of the camp. Elderly, wise, and sentimental, Sophia adored Aunt Golda.

Sophia was a short, pudgy woman with a dark complexion, gray hair, and flashing brown eyes. Aunt Golda had been as stick thin as Sophia was rotund. Golda had been as friendly as Sophia was withdrawn.

"Sophia, I dropped by to see how you're doing," Fleur said as she patted Sophia's shoulder. She took a seat next to her great aunt's best friend. "Are you doing well?"

"Fleur. Little Fleur. Is Golda with you today?"

"No, Sophia. Remember? We lost Golda. She passed last week."

Sophia's head bobbed as her eyes filled. "Yes. Golda is gone. My poor friend, Golda. Are you being cared for?"

"Yes. I'm fine. I wanted to ask you some questions. About the past. About my past. Aunt Golda told me my parents were killed in an auto accident. Today I received a call claiming their deaths were murder and suicide."

Sophia's eyes flashed recognition. Her mouth pressed into silence. Her body shook violently for a moment, and her head pivoted away from Fleur. "Ask your Aunt Golda. I wasn't there."

"I can't ask Aunt Golda, and I desperately need to know. It's important. If you can't clear up the mystery, I'll have to go to California. A stranger called this morning. He told me my parents hadn't died in an accident. And that Aunt Golda wasn't my actual aunt. I've got to know the truth."

Sophia leaned back. "Finding yourself isn't as easy as looking at the last place you were. I don't know your answers."

"Of course you do. The two of you shared everything. If what he said was true, Aunt Golda would've told you. No secrets now. Please tell me." Fleur pressed her hands together.

"When we were girls, there were small weeds growing beside the buildings. Barracks. Coops. We always looked for the colors of petals. One day Golda saw one was beginning to bloom. There wasn't enough water to keep it alive, so she spat on the ground above the roots, watering it so we could see it blossom into flowers. We really wanted to know what color it would be. I told her not to do it, that her mouth would dry out and she would suffer. She said she didn't care. She wanted to help the flower. It had, she told me, survived in adversity. It had to be careful to grow in the shade and not be trampled. And that was what we must also do."

Fleur wanted to keep Sophia talking as long as she was rational, so she said, "The camps were tragic."

"But we had the careful flowers. They helped us." Tears filled the old woman's eyes and dripped over her lower lids. "I'm an old leftover now. Our families were killed. For those of us without family, friends became our tribe. Golda and I were French citizens. Her mother was Jewish, and both my parents were Jewish. In 1940, the Vichy regime passed the Statute on Jews. Between 1942 and 1943, the regime worked with the Gestapo to round up Jews. We thought we would be safe. We thought we could get papers, but we couldn't. They took us away. Golda and I became part of the tribe of those who remained alive. Twenty-five hundred of us who went to Poland survived. Out of seventy-six thousand. We were starved and in constant fear, but Golda and I lived. Like careful flowers."

"Aunt Golda loved flowers. Perhaps that's why I'm a botanist now. We often went to the mountains to hunt wildflowers." Fleur remembered those days as if she might reach out to touch them and they would be there. "She'd tell me about the flowers. The saxifrage grew from a crevice in the rocks, and we'd say they had to be careful. I'm still always searching for those out-of-the-way species."

Maybe, Fleur considered, she was endlessly searching for courageous plants. The study of plants had instilled in her that life was random. Happenstance was where the strategy of life was best understood. Good fortune was when love and kindness landed on their feet, just as bad fortune was when kindness hid.

"Sophia, it's important that I know if there was a secret. It would've been something Aunt Golda told you about when she lived in San Francisco. It would be a secret about my parents."

"Secrets!" Sophia cursed the very word itself. "There were secrets. And when we wrote letters, we encoded our secrets."

"Letters? There were letters you wrote? You and Aunt Golda?"

"When she lived in California, she sent letters to me in Denver. We carefully scrambled the code."

"But it was after the war. You were both safe in the United States."

"No. No, we were never again safe. There might have been agents spying on us."

It occurred to Fleur that the years had embedded fear within the core of these women. She asked herself if those who had endured the war could ever truly be survivors. "Sophia, the letters you spoke of, do you have them? I know Aunt Golda didn't leave letters behind with me."

"I kept her letters, the ones she wrote to me. A few only. Three. Yes, there were three of them."

"Where are they now?"

Sophia's gaze nervously darted sideways. "No one knows but me, and I'm not telling. Don't worry, the letters are safe. And they're secure. We made certain of that. I've kept them all these years."

"Can you tell me what they say?" Fleur didn't want to rush Sophia, nor did she want to pressure her. "Maybe they talked about the flowers?"

"Yes. When we couldn't find the careful flowers in the camp, we would draw them. We would take sticks and draw them on the ground, in the dirt. We called them earth flowers then." Sophia's furtive side-glance made it clear that she was hiding something.

"Aunt Golda would want me to know about the flowers. And about the letters. Did the letters tell about flowers and about the war?"

"Yes. That's why we hid the words."

"The words were about the attempt to annihilate an entire people? So you wrote about the atrocities?"

"Golda said souls were erased."

Fleur's frown deepened. "So you hid the meanings of the letters in code so that the words couldn't be erased?"

"Yes, hidden. The next time you visit, please bring Golda. We could play cards to pass the time. Abby plays cards with me, too. Yes, bring them both."

Their dialogue withered to Sophia's mumbling, unintelligible utterances. She had retreated into a trancelike state. Fleur hugged the old woman and left her with her magazines and her memories. She felt Fate was weighing her to the ground. Aunt Golda had often said comedy and tragedy are known to intersect. This was a day Fleur understood the wisdom in that bromide.

Chapter 3

Fleur sat at the kitchen table and rushed her announcement to Abby. "I'm certain Sophia was concealing something."

"There wasn't any accident with four fatalities named Hamilton that summer in San Fran. But…" Her monotone voice was barely audible. "There *was* a suicide and a homicide. The names are different, though."

"That would support Golda and my parents not being related. I'm going to book the next available flight. I can pack enough clothing and sundries for a few days, and I can leave right away."

Abby leaned toward her lover. "Think it over. Take tonight to think about it, and you can leave in the morning, if you decide to go."

"I've made my decision." Fleur's voice was firm. "I've got to find out."

"Are you certain this is what you want to do? You've got a great deal at stake. You're putting your grant in jeopardy. You haven't even started your evaluation report. And you've worked so hard on it. It's a big decision."

Fleur recognized Abby's censuring tone. "I've got the notes. I'll deal with the report when I return. I know the trip is impulsive, but it's something I need to do."

Abby crossed her arms, and her fingers dug into her upper arm. "Impulsive is an understatement. Come on, be realistic. You've been off the last week for the funeral. You know you're busy at work. Losing your job at this time wouldn't be wise. There's Aunt Golda's burial expenses plus other financial concerns, Trips are expensive."

"Abby, I have to do this. I never attempted to unearth the history of my parents. There was no reason to doubt Aunt Golda. The idea of my parent's death being so violent disturbs me."

"You couldn't get Sophia to open up today, but maybe tomorrow…"

14

"She knows something, but you should have seen her clam up. She's not going to relinquish her best friend's secret. She rambled on about letters. Apparently Sophia has three letters written by Aunt Golda. And she says the secrets in them are hidden in some code. I know there's more to this, and I've got to find out."

"Sophia is often delusional. You know that. She tells you about some coded letters written by Aunt Golda, and you believe it? Sophia says there are secrets, but it's probably all in her head. None of this makes sense. And why does it matter? It's over. Time has passed. We need to go on."

Agitated, Fleur slapped the tabletop. True, the graves were long ago closed, and Abby was being both pragmatic and frugal. But... "I need to get to the truth of all this. I won't be satisfied until I do. Would you mind dropping by to see Sophia tomorrow? Maybe you can get information on the letters."

"I have time to drop by before I go to work. I'll try to get her to open up."

"Thank you. It may be that the letters, if they exist, include something about my parents."

"Won't you reconsider this? What about your future?"

"I've got to find out about my past so that I can go on with my future. I'm going to San Francisco."

"Please do one thing for me."

Fleur glanced into her lover's bronze eyes. Abby gave an impatient press against her short, graying, reddish hair. Her face was flushed. Fleur recognized that her anger was building. "Ab, I do everything for you. Right now, this is for me."

"It doesn't make sense. Think about what this trip is going to cost. Plus you'll be losing at least a week of pay."

Fleur was becoming irritated at Abby's constant reference to money. "I'll use my vacation time. And besides, it's my money that will pay for it."

"We were going to use our vacation time to go to Canada next spring." Abby's words were more pouting than confrontational. "I suppose our trip will be cancelled."

"It's only early September."

Abby turned her coffee cup around several times, as her frustration surged. "This is nuts. You're running off to meet with two strangers. One is a man you've only talked with on the telephone. The other person you haven't even spoken with."

"Why aren't you being supportive of my decision? For once it wouldn't hurt you to bolster me." Fleur heard her own deep sigh. "Can't you back me up?"

"I've been backing you up for sixteen years. Last week I did everything I could to help you. There's your experiment to consider and your grant. Plus, we've got Golda's house to get cleaned out and ready to sell. And you want to go off on some useless wild goose chase. I'll be taking care of the lab plants, the research records for you, and the houses. And our dogs, as well as Aunt Golda's dog and cat, need to be cared for. That's in addition to my busy work schedule. You're chasing some weird story that might not even be true. Besides it was four decades ago, so how is it relevant now?"

"To me it's more than relevant. It could turn out that one of my parents was a murderer. That's my concern. I'm sorry to put extra burden on you, but I'm going. Finding out about my past is more to me than a wild goose chase. And don't bother with Aunt Golda's house while I'm gone. I can handle it when I return. I know you'll be plenty busy with your own work."

"And what about your grant work? If you don't have your report finished by the deadline, you're going to lose your research grant. Then your job will be in jeopardy. We could manage on my paycheck, but you wouldn't be happy having to be dependent on me. You already accuse me of being controlling."

"It's because you do try to be controlling. It's as if you *need* the power. To you, our relationship is about your controlling it."

"Fleur…" Abby's hand became a fist as she tucked it into her pocket. "It's always about you. All I'm good for is planting trees and taking care of the slug work. The animals, the house, it's all hired handwork. You're the intellectual."

It was a standoff. Abby would outmaneuver her. She would argue, cajole, and make a play for sympathy. Fleur avoided any further verbal fencing. "I'm flying out of Denver tonight."

"You know you can't sleep on the plane. If you insist on leaving, at least go tomorrow, early."

"I can rest in the morning when I get in to San Francisco. Why should I wait?" Fleur scowled. "Because *you* insist?"

Abby's tone softened. "Is there something wrong with me wanting to have a say in this? We've just lost Aunt Golda. We should be together. It's ludicrous to go off on a crazy search when we're so busy. Going out to the airport when it's dark and getting in to San Fran when it's still dark isn't safe. Please reconsider. Aunt Golda wouldn't like that you're going out after dark."

Fleur combed her fingers through her curls. "Okay, I'll leave early in the morning."

"It'll give us time together. I need to hold you tonight."

"Abby, I knew it would come down to the truth. *You need* to hold me. You need!"

Abby's jaw clamped as she turned away from Fleur. "I'm feeding the pups and kitty. You do what you want."

"I said I'd wait until morning, but I *am* going. You're not changing my mind."

"Of course not," Abby said with sarcasm. "Permission to be concerned about my mate's safety, please?"

"I'm too wiped out to argue. I'm staying tonight. We can hold any further discussion when I return. And I do appreciate your helping with the pets and the plants. I do."

Fleur could hear her great aunt Golda chastising her as she had whenever Fleur became upset with Abby. Golda recognized Abby's cynical tendencies, however she encouraged Fleur to be patient. She would say, "Some plants are wonderful, but they need pruning. If a gardener excels, a lovely plant, and self-satisfaction at having tended the plant, are the rewards." Fleur often wondered how patient she could be.

As for Abby's allegation about wasting time, perhaps it had some merit. But Fleur didn't consider a search of her past to be wasting time. There was wisdom in an old saying that wasting time is not always time wasted. Every version of her life provided a different vantage point. It could be, she thought sadly, that she and her mate might not always understand what one another was thinking; they might not know what one another was feeling.

Fleur didn't want to be controlled by another person's ideas and decisions. Abby didn't approve of most of Fleur's decisions, no matter what Fleur's reasons were. Still, in this case, Fleur refused to be deterred. She intended to go to San Francisco not only to search her past, but to find her future.

When Fleur stood, Abby reached for her hand. After a quick squeeze of their interlocking fingers, Fleur moved away. She went to Aunt Golda's desk. In the top drawer, where Golda had lovingly placed them, was a packet of photos. She pulled the aged photos from the envelope and examined them. One was of Golda, holding Fleur and flanked by Fleur's parents. Another showed the two mod-looking hippie parents posing with their newborn.

Her father looked to be a serious young man. Shane's hair was straight and shoulder length, tied at the base of his neck. His clothing was loosely fitting khaki. Her mother's smile was broad and beaming. Maggie's thick, long, dark, curly hair flowed outward from her pink face. She wore a wildly colorful, printed, over-blouse, a Navajo skirt, and high-top boots.

Fleur attempted to look deeper into her mother's expression for the first time. Holding her infant, Maggie's face reflected joy. Beside them, Shane's lips lifted in a half smile. They looked to be in love.

In other photos, Golda posed with her beloved husband, Walter. One photo had been taken just before he'd suffered a massive heart attack. Aunt Golda had told Fleur it was sad that he hadn't lived to see baby Fleur.

Fleur recalled how she'd once carefully examined the photos for any resemblance between her and her family. Strangely, she'd seen her own eyes in the eyes of Golda's husband. She'd always been told by Aunt Golda that she had gotten the Hamilton blue eyes. Now it appeared that had been make-believe.

Fleur lifted her head when she heard Abby calling to her. Sticking the envelope into her handbag, Fleur said, "I'll be there in a moment."

She and Abby had always enjoyed showering together. She hoped it would bring them closer now. *If even for fifteen minutes.* The rushing, tranquil waters usually eased their tensions, their individual anxieties, as well as the strain between them.

As she disrobed, Fleur felt the shower's steam billowing with humidity. Although their shower was brief, the women's touches were tender. Abby rested her mouth on Fleur's shoulder, then her tongue traced the length of her lover's clavicle. Abby raised her head slightly, and her kiss traveled up along the neck until her lips reached Fleur's mouth.

Abby's soft, warm kiss was followed by a deep kiss that enticed Fleur. Their bodies merged together under the raining waters, as Abby wound her arms around Fleur and then slid her hands down over Fleur's buttocks.

Fleur often wondered why Abby's personality didn't match her lovemaking.

Fleur attributed the lack of passion that had once soared to their advancing years. Not so long ago, the snug fit of their bodies and their heartbeats made her feel as if they were one. Fleur had hoped that would remain forever. But now, something was missing.

Their nude bodies slid beneath the sheets. One of their small gestures of love was that their hands twined throughout the night. When Abby's fingers squeezed hers, Fleur cuddled nearer, then Abby withdrew her fingers and moved away.

"You're still upset about my decision, aren't you?" Fleur asked.

"We've just lost Aunt Golda, and we should be closer than ever before. But we aren't. Life seems to be coming apart."

"After all these years we've been in love, I'm supposed to be your life. You're my life. Aunt Golda was a part of our lives, but you are my life. I want you to be supportive."

"Because I'm against something that isn't in your best interest, I'm not supportive? Look, I recognize how much we're both grieving over Aunt Golda. I'm trying to protect you." Abby caressed Fleur's face. "Please, let's end the night with love."

Feeling Abby's kiss on her fingertips, Fleur relented. "I want to share our love. I do." She wrapped her arms around Abby and immediately felt the warmth of Abby's kisses on her lips. Arousal built. Abby knew Fleur's body by heart, and each touch was a sensual mapping. As if molding soft, silken clay, Abby's hands caressed her lover. The press of their bodies against one another was gentle. Each rocking motion, each touch they shared was perfection. They lifted one another to a throbbing orgasm.

Clasped together for many moments, they each caught their breath as their heartbeats resumed a normal cadence. Fleur rested her head against Abby's shoulder. The excitement of their love-sharing, that rush to climax, always stirred Fleur. It was as if Abby perfectly choreographed their love.

Abby moved away with a quick roll across the bed, and her head settled back against the pillow. Several moments passed before she spoke. "I reset the alarm for six. I know after a good night's sleep, you'll change your mind about San Francisco."

Fleur lifted herself onto one elbow. She reached across to the nightstand and pressed buttons on the clock. "I'll be leaving early."

"Come on, babe—"

"Enough!" Tears burned Fleur's eyes. Blinking wildly, she felt them build. Her eyes shut quickly and reopened, as if slapping her tears dry.

Moonlight seeped across their bodies. Through the slightly opened window, the chirring crickets interrupted Fleur's thought. Love was still, and its motionless imprint frightened her.

Fleur considered the theory of parallel universes. Certainly this moment created her own personal alternate reality. She wondered what part of which universe her mate might belong to at this moment. A glance through the window showed the dome of heaven. The brightness of Colorado stars seemed to be acknowledging that life had been remodeled. The passing of Aunt Golda had wiped away a great portion of her universe. Her great aunt's resonant voice—that voice of reason—was unavailable to her. And there was nothing she knew with certainty.

Chapter 4

During the trip to San Francisco, Fleur checked her memory for what she had hurriedly packed. Worried she might miss her flight out of Denver International Airport, she had hastily thrown things into her case.

She then made notations in her journal. What little information she had—about his allegation and the name of Gemma Rae—came from Bernie Maylor. She listed questions she wanted to ask them both. She didn't have enough information to properly formulate the in-depth questions she would have liked. She assumed there would be many more questions after she met them.

The thought of investigating her past was daunting. She'd never been inquisitive about her past. It hadn't seemed important. Now finding out about it was the most important thing in her life.

When the airplane landed in San Francisco, Fleur glanced at her wristwatch. It was early afternoon. She'd booked her reservation in a moderately priced hotel in the city's center by using the same area code as Bernie's telephone number. She guessed that would at least put her in the vicinity of Bernie and Gemma Rae. She took a cab directly to the hotel, checked in, and quickly unpacked her suitcase.

She called the number Bernie had given her and recognized his voice when he answered. He gave her directions on how to find his small bookstore, Maylor Books, and she realized it was only blocks away from her hotel. It could be walked easily and probably more quickly than searching out a cab. She sternly cautioned herself that she might be unprepared for either the physically or mentally frightening adventure. One for which she could not prepare, nor had she ever needed to prepare.

As she walked, she felt a compulsion to run in the opposite direction. She nervously twisted the straps of her large handbag. It was habit for her to bring her laptop. She had most of her important research information on it, and hence she felt the need to keep it near her.

Entering the shop, she noticed Maylor Books was well-kept, though time-weathered. A group of young people was gathered around a corner table, vehemently discussing Keats. Stacks of books were on the opposite side of the room. Filled with rows of both new and antiquated books, the shelves stood as if they were bastions of literature.

From behind the counter, a man who appeared to be in his seventies looked up at Fleur as she entered. He was short, thin, and bent. Fleur noticed a cane beside the counter case. Bernie Maylor appeared sickly, but a spark of energy still emanated from him. He was bespectacled, with gray-green eyes behind the metal frames. His face was lined and gaunt.

Seemingly still on the fringes of the famed "hippie era," Mr. Maylor wore a bright red beret. His suit was outdated, and the bowtie perhaps older still. The neck of his shirt was like a loose circle. The clothing sagged around his frail frame. When he lifted the beret with an accompanying nod, Fleur noticed a fringe of snow white hair around his head. His voice was hoarse, and he spoke softly. "Welcome to Maylor Books."

"Mr. Maylor, I'm Fleur Hamilton," she said, holding out her hand.

"Bernie, here, just call me Bernie. And please don't shake my hand too vigorously. I've got severe arthritis."

Her touch skimmed his outstretched, claw-like hand. "Thank you for calling. If you hadn't phoned, I would never have become aware that my parents hadn't died in a car crash. Before I left Denver, my partner did a cursory search on the Internet. And I did some research while I was waiting for my flight. Neither of us could find anything in the historical archives about an auto crash at the time it might have taken place. Not a thing. And there *was* a story about the deaths of a young couple, so there might be some validity to your story. I'm just not certain what I should believe."

"I assure you," he said tentatively, a glimmer in his eyes, "although I love literature, I am not nearly creative enough to make things up. I'm also sorry I was the one who told you about it." Examining Fleur's face, he said slowly, "You look a great deal like your parents. You have your mother's hair—curly and dark. Maggie's was extremely black, though, while yours is a dark brown. I believe you have her smile, as well. You have your father's eyes.

Exactly, yes." He studied her. "You're taller than your mother, but not nearly as tall as your father was."

Bernie pointed to a small desk in the back room, and she followed him to it. "Thank you for taking this time with me."

They sat, and he held up a yellowed front page of a newspaper. "This newspaper clipping tells about the killings. I've saved this for forty years. I'm uncertain as to why I've held on to it. Most probably because it was the only time I've ever been interviewed by the press." He handed it to her. "You may keep it, if you like. I have no use for it."

"Thank you." Fleur unfolded the sheet carefully and skimmed the headlines telling of a double homicide—murder and suicide. The subheading mentioned a hippie couple had died. "Horrific. What a grisly scene it must have been. And you were their friend?"

"Yes. I was over a decade older than they were, so I wasn't on the commune with them. I didn't know them until they moved into the apartment building. I was much closer to Golda than I was to your parents. Golda and I often played canasta and bridge with a neighborhood group."

"In Denver, Aunt Golda played cards with her friend Sophia and their friends."

"She made mention of Sophia. Said they met in the concentration camp. When talking of their imprisonment together, Golda would say that life isn't a certainty."

"You said my parents lived on a commune."

"They did until your Golda intervened. Maggie, your mother, was Golda's piano and voice student. Golda always helped the young people. Especially hippies. Maggie had a marginal voice with very little range."

"Aunt Golda said my mother's voice was not for traditional music."

Bernie chuckled. "Golda was the finest with euphemisms. She'd call Maggie *flighty*. In actuality, although Maggie was sweet, she was erratic, impulsive, and had a penchant to treat the words 'fun' and 'crazy' as interchangeable. Poor, dear Maggie was without great musical talent." He paused in thought. "Yes, and Golda called Shane *severe*. He was, in fact, a raving radical. He'd been in Viet Nam in 1967 and 1968 and found it a vulgarity. As is all war. Being part of the hippie movement was his revolution. At any rate, Golda helped the young couple."

"How did Aunt Golda help them?"

"When Golda discovered your parents were living on a commune and Maggie was pregnant, she tried to convince them to get an apartment. They declined, until you were born, then they accepted Golda's help. I'm certain Golda talked the landlord into taking them as tenants, and she probably paid for the apartment."

"I was born in a commune?" This was a staggering concept to consider.

"Yes. But immediately afterwards, Golda insisted you have medical care, be checked. They took you to a small free clinic where no one asked questions."

"Golda was always watching out for those around her. She always made certain to care for me. Perhaps that's the part of this that bothers me most," Fleur said. "Apparently Golda isn't my great aunt."

"In the early years, she was everyone's aunt, it seemed. She generously gave food and shelter to those in need. When I needed to talk, she'd put on tea and music, and she would chat with me. When you were born, she was a caregiver, and you needed care, so it was a perfect fit. It was Golda who cared for you. Your parents were so young, and youth often gets it wrong. They weren't interested in being parents."

"You're saying they were rotten parents." Fleur watched his expressions intently.

"Well, with drugs, and with their histories, they weren't cut out to be parents. No. Not at all. They were too young and immature to be up to the responsibility."

"Although Aunt Golda told me a few things about my parents, her reminiscences were minimal. It didn't occur to me to question what I'd been told. No question went without answers, but nothing additional was offered. Aunt Golda kept answers simple. My assumption was that the painful memories were difficult for her to talk about. But she did mention that my father was a soldier."

"A Marine. And he was wounded in Nam—head wound, leg wound. He was in pain much of the time. And whether his drug dependency began with pills for his pain, or if he'd started using them before he was injured, I can't tell you. I know drugs were at times used by soldiers during the war to deal with war's atrocities."

"I've read about the Viet Nam War, as well as the peace movement."

"Yes. There was a resistance to the military's induction policies. Back then, there was the draft. If their number came up, young men had no choice but to serve. And die. Disposable bodies,

Shane once called it. In another of his speeches, he talked about thinking every night might be his last glimpse of the moon. Many other young men felt the same. So the demonstrations began. Recording artists like Joan Baez were jailed for antiwar demonstrations. It was very sad. Your father, as most do, found killing an atrocious act. I also find war onerous. I believe the reason Shane didn't want children was that he believed everyone was in immense danger. Rather a paranoid fear, but there you have it."

"I wonder how much he could have loved an infant if he didn't want a child."

"Had he been a man of today, he probably would have been able to better show his love for his child, but those times were sad and very confusing. The era was filled with youths still tasting blood. I recall once I spoke with him about the battlefield. He told me when he was in battle, the air was thick with the smell of blood. He couldn't get the metallic taste of blood out of his mouth. Even after he was safe in his homeland, he still tasted it. Their anguish reverberated through our culture."

"And what was my mother's excuse for not loving me?"

"I didn't say she didn't love you. She was unable to care properly for you, but she did leave you with Golda most of the time. She knew Golda would take care of you. Golda loved children, and she certainly loved you. She taught you patty-cake. Of course, you were too young, but when you lifted your small hands, it convinced Golda you'd learned. She was ecstatic when you would show off for her visitors."

"Yes," Fleur said. "She encouraged me to excel. Her great joy was backyard discoveries: trees, plants, flowers, rocks, birds' nests—all the mysteries of nature. It pleased her when I could name species and subspecies. And when I would talk about dendrite, the most complex snowflake, she would take pride, as though I was her student. We saw snowflakes by the ton in Denver winters. Although she had limited funds, we always took a summer vacation to some exotic place. She often said our intelligence, along with knowledge, is the bond between us and the world. She wanted to open up the world for me to see—from backyard snowflakes to European vacations."

"She was originally from France."

"Yes. She took me to France, to the area that had been her childhood home. The entire neighborhood had crumbled with time, or maybe it was leveled by the war. At any rate, it had been rebuilt.

All that remained of the original town were her memories of how it had been."

"Golda's sensitivity for her country, and for an infant, was part of her love. Maggie knew you would be safe in Golda's company."

"How could my mother have wanted me, if she passed me on? Even to the kindest-intentioned person."

"You were loved by both Golda and your mother, and Maggie recognized it was in your best interests to be with Golda. Maggie often used drugs. Our era was one of experimentation, where mind-alteration was a constant. The world saw an explosion of moral conviction, of hallucinogens, and of 'different drummers.' I'm not certain that there'll ever be another time where the confluence of drugs, war, art, and love will come together as it did then."

Fleur's eyes closed for a moment. "The times were so unsettling for everyone. Aunt Golda blamed wars for the spread of hatred."

"Wars make countries into something other than what they might have been. We're the land of today because of both the courage of those serving, and those who harbored a divisive opposition to war. We import our beliefs from those who've gone before. Literature has recorded these facts and divulged them to us."

"The hippie era produced its own revolution."

"Yes." With a mournful sigh, Maylor added, "There's much to thank the people of the hippie generation for and perhaps equally as much to condemn them for. And as for Maggie's excuses, I don't know the full story. Gemma Rae was her closest friend. You might want to check with her for the answer to that question."

"Her shop is near?"

"Three blocks north and two blocks down. I'll write down the address for you. I would accompany you, except I have my poetry group here this afternoon and evening. Last session, we explored Dickinson, and this session is devoted to Keats. And who can turn their backs on Keats?" His eyebrow lifted. "Other than Gemma Rae. She once said she would gladly moon most of the poets of old."

Fleur's spark of a laughter turned up her lips. "She's not keen on Keats?"

"Not at all." His face held empathy mixed with teasing, "The poetic arts are lost to her. When I became dependent on a cane, she began calling me 'Zippy the wannabe hippie.' So the poor dear has some rhyme within her soul."

"Was she being unkind?"

"Not at all. Her spirit is kind. She has become my friend. During the psychedelic years, I was very much off to the side of the revolution. Even if I hadn't been slightly older than the youngsters, I probably wouldn't have been in their subculture. I'm looking back from another perspective. We should ask the aged about yesterday, and the youth about tomorrow."

Fleur took a deep breath. "I'm in the middle, so clarity escapes me. Maybe the perspective of an older person might help me." Her smile was subdued. "Gemma Rae was my mother's best friend?"

"Yes. Yes. If you contact Gemma Rae, I'm sure she can give you much more information. However I can help, please let me know."

"Thank you, Bernie. I appreciate your help. Since you called, I somehow have felt lost."

"Golda could never have raised a lost soul. You'll find your way. We're all here to help you."

"I appreciate that."

As they walked toward the door, he asked, "I'm curious, Ms. Fleur. What profession have you chosen?"

"I'm a botanist. I work in a medical science lab. I'm also working on a grant proposal to experiment with plants. Although this trip may terminate my future plans."

"We find our own purpose somehow. Perhaps that's our life's true responsibility. Nothing more, nothing less."

"Perhaps." Fleur looked at the directions Bernie had carefully, painstakingly written. "Thank you for your help." *What would Gemma tell her?*

Chapter 5

Gemma's shop was a two-story storefront on a corner of an intersection. Rainbow signage above the entryway advertised *Gemma Rae's Earth*. To the side of the door, a multicolored flag bucked and snapped wildly in the breeze. Fleur crossed the street and hastened toward the small metaphysical shop.

Bookstores of a certain age had a familiar ambience. Aunt Golda often called it the mystique of word-friendly areas. Maylor Books had reminded her of the many visits she and Aunt Golda had made to bookstores and libraries.

This bookstore had a slightly musty smell. She also recognized another fragrance from her past—the smoky scent of floral incense combined with the smell of freshly brewed coffee. She inhaled the aromas of a variety of java flavors and spiced teas. She saw a coffee and tea bar and pastries under glass. Beyond the coffee and tea bar area were counters of new-age trinkets, books, decorative items, and lovely hand-thrown pottery. The glazes on the pots were swirls of color and design.

"You're Fleur."

The woman who greeted her was in her early to mid-sixties, of medium height, with a wide girth around breast and belly. She was dressed like a hippie. Her tie-died muumuu, that nearly reached the floor, was done in patterns of neon green, neon yellow, tangerine, and shades of aquamarine. Thick, strawberry-blonde hair streaked with gray fluffed in a cumulus cloud around her head. A bright, multicolored headband failed to restrain the bushy hair.

Huge golden eyes shone from Gemma Rae's round face. Her plump features were attractively proportioned. Circular globe cheeks were crocus pink. Bursting from her grin, her large front teeth were the size of Chiclets. Gemma Rae took Fleur in her arms and twirled her.

"Maggie's baby girl. I've been expecting you. Bernie said you'd come. Can I get you something to drink? Coffee or tea? Please sit at the corner table over there. Would you like a tea cake?"

Fleur smiled at the woman's enthusiasm. "Coffee would be wonderful. Black, please." She wondered how drab she must appear to Gemma Rae. Wearing a lightweight, ecru and cocoa-brown print blouse and matching ecru slacks, Fleur admitted her attire paled in comparison to Gemma Rae's outfit.

Gemma Rae motioned a slim young man forward. His handsome features indicated he might be oriental or biracial. She introduced him as Rolly Li, her assistant and barista. "Rolly, Fleur'll have a cup of our finest coffee. And please bring a lemerald tea for me." She turned to Fleur. "Lemerald is lemon in green tea. Love exotic names. I drink coffee and tea based on whatever name suits me at the time." Her sentences rushed together. "I can't get over how much you look like Maggie."

Rolly placed a ceramic mug of steaming coffee on the table in front of Fleur and another of tea in front of Gemma Rae. "Coffee and Lemerald," he said. Steam rose from both cups.

"Rolly is bickering with his boyfriend, so don't expect a hell of a lot of conversation out of him," Gemma Rae said. He forced a smile for her, which drew a deep belly laugh. "For the sake of my friendly establishment, I hope to hell they make up soon." Turning back to Fleur, she patted her own voluminous chest. "I can't believe you're Maggie's baby. Over the years, I've stayed in contact with Golda. What a gal! Back in the sixties, we all loved her. When I heard she'd passed, I was heartbroken. Cried the entire day. Back when I knew her, she was a mother figure to the hippies."

"Aunt Golda was special."

"She was a wonderful woman. I loved her humor. It was kind, never mean-spirited."

Fleur added with a glint of reminiscence, "She was always generous, both in spirit and in actual giving."

"That's true. She used to say that if she had anything left over, she hadn't given enough away."

"I remember her saying that."

Gemma Rae poured honey into her tea. "This reminds me of something else about Golda. She used honey as a magic remedy. I remember when you were an infant and wouldn't take your bottle, Golda put honey on the bottle's nipple and you'd lap it up. She knew things. She'd lived on a commune of sorts. A terrible commune."

"I know. I often thought that since part of her childhood had been so horrible, from then on, she tried to make everything better, more fun."

"Whimsical. The old girl loved whimsy." Gemma Rae's fingers fluttered as she spoke.

"Yes, she did. Last year, my fortieth birthday was a magical outdoor birthday party. When I was a child, I loved bubbles, so Golda rigged up a couple dozen bubble machines. The backyard was filled with bubbles throughout the afternoon. They were the highlight of the day."

"She always used to say how some of life was awful, and some awfully good, it all depended on how we interpreted life. I'll bet you miss her."

"I do. She was always so tranquil." Fleur looked away a moment as she sipped her coffee.

"Golda was one in a million. I was shocked when Bernie told me you were actually coming here."

"I have so many questions about my parents."

"We all had questions about what happened. None of it felt legit. I get these feelings, and I can tell you, it jangled me."

The woman seemed completely credible, but Fleur reminded herself of one of Golda's primary lessons: Things aren't always as they seem. Everyone has an agenda. Fleur watched Gemma Rae's expressions carefully as she said, "You think my father murdered her and then killed himself?"

"Sure. What else? He was the gun expert, an expert shot. He'd been in Nam a couple of years. He had a gun he carried on him all the time. It was his gun that killed them. Maggie didn't even know where the fucking trigger was. I mean, she was scatterbrained as hell. She could flare up, but kill someone? Not Maggie."

"Golda wouldn't have assigned blame. Having been raised by Golda, I've probably assumed her mellow ways. I realize my spirit doesn't resemble my mother's. I'm much more like Golda— reserved."

"Maggie was her own person, for sure, but we were all pretty ragtag back then. Hell, I still am. But I'm a little less agitated and a lot more fluffy." Her blustering laugh boomed. "Maggie was usually loaded up on drugs, but she was fun. We didn't think we were lascivious and wanton, we thought we were Renaissance women. Sure, she was boy crazy, but she settled down when she went nuts for Shane. And she could be empty-headed. When she was tripping, she would have needed a recipe to make ice cubes. But we were all wild then. There was nothing G-rated about the sixties. There was only wide-open living. We made it up as we went along. We were part of an era of revolution. You might say we were just a tad above being a Bohemian enclave. The Haight was a spectacle that was either an energetic rush or toxic."

"For my parents it was toxic."

"No doubt about it. Maggie and Shane were in love, but they weren't right for each other. Maggie's favorite songs were all things Janis Joplin, but she also adored Tommy James and the Shondells' 'Crimson and Clover.' Shane loved the Animals singing that old song, 'House of the Rising Sun.' Go figure. Always ask what a person's favorite song is. Their answer will tell you if you're compatible."

"Probably."

A profound ache overwhelmed Fleur. She and Abby had both had the same favorite song when they were getting together over a decade and a half ago—Elton John's "Can You Feel the Love." She took a sip of coffee. "Did you know my parents' backgrounds?"

"Sure. We all knew each other's pasts."

"I tried to check via the Internet, but I couldn't pull up any Shane Hamilton. Bernie gave me the front page newspaper story about their deaths. Both my parents had different names than Hamilton. So I'm wondering whether the newspaper was accurate."

"I can help you," Gemma Rae said. "I'll tell you whatever you'd like. I don't know everything about Maggie, but I probably knew her better than anyone else. She trusted me. Maybe Shane knew her as well as I did. Hard to say what he knew and didn't know. He was sullen, but he was also a rascal."

Fleur pulled out her small journal and pen. "For instance, I wasn't aware they hadn't married, much less that their names weren't Hamilton."

"They lived together, but there was no official marriage license, so they had different names. And neither of them was Hamilton. That came from Golda's husband, Walter Hamilton. I think she said his name was Walter. And his middle name was W-something. A little alliteration going on. Anyway, he died a year before all this happened. Your father's name was Shane Bradley. Your mother's name was Margaret Heywood." Her melodic laugh was inserted between every thought change. "When she used to get high as a Georgia pine, you know, all stoned, I'd call her Maggie Haywire. Her great big green eyes would stab me. She had this pixie face and wild black coils of curls. Her small, voluptuous figure drove the men wild. Haywire. And Shane's last name was Bradley. When he pissed me off, I called him Shane Badley, instead of Bradley."

"Fleur Bradley," Fleur said softly, as if she were meeting herself for the first time.

"No. Your mother named you Flower. No middle name, simply Flower. Right after you were born, we held a naming ceremony on the commune. What a gas!" Gemma Rae reflected a moment. "The weed was really burning for that event. The best lid of grass we could find. Wine and weed." Gemma Rae's eyes squinted as she recalled the ceremony. "Anyway, she named you Flower."

"The grass must have acted as her epidural," Fleur said.

"Yes." Gemma Rae laughed. "Flower was a song she sang to you. 'Flower, Flower, please don't glower, or be sour, little Flower. Growing bigger by the hour. Flower, Flower, please don't cower, little Flower, Flower.' She would sing it over and over again. She could scream lyrics loudly enough that she could have blown out the fillings in her teeth, but when she sang to you, it was all mellow. Then she would want to get high, and she would park you upstairs with Golda."

"Flower. And how did I get the French name Fleur?"

"Immediately after your parents died, Golda had to think fast. Since she was originally from France, she changed Flower to the French *fleur*."

"Yes. She was a polyglot. Spoke fluent French, English, and German, plus enough to get by in several other languages. She was originally from France and then was transported by the Nazis to Poland during the war. When she was freed, she came to this country, where she learned English."

"She spoke precise English when I first knew her," Gemma Rae said. "Golda had a good ear, maybe that's what made her a good musician. Probably also gave her the ability to learn languages. She was a brilliant lady, that's for sure."

"I can see where she'd need to think quickly when my parents died."

"That's right. The fuzz would have taken you to Social Services. Even before she renamed you, she'd called you her sweet little *fleur*."

"Didn't I have grandparents? Aunts or uncles?"

Gemma Rae turned her head toward the wall. "Look, kid, this isn't an easy story. And if Golda was alive, I'd never be talking with

you like this, out of respect for her. She may have broken the law…
Well, she did break the law."

"There must have been a reason."

"Okay, here's how it went down. Maggie had a hell of a life.
Her old lady was a crazy whore who was always lit up with booze.
She was a fuuucking"—Gemma Rae stretched out the word for
emphasis—"mental case, always drunk and belligerent. She was a
bad woman and a worse mother. Negligent, yes, but she was also
cruel. She mistreated her kids. She was evil, and evil people are
jumbled up with major glitches."

"So, my mother had a terrible childhood." Fleur felt sadness.
The childhood years should nurture one's soul. Mapping the human
heart is difficult. She felt compassion for her mother, as well as
understanding. "I wish she'd had at least one good parent."

"Her crazy mother had no idea who Maggie's dad was. She
told Maggie her father was Puerto Rican. He might have been,
because Maggie's hair was curly black, curlier by far than yours.
Yours is sort of wavy in comparison to her absolute curl."

With a chuckle, Fleur said, "I'm glad I have a diversified
heritage. Aunt Golda always said I'm primarily English."

"She was probably correct. Shane's parents were English.
Anyway, Maggie left home at fifteen because her mother's men
friends were trying it on her. She ended up a hippie, but hippie
living was a step up from where she'd been. Whoever her father
was, he'd been long gone since Maggie was a kid. So Golda knew,
for all practical purposes, Maggie had no family. None who would
have cared for you. None that Maggie would have wanted you
anywhere near. She trusted Golda with you."

"What about my father's family, the Bradleys?"

"They were a bunch of tight asses from New York. Shane's
mother was a venomous society bitch. The old man was a hotshot
advertising executive. They'd kicked Shane out. And when he
announced he was going to be a father, they claimed Maggie was a
slut. Told him not to marry her, that the kid probably wasn't his.
Back then they didn't have DNA tests, and Maggie's word wasn't
worth a goddamn dime." Gemma Rae turned her cup around several
times. "Needless to say, they wouldn't have taken you in. But you
got his eyes—bedroom eyes, they used to say. And you're lean like
he was."

"I always thought I looked exactly like Golda's husband,
Walter. He had blue eyes like mine, and he was lean." Fleur tried to

take it all in. To prove parenthood, she would need to track down her father's family and convince one of them to take a DNA test.

"Well, I can tell you, your eyes are the spitting image of Shane's. He was a hell of a good looker, but his temper was terrifying. Hope you didn't get his temper," Gemma Rae said with a grin.

"No," Fleur answered shyly. "I'm more likely to be accused of being too soft. I probably should be more confrontational at times." She considered Abby's assessment of her. She'd often called Fleur a floor mat with an inability to stick up for herself. "I always thought it was another part of Golda's husband's genes I'd inherited. Both Walter and Golda had tranquil spirits. She was never aggressive and always flexible."

"Probably her years in the camp made her resilient. Probably saved her life," Gemma Rae said.

"Thankfully. Otherwise who would have cared for me when I was a baby?"

"Yeah, that's the truth. All of us back then were too messed up to take a kid." Again Gemma Rae studied the tea residue in the cup before she took a final swig. "So when the tragedy played out, something had to be done to protect you. It was a lie, but better a lie than you being endangered."

"When was the decision made to fake my identity?"

"That was the same day as the shooting. Bernie rushed down to the apartment because he heard shouting, then gunfire, then total quiet. He banged on Maggie and Shane's door. Nothing. So he went across the hall and woke the superintendent. They opened the apartment up and found Maggie and Shane lying there. When the cops arrived, the super told them there was a baby. Bernie said you were probably up at Golda's, so he took the cops up there. Golda had been playing music, so she hadn't heard any shots. They had to tell her what had happened. When the cops asked her if she had the baby, she said yes. Bernie, bless him, piped up, said Golda was your great aunt. The cops figured it was less paperwork—family had the baby, end of story."

After a moment of deliberation, Fleur asked, "But what about documents? I have my birth certificate that says Fleur Hamilton."

"Bernie took care of it. He acts like a little milquetoast, but he's got a set of balls somewhere. He'd always been in the book business and knew tons of printers. He had one of his friends fake the paper. Gave it to Golda so you had official-looking documentation. That's what I meant about Golda stepping outside the law."

"My papers are all fraudulent?"

"But I'm sure they were done by the very best printer in town." Gemma Rae's face grimaced into a comedic frown.

"Whew!" Fleur shook her head. "That means all of my credentials are fraudulent."

"Not if no one knows. That's always been my motto: it isn't illegal if you don't get caught." Gemma Rae chuckled. "No one has ever caught you. Probably the reason Golda decided to move to Denver where her friend Sophia lived. You know, to cool the trail. There would be fewer questions. And she'd always wanted a baby, but she couldn't have children. My guess is it was because of the concentration camp's bad nutrition and bad everything. So having a child was manna from heaven. She was determined to raise you."

"And she did. She took such wonderful care of me. But why didn't she go through the proper channels? Why the charade?"

"Working with city hall is a toss-up. She was over forty, middle-aged, no husband. It wouldn't have been a given. Dicey. She'd lived under the Occupation and in a concentration camp. If anyone knew authority's perils, it was her." Gemma Rae laughed and slapped the table. "Hippies know the lesson by heart: never trust the 'oink,' and you can't go wrong."

"I see what you mean." Fleur joined in Gemma Rae's laughter. "Trusting the power structure would probably have put me in foster care for my entire childhood."

"Well, into late adolescence anyway, if you lasted that long. Golda didn't want your future to depend on a crapshoot. None of us wanted that for you. And after all, she'd practically raised you those many months. Maggie's mother was gooney garbage, and the Bradley parents were haters. They also tried to raise haters. No matter, because they refuted Shane's paternity, so they weren't an option. There was only Golda. No one else seemed interested in you."

"With the exception of my mother, when she sang to me." Fleur's voice dipped with gloom. "When she sang her Flower song to me, she must have loved me."

"She did. She sang it with love," Gemma Rae said. "Sometimes it was as if she was singing a prayer." She patted Fleur's hand as she ruffled her own hair with the other.

"Did I act as though I believed I was loved when she sang to me?"

"Sure. You were probably her *best* audience," she answered. "You'd smile. Or maybe you needed to be burped. Anyway, Maggie's chops sometimes sounded okay, if the band was loud and the acoustics were really bad."

Chapter 6

Fleur's iPhone rang. She knew it was Abby, because the ringtone was their Elton John song. "Gemma Rae, I'm going to step outside to take this call. It's a little noisy in here."

Gemma Rae's smile lifted in amusement. "We call it music, but it is distracting."

Outside on the sidewalk, Fleur pulled the cell phone from her pocket and answered, "Hi, babe." As Abby's words rushed out, Fleur seated herself on the small bench that leaned against Gemma Rae's storefront. Holding her head, Fleur gave a sigh. "Can you slow down, please?"

"I just finished visiting with Sophia. After yesterday's zip, zilch, today she gave me one of the letters written by Aunt Golda. It is definitely her handwriting."

"What does it say?" Fleur asked impatiently.

"I don't know. It's in two or three languages. That must be what Sophia meant by it being written in code."

Fleur was perplexed. "She obviously only wanted Sophia to read it. Abby, would you shoot photos of it and send it to me via e-mail?"

There was a hesitation on the other end of the line. "You know how I hate all that computer crap. Can't it wait until you get back here?"

"Work with me on this, Abby." Fleur rubbed her temple. "Please."

"I'm working on my job, on the house, on your project, and chasing after letters that are nonsensical," Abby snapped. "I think I'm flipping working with you."

"Sorry. If you'll take the photos, I'll guide you through the download and loading it onto the e-mail as an attachment."

"What you just said about the tech stuff is like a foreign language to me."

Fleur found Abby's resistance to working with computers infuriating. Abby was able to do spreadsheets for her business and utilize the simplest computer basics, but nothing beyond that. She would often ask Fleur to do any technical work she had no interest in learning. "You're going to tell me you don't do tech, but you're going to have to learn to e-mail me a photo of the letter. As an attachment."

"Like in everything else, your skills are far better than mine." Discouragement and frustration mingled in Abby's voice.

Exasperated, Fleur said through her teeth, "Please don't start with me. I don't want to fight with you. And your skills are fine when you apply yourself."

"Apparently not so much, even when I apply myself. Like last night, that didn't go so great. It was as if we went from unabridged to emotionally abridged."

Fleur inhaled deeply. "I don't know what you're talking about."

"You must have noticed how distant we seemed when we were making love."

"It's your imagination." Fleur clutched the iPhone tightly. "Admittedly I'm tense right now. We lost Aunt Golda, there's the grant for my research project, and now I'm face-to-face with unimaginable discoveries about my past."

"You didn't mention our relationship."

"I don't consider our relationship a problem," Fleur said, but there was an edge in her voice.

Several seconds of silence passed, finally broken by Abby's deep sigh. "I'll find the camera and take pictures, then you can tell me what I'm supposed to do."

Fleur waited while Abby found the camera and took photographs of both sides of the letter. When the photography was completed, Fleur instructed her on how to download the images to the computer and make an e-mail attachment.

"That wasn't too difficult, was it?" Fleur asked.

Again there was a hesitation. Finally Abby said tersely, "No."

"Thanks. I appreciate your help." As the photographs appeared on her phone, Fleur examined them carefully. "I'll study the letter when I get back to the hotel and can use my computer. Wish I had paid more attention to Aunt Golda's language lessons."

"At least you know more than one language."

"I only know smatterings of a variety of languages. I'm hardly a polyglot."

"A polyglot…"

"Multilingual."

"I know what the hell polyglot means," Abby stated angrily. "I need to ask you about the plants. Do I put down the genus as *Ammi* on both sections of the samplings?"

"Yes. And on the trays on the blue side of the room, it should be Species: *A visnaga.*"

Abby's voice became angry, unfeeling. "Right. As a synonym, we could say *visnaga daucoides.* Family would be Apiaceae. Kingdom would be Plantae. Anything else?"

"If you'll just take care of the clippings and the slides, I can finish the rest if I get home in time. Listen, Abby, I do appreciate you helping me with this, but you snipe at me and then think we're going to be perfectly fine in bed. It just doesn't work that way. You know how important this study is, not just getting the grant, but doing something meaningful."

Just as Fleur was about to say something to break the uncomfortable silence on the line, Abby blurted, "I've got to go. I'm too busy for this Doc Phil crap."

When Fleur heard the click and the sound of dead air, she disconnected to escape the annoying hum coming from the phone's receiver.

She remained seated on the bench, her eyes closed. Abby could pull up names of every botanical species known. And more, she would know how to save the plants. She would understand the fragility of them. But when Fleur explained RNA transcripts and their encoded proteins, Abby's wall went up.

Fleur recalled the day she'd found out about *ammi* being mentioned in the Hebrew Bible. It was a sage mentioned in the Mishnah and Talmud. When she'd told Aunt Golda, her great aunt had seemed pleased to know the history. And pleased that it meant so much to Fleur.

But when she'd excitedly mentioned it to Abby, her lover had merely dished another helping of vegetables onto her plate. She then muttered that her day had been busier than usual, as she was trying to save a grove of aspen at a new construction site. She complained that the water pipes were supposed to have been working, but they weren't.

She'd gone on to explain to Abby how the active ingredient from the weed called ammi yielded a plant-derived chemical called psoralen, which became activated when exposed to light, and could be used to treat some forms of cancer with photodynamic therapy.

Fleur had attempted to explain epigenetics and genomic imprinting. She wanted the woman she loved to understand her quest to locate a more productive, efficient way to grow a very important plant life. If her hypothesis was correct, the plant could be made more potent. Her experiment could speed up the development of a potential cure for one of the major diseases of this generation. Fleur could still see Abby's mind veering from her information, as if Abby had completely turned her hearing off.

Shaking her head at the thought of Abby's past insensitivity, Fleur stood. Her steps became plodding as she returned inside Gemma Rae's shop, a low-grade anger collecting. Her face was flushed and burning.

As her frame slumped into a chair, she wondered whether her happiness hadn't died with Aunt Golda. The things she had once believed in were now unraveling. And her research experiment, which she so enjoyed, was in the hands of a woman who viewed it as a task.

Fleur wanted to run, but was unable to think of where she might run to. Home had always been with Aunt Golda and then with Abby. Those two women were no longer her home.

"You doing okay?" Gemma Rae asked.

"The flight was tiring. My emotions are still raw from losing Aunt Golda. Her dying has taken a toll on Abby and on me."

"Tattered nerves are the pits. Back in the day, that was the nice part about staying high. For some, it was a hiatus from reality. It was some psychedelic chaos."

"And for others?"

"Hell, drugs were a free-pass therapy for out-of-control hormones." Gemma Rae smirked.

"It worked?"

"When lit up and having a crackerjack orgasm, nobody knew if they were on the edge of an abyss. Nobody cared."

"My parents?"

"From what Maggie said, Shane especially liked getting a little after he'd spent the night in jail. He called jail his penalty box, his disturbing-the-peace penalty box."

"Did my parents love each other?"

"Your mother said that love spins your heart around. Your father, well, he never talked much about love. He wouldn't make plans to legally marry your mother. He always said life is what happens while we're making other plans."

Fleur stared across the table into Gemma Rae's eyes. "But did he love her?"

"Sometimes he must have. And I say that because at least one time he didn't. When he killed her, he couldn't have loved her."

Chapter 7

At seven o'clock that evening, Gemma Rae and Fleur were still talking. Fleur found the conversation not only informative but enjoyable. As Rolly pulled down the door shade, he called to Gemma Rae, "Want me to lock up on my way out?"

"Sure." Gemma Rae looked back at Fleur. "We can go upstairs. I'll fix us a sandwich and a glass of wine. I'll give Bernie a call and ask him to come over after his group dissolves. He could walk you back to the hotel later."

"I'd appreciate it. What a nice thing that he has the poetry groups."

"Poets. Old Poets." Gemma Rae rolled her eyes. "All those old buggers bore the hell out of me. Keats, ode to this and ode to that. Shelley, Wordsworth, Whitman… Bernie goes for all of them."

"I have to confess, I love poetry. Aunt Golda always had a penchant for verse. I think she could appreciate poetry the way it was intended. She could hear the melody of the words. That's how she presented it to me. Good poetry, she used to say, should be like song lyrics. It needs to be musical. And I ended up loving it."

"It would take a hell of a lot more to get me interested. Those words could jump out of the book and smack me, and they wouldn't get my attention. Funny." She frowned. "I had no idea Golda dug poetry. Your mom did. I think Shane wrote her some poetry early on. Anyway, she liked poetry. However, do me a favor. Tonight, please don't get Bernie started on any of those prissy old poets. He'd go on forever."

"I promise," Fleur said with a quick laugh. She watched as Gemma Rae went around the counter to telephone Bernie. The evening with Gemma Rae and Bernie would offer Fleur an excuse not to check in early with Abby. She was certain Abby would be cross. Or, as Aunt Golda would say, be a fussbudget. Anyone angry, crabby, or bitchy fell into that category.

Gemma Rae led the way up the narrow stairway and opened the door. Fleur was amazed at the hominess of the small apartment. A rustic pioneer-style was blended with contemporary. Gemma Rae's interior was a living room adjoining the dinette kitchen area. Hanging beads, like sparkling fringe on the doorway, separated the living area from the bedroom. Gemma Rae's taste ran to an eclectic mixture of Victorian and utilitarian. The cardinal-red sofa was sleek modernity. The remaining pieces of furniture were a combination of steel strike leather and functional pillows.

Gemma Rae waved her to the sofa. "Sit. I'll prepare some chow."

"Can I help?"

"Nope. I've got it under control." Gemma Rae opened a bottle of merlot and passed a glass to Fleur. "I've limited my highs to a couple glasses of wine. Age is the shits. Back in the day, it was grass, hashish, and loads of wine. Not now. I lost my appetite for high-powered drugs when I took an acid trip. Almost didn't leave me with a return ticket. Thankfully, I went back to the less dangerous drugs."

"Did my mother ever overdose?"

"She was more cautious than I was. She stayed clear of hallucinogens and intravenous drugs, but she sure loaded up on the smokes and booze." Gemma Rae packed slices of a variety of grilled vegetables onto wheat bread, then slathered the veggies with spiced olive oil. After sprinkling them with shredded cheese, she finished by placing the sandwiches in a pan to toast them. "I'm a vegetarian, hope that's okay."

"It looks lovely. Was my mother a vegan?"

"Not so much. She loved all forms of exploration. She'd try anything once, twice if she liked it." Gemma Rae's laugh escaped from her lips. "We were pretty damned wild back then. We were high, but not high on middleclass morality. Hell, my parents were okay. I was a wild daughter with wanton ways. We were never on the same wavelength. I wasn't about to have some miracle conversion to their ordinary lives."

"Did they disown you?"

"Nope. The break from them was a matter of not having corporate sponsorship. They would threaten to cut my funds, hide me off to the side when I'd go back home to Nevada. One time, my mother took me aside to inform me I was too liberal for them, and I should change my glitzy wardrobe, get new threads. I told the old battle-ax I was too old to pick up any more bad habits, so I'd keep my wild colors. They cut my small allowance down to a water, bread, and potatoes pittance."

"And did that end the relationship?"

"Not completely. They held out hope for me. They visited me once in a while, but my hometown did without me. My mother told me I 'stuck out' in a small town. They died a few years ago. Burying parents connects us to the reality of life being temporary. My mother *still* haunts me as best she can, but as you see, her spirit entity doesn't have any more impact than she did when she was alive. I still dress like a tramp that rolled across a wet Jackson Pollock painting." She smirked and her eyebrows lifted. "A regular *objet d'art.*"

"I like your clothing. Abby aggravates her mother because her garb is usually androgynous. She always gives the excuse that she makes her living in the dirt and isn't about to doll up to pop a tree in the ground." Fleur sampled the sandwich. She enjoyed its tartness. "Very good."

Gemma Rae chomped at her sandwich. "Not bad. Maggie loved dressing up. Fancy, fun, it didn't matter. We shopped at the thrift stores to find wild outfits. Maggie's threads were sparkly, dripping with spangles. Today we would call it blinged out. She loved dressing as if she was a rock star."

"I can't visualize being the offspring of a rock star."

"One time I remember Maggie said to Golda how she wanted to be a rock star, asked if Golda thought she could. Golda answered, 'It's possible, because there's an *immense* difference between being a rock star and being a musician.' Poor Maggie thought it was a compliment. Golda was so kind, she'd always tell Maggie to keep working, never give up on her dream."

"Golda was encouraging," Fleur said. "She believed there was great emotional and mathematical accuracy in music. I wish I had been more adept at it."

Gemma Rae cringed. "You couldn't be much good if you got Maggie's aptitude for music. She'd smoke a joint before singing with a group."

"Did she work with a group?"

"Not even. I mean, not *with.* Sometimes some of the groups would let her sing with them—warm the audience up, sing a couple songs. But no, most of the bands had their own singers. She never would have made it to their key, because she never sang on key." Gemma Rae snickered. "Once she told me *all* the musicians were playing off key."

"What would I be good at if I had Shane's aptitudes?"

"Shane probably would have ended up a politician. He was always on his antiwar soapbox. He'd yell out how the United States fills its holsters with nukes to kill the world. He'd give his speech with gusto. He once said he felt invisible when he was in front of a crowd, but when he was dodging bullets in Nam, he felt as though he was being seen by every set of Viet Cong eyes. He wasn't optimistic about humanity having the good sense to stay war-free."

"He was a good speaker though?"

"Hell, yes. Maggie was around and singing, but when Shane was around, no one noticed her much." Gemma Rae squeezed out each word. "She was filled with light, but he blocked out her sunshine. Finally, he extinguished it all together."

"I don't understand why he would murder the mother of his child."

"To be honest, he didn't want kids, though he was okay with you. I mean, he'd hold you and play with you. But when Maggie told him she was pregnant, he wanted her to get an abortion."

"And my mother considered it?"

"No. Not even. She didn't believe in it. I repeated the old saying that the people who say abortion is murder need to consider that would make a blowjob an act of cannibalism." Gemma Rae's head shot back as she chuckled. "Maggie was absolutely insistent on having you."

"Did she resent him for wanting her to get rid of me?"

"She understood Shane. He didn't want his kid to see war. He'd seen what happens to kids in war. He got real riled over it." She looked at Fleur and then away quickly. "But he was never hostile to you. I heard him say only Maggie and you could make him smile."

Gemma Rae heard a knock on the door and went to answer it. Fleur scoured the room for anything providing a glimpse into the world of her mother's best friend. Her glance froze on a framed photograph. It was of her mother and Gemma Rae. Both were wearing large floral diadems on their heads. Flowers trickled down onto their foreheads. They were smiling, their cheeks pressed together. Their lips created huge smiles, filled with teeth and joy. Their clothing was outrageously colorful, and they were barefoot.

"Ms. Hamilton," Bernie Maylor said.

"Fleur, please."

"Fleur, it's so nice to see you again." He sat as Gemma Rae poured him a wine and began to fix him a sandwich. "Have more of your questions been answered?"

"Many more. I thank you both."

"Has Gemma Rae told you all the tawdry tales of commune living?"

Fleur joined in their jovial laughter. Gemma Rae gave him the peace sign and immediately flipped him the bird with the other hand. She noticed Fleur was gazing at the photo. "That was taken when we were young enough to remember what we were doing but unfortunately were too stoned to remember."

"The photo is lovely."

"I want you to take it." Gemma Rae handed it to Fleur. "Back then I was thin as a toothpick. Look at that figure. Back then," she said with a laugh and a hearty shake of her large breasts, "I had great jigglers. Silicone free! Even more to them now," she said with a naughty giggle.

Bernie added dryly, "You have more of *everything* now, Gemma Rae."

The three laughed and chatted together until Fleur glanced at her wristwatch. "I should be leaving. I'd like to get back to the hotel in time to call Abby. She has a small landscape company, so she gets up early. Daybreak, actually. And Denver time is an hour later."

After thanking Gemma Rae for dinner and the photograph, she walked with Bernie back to her hotel. They parted with kisses on the cheeks, and he gallantly tipped his beret.

Chapter 8

On her way up in the elevator, Fleur clutched the photo and her journal. She'd filled several pages in her journal with information she deemed important.

She sat on the hotel bed, wishing she didn't have to call Abby. With the wine, the full day, and the travel, she was exhausted. She pressed the button on her iPhone, then realized immediately that she'd awakened Abby. After profusely apologizing, Fleur rushed out the news of her parents.

"For god sakes, Fleur, you're wasting time chasing ghosts. Let it go. You're usually so sensible, so pragmatic." Abby's annoyed sigh puffed through the phone.

Fleur's voice became serene. "If all this had been dropped on you this morning, you would be excited to find the truth."

"No. That's the difference between us. I wouldn't give a damn about it. It's history. It's over. Gone."

"You've got your family."

"*Our* family, Fleur. My parents love you. My sibs love you. And if I hadn't had them, I wouldn't know the difference. I wouldn't give a flip about the entire thing. Let's live with what we have, not what we might have had."

Fleur's eyes closed as she fought back tears. "Aren't you curious about any of this?"

"Not really. I don't know those people and neither do you. We both knew and loved Golda. I miss her. All day today I wanted to talk with you about Aunt Golda. But you weren't here."

"Both Bernie and Gemma Rae thought highly of Golda. They said everyone here back in the late sixties loved her."

"She was an exceptional woman, of course they loved her. And she loved you. She absconded with you in order to give you a normal, sweet, kind life. These other people were blips on the screen of your life."

Sometimes, Fleur considered, Abby was too matter-of-fact. Maybe Abby didn't want unknown ghosts from the past to diminish the love Fleur had for Golda. And there was no doubt Golda had held Abby in high regard. She respected Abby. Abby's love of growing plants was phenomenal. She had a way not only with landscapes, but with all plants. She would tenderly care for plants in Fleur's minilab. The space on the second floor had been devoted to Fleur's research, but it was Abby who had the "green" touch with the plants. Fleur knew that Abby had a special way with both plants and animals. Dealing with most people, on the other hand, wasn't her strong suit. Unless she liked a person, Abby put no effort into being pleasant.

"I have questions that require answers."

"I don't understand you, Fleur."

"Don't make understanding me your life's work, damn it."

"You used to be so mellow."

"Don't interpret mellow as being marshmallow. I'm usually tranquil because I was raised by a tranquil soul. But maybe I have my father's dissatisfaction from time to time. I want to know about them so I can put myself into focus. I'm searching for something to complete me. If it upsets you, so be it."

"I applaud your effort. If I recall correctly, it was Aunt Golda who completed you. And I'm sorry you find my love so flipping restrictive. Right now, I'm in the middle of a hundred messes. I'm trying to take care of everything. And I miss you, and I'm grieving Aunt Golda. We've been apart before, when one of us has gone to a conference or whatever, but I always had Aunt Golda."

"You have *your* family."

"I love my family, but I always preferred spending time with Aunt Golda. Come home. Please?"

"It's been a long day. I want to look over Aunt Golda's letter, then I'm going to shower and try to get some sleep."

"The words made no sense to me. I'm not even sure which language was which in some cases. But I'm sure you'll know."

"I'll translate what I can. I can probably handle the French, and I have friends who are fluent in German. One of my college friends in New York is a linguist. I'll try her first if I run into problems." Fleur pulled pajamas from her case. "I'll call you in the morning."

"Fleur, when do you plan on coming home?"

"When I've finished exploring my past. When I have enough answers to my questions. I'll come home when I'm ready. Goodnight." Fleur clicked off her iPhone. She felt anger at Abby, then at her parents. She placed her computer on the small hotel desk, pulled up the e-mail, and studied the tattered old letter. Marked with brown discoloring, its paper looked fragile. She realized that Sophia had probably read it often, as the folding and unfolding had left creases in the paper.

As she read the letter, she would hone in on specific words to try to understand, as best she could, what they were saying. Even the words and phrases she quickly translated made little sense. It was indeed coded in some way. She searched for words that looked as though they might be related to one another.

Aunt Golda had written about being called a "Christ killer" by guards. They'd been loaded into the cattle cars. She'd felt the music in the beat of rhythmic steel rails as the train sped through the darkness.

Fleur wiped away a falling tear. Aunt Golda was being herded to the unknown of hell's entrance, and she was hearing music. Cramped, struggling to survive, Aunt Golda's huddled heart found sound, tempo, and song.

Glancing through both sides of the letter, Fleur realized she'd need help with the translation. Many of the phrases were disjointed. Some of what she deciphered told of sadistic, savage beatings. They terrified Golda, just as the dogs terrified her. Hunger, her aunt had written, was a torture because she remembered her mother's lovely meals.

Through the written words, Fleur was reminded that with an empty stomach, Golda would think of a traditional Jewish cookie. *Hamentaschen* was a cookie made for the holiday of Purim. Fleur relished them whenever Aunt Golda baked them. Shaped to resemble the hat worn a by villain in a holiday story, the cookies were made with various fruit fillings.

Weary, Fleur could go no further. She exited the letter and closed the laptop. After undressing, she stepped into the shower. With the water beating down, she leaned against the corner of the shower and sobbed into the washcloth.

After slipping into her nightclothes, she sat on the bed and picked up her journal, where she'd written hasty notes about her parents. At least those, unlike Aunt Golda's words, were intelligible and easy for her to understand.

Her anger at her parents was building. Not knowing what had happened was annoying her. She yearned to understand, but it seemed impossible.

According to Gemma Rae, her father had murdered her mother and then killed himself. Drug-induced murder was certainly possible. She wondered what had been the flashpoint. She also wondered if Shane was even her father. She'd begin her search in earnest in the morning.

She'd look at police records and search the Internet again for anything that might help in her quest. There must be newspaper archives on the net. Probably there were follow-up stories to the page one clipping Bernie had given her. Newspaper morgues should tell more about the killing. For whatever answers the net didn't provide, she would expand her search. No matter what, she vowed, she would get the answers she needed.

By the time Fleur succumbed to exhaustion, the night was half gone.

She slept until midmorning when the bright California sun shone in. Her eyes blinked open, and she reached across the bed for Abby. Then she realized her being in California wasn't part of a dream. Fleur had never experienced such an emotional storm. She had no idea how she could face it. For a brief moment, she wondered if she truly wanted to explore the history from which she had come.

She thought she knew about the Fleur she was. Now she wanted to investigate the history of the infant, Flower.

Chapter 9

"Good morning, Fleur," Bernie said as she entered his bookstore. "You're just in time to accompany me to Gemma Rae's on my midmorning break."

"That sounds great. Are you up to the walk? I feel badly that you escorted me all the way back to the hotel last night."

"Oh, yes. Exercise is good for my arthritis, though it does slow me considerably. Gemma Rae has delicious wheat bagels that make the trip worth it. She always saves one for me." He took his cane, pressed the beret on his head, and motioned toward the door.

Fleur flung back the door and waited for Bernie to slowly move outside. As they walked, she said, "What a beautiful autumn day."

"Your Aunt Golda always loved spring and autumn. She'd remark about the colorful flowers. She saw beauty as no other person I've ever known."

"Yes. She watched each spring for buds and for the trees to fill the landscape with leaves. And in the autumn, she watched the colors of the leaves turning. Over the different seasons, we'd collect leaves from the same trees as the colors changed." Fleur found herself wishing that Golda was with her to share the colors of this autumn. "There are so many ways I miss her."

"I'm sure. And how is your search going this morning?"

"I've been attempting to find everything I can online. This morning, I found the names of the police officers who took the call when my parents died. They're probably retired now."

"The police precinct and maybe even our county courthouse might have some documents. I wish I could be of more help, but I wasn't as involved with your parents as I might have been. We were on friendly terms, but I never knew much about their past lives. As I mentioned, Gemma Rae was Maggie's best friend, so she should be an excellent resource."

"When we talked yesterday, she gave me insight into so many things. Gemma Rae is terrific."

"Absolutely. She never ceases to be a *completely* euphoric 1960s femme fatale. And her memory is excellent. I presume she gave you some viable information?"

"Yes. In fact, I'm going to attempt to contact the families of both my mother and my father. Until the murder and suicide aspect came to light, I'd never given my history much of a thought. I figured I was blessed to be with Aunt Golda. She always believed things turn out as they're meant to be. But the murder part of it really bothers me. Having been raised by the gentlest woman in the world, I find it impossible to think I have the DNA of a killer coursing through my veins."

"Keats talks about noble natures and gloomy days in his 'A Thing of Beauty.' He says there's an endless fountain of immortal drink poured down from heaven. As individuals, we are poured through our parents. Naturally, they are of interest to us. Well, that's paraphrasing with great liberty. But I understand your desire to find your past. I'd guess that's now the part most important to you."

"For some reason I can't fathom, it *is* the most important thing in my life right now. I've put everything else on hold. Everything, and that includes my relationship. My job, my home, and a research study are imperiled."

"Do you have someone looking after things for you?"

"I do. Abby is my lover of sixteen years."

"You're lesbian?"

"Yes. Abby is taking care of our two dogs, Golda's Chihuahua named Fezzy, and what Golda referred to as her antique cat, Sugarplum, who came to us as a stray."

"How did Golda react to the news that you and Abby were together?"

"I was in my twenties when I realized I'm Sapphic. When I told Golda, she was accepting. She wanted me to be happy. She did remark that a child is a unique gift, and she hoped I might experience that gift, but it was my life to live as I saw fit. She knew all about bigotry first hand. She would have been the last one on earth to object to anything on the basis of prejudice, including the people she'd seen wearing pink triangles in the concentration camp. She was accepting of all people."

"That sounds absolutely Golda-esque."

"My first couple of flings weren't serious, so perhaps she thought I'd outgrow it. She was much more at ease about it after she met Abby. She knew it was a serious relationship, as Abby was the first woman I'd introduced to Aunt Golda. My great aunt was expecting a shameless hussy, and Abby was affable and decent. She and Golda got along so well, Abby could have been male or female and Golda would have approved. Over the years, Abby was always so good with both Golda's garden and her pets. Funny, Abby gets along far better than I do with pets, kids, and the elderly. It's only certain people she has problems with. Including me."

"Your Abby has a difficult personality?"

"Very much so. And I'm not sure why. Her family is delightful. However, over the years she's become bossy, critical, and cynical. Maybe I haven't made her life happier. I wish I had."

"And why did you fall in love with her?"

"I'm not sure. I'm even less sure now than before."

She had met Abby Vance at a conference on medicinal properties in the botanical world. It was an immediate attraction that didn't fade. Nor had it been shaken for the first decade. Then, slowly, it began to be a matter of them growing apart. This current fissure, Fleur admitted to herself, was a rift so great that they might not be able to mend it.

She took a deep breath. "If there's a poem to describe how I feel, perhaps it would be an Auden poem. I especially like one of the lines about love that says we don't know the where or the why. Well, that's me right now."

Bernie smiled. "Ah, yes. Auden's 'Law, Like Love' depicts internal questions. Poets are usually correct about love. I believe love is a law unto itself. I've never found the right woman. God knows I've looked, and sometimes been near, but the women I loved never loved me back. I've always been a rather trapped soul. I have never given my emotions free rein. Unfortunately, women and I never mixed well romantically, but they like me as a friend. I envied your father back then. Women absolutely adored him. It was more than his rugged good looks. There was a sexy broodiness about him that drove the girls crazy."

Fleur felt relief being with Bernie. He had a sensitivity about him. As they neared *Gemma Rae's Earth*, she slowed. "Bernie, I want to thank you for your help. I really appreciate it."

"I'm not certain this kind of shock from the past can be considered a help. I honestly figured that when you became an adult, Golda would explain the past to you. She was a stickler for the exactitude of reality. Perhaps it was too difficult for her."

They entered Gemma Rae's and were seated by the young barista.

"Gemma Rae is out shopping. She'll be back soon," Rolly said. He turned to Bernie. "I kept a wheat bagel back for you," he said. Addressing Fleur, he teased, "I might be able to find another one, if that's what you would like."

"I'd love one."

Fleur was glad when the coffee and wheat bagels were delivered. She'd hurried through the initial part of her morning without taking time for breakfast. The scent of the steaming hot bagel made her realize how hungry she was. She quickly slathered cream cheese over it and bit into it. Its chewiness was perfect. Suddenly it was as if her thoughts were with her Aunt Golda. Flashing before her was the girl Golda, famished and on a terrifying train ride. Startled, she dropped the bagel onto the plate.

When Bernie noticed her ignoring the bagel and coffee, he remarked, "You must eat. I know when you lose a loved one, it's difficult, but you mustn't get run down. That will just lead to you becoming ill."

"I know." She picked up the bagel and nibbled at it.

"Golda wouldn't like you becoming ill. And she wouldn't like wasting food. I recall once when I was eating a plate of pasta that was much more than I could eat. I'm not a large man, nor did I enjoy overeating. I pushed my plate away with half the serving still on it. She pushed it back in front of me and insisted I finish it."

"Yes," Fleur said. "She was a stickler for that. I was raised to take small portions, none beyond a child's capacity." She smiled briefly. "She would say that food was to be honored. Without it there could be no life." She resumed eating her bagel.

For the next half hour, Fleur interrogated Bernie. Bit by bit, she gleaned more of the story of what had happened in the lives of the young couple after they had moved into the apartment building. As soon as Bernie had finished his midmorning snack, he left Fleur to return to his bookstore.

Fleur waited to ask Gemma Rae the questions she'd written down during the previous evening. The answers would better prepare her for her next visit. Next on her agenda was an afternoon at the Haight-Ashbury police precinct. Although some of her search was to be conducted via the Internet, much would be legwork.

She'd just finished writing her "to do" list, when her phone rang. It was Abby. Knowing Abby would probably persist in pressuring her to return home, Fleur hesitated before answering.

Abby sulkily began with asking about when she would be returning. "Do you have a guess? Your deadline for the grant application is fast approaching. Your entire research project is on the line. I mean, if we're talking the end of the week before you get home, you're right up against your deadline."

"I'm just not certain, Abby. I've got to get to the bottom of this. Don't you understand, yesterday was life-changing. I need to resolve the questions I have about my family."

"I absolutely don't understand. You don't need to get it worked out. And life doesn't need to change. You're changing it. You want to work out something that two days ago meant nothing in our lives. I can't make you understand it's all irrelevant."

Fleur's jaw twitched as she attempted to suppress her anger. "It's difficult to come to terms with the fact that one of my parents was a murderer. From photos, they look to be typical hippies of the era, like a couple of kids in love."

"Killers usually look exactly like victims. Your parents got high, and they died. In life, people either contribute or destroy. Sometimes they do both. What matters is that our relationship stays intact. This decision impacts both our lives. I don't think love requires falling on a grenade for one another, but I think we owe each other some input."

"Love also requires a simple empathy for one another. Not being abusive to the other because she has a differing opinion."

"You surely can't be saying we're abusive. My company works with abused women shelters. One of the sayings is 'never be rough with a woman, or she'll think you're a man.'"

"I'm not referring to that kind of abuse. You've always been physically tender. Verbally, you attempt to batter your way through my feelings. You want me to agree with you. This time I don't. You don't seem to understand me, or what I'm going through. Maybe there are times when human beings need to be singular. We don't need to be perpetually in sync."

"Fine. I realize there's no such thing as perpetual agreement, but you're going to extremes. In your field, you chase question marks. That's part of science. You chase something with a low probability of finding a definitive answer. Surely you can see this search is probably irresolvable. You know as much as you're going to know. Your parents are dead. Come on, Fleur, you've got responsibilities back here. Now is not a good time for you to be taking off."

"You're upset because you're doing all the heavy lifting. Sorry I'm such a burden. Jeez, you can be so dictatorial."

"I'm not being a dictator in the least."

"You're being this authoritative commander," Fleur insisted.

"It's all falling apart here. One of the company SUVs broke down, and my own butch bus is showing some distress. Everyone wants their autumn cleanup done, now. Everyone needs trees planted, now. With all that's going on, I'm overwhelmed."

"I'm not going on some guilt trip over your panic. So shove your damned Saph wagon where the sun doesn't shine."

"Butch bus. And when did you find it in fashion to swear?"

"I'm angry. I'm fucking angry. Right now, I'm in the middle of a nightmare I could never have imagined. I'm concerned with uncovering my history. Not simply because it's my history, but because there was a murder. One of my parents killed my other parent. I'm searching for the truth, no matter what it requires. Is that simple enough for you?"

"I wish there was a way to get through to you. It's like you're having a nervous breakdown. If Aunt Golda was alive—"

"If Aunt Golda was here, we would both be better able to cope." Fleur closed her eyes and envisioned her sweet aunt. The diminutive woman with a halo of cottony gray hair, tender, round brown eyes, long nose, and protruding chin could fix any and all problems with a few wise words. Her eyes filled with tears. "She would understand."

"Look, I'll go back and talk with Sophia tomorrow. She was going to find the other letters. She hides things. I asked if she wanted them returned. Sophia said her daughter destroyed most of the letters between her and Aunt Golda. Her daughter claimed they made her mother too sad."

"Her daughter destroyed a survivor's letters about the concentration camp?" Fleur asked incredulously.

"That's why Sophia hid them. The daughter said they were of no use and didn't make sense. Yes, she destroyed them. That's why Sophia only has three left."

Fleur swallowed away the burning in her throat. "Good God! Does her daughter have any idea what she's done? She's thrown away history. They all should've been donated to the Holocaust Memorial Museum. It's where I think we should place any letters we get from Sophia."

"Would her daughter have any standing to dispute that?"

"They are Aunt Golda's personal property. They were written by her. They're going wherever we say. Sophia's daughter has destroyed enough."

"Maybe she didn't want her mother to have to go through continually remembering it."

"We've got to remember it. It happened."

"Fleur, I understand why you want it remembered. I don't want people forgetting, either. I'll put away this first letter in a safe spot, and I'll do everything I can to get the other letters. If Sophia has them, I'll help her find them."

"Thanks, Abby."

"Hope you come home tomorrow."

"I'm sure it won't be tomorrow."

"We can conduct a search from here. You can talk with Gemma Rae and Bernie on the phone. Please be sensible and come back."

Fleur gripped her cell phone tightly. "I've got work to do. I'm hanging up."

"You think you've got work to do—"

With a burst of anger, Fleur pressed the power button on her phone. She sat staring into her coffee cup for several moments, then shut her eyes. She felt like collapsing into a heap and crying until the last tear disappeared. She wanted desperately to talk with Golda and couldn't.

A sudden, unexpected memory appeared. Each year, cottontail rabbits made their home in Aunt Golda's backyard. Aunt Golda would scope them out every morning, saying they'd made it through the night without being attacked by a roaming fox. Spotting the little bunnies out on the grass was always a treat for both Aunt Golda and Fleur. One day, the child Fleur asked why the bunnies came to their yard. Aunt Golda had answered that the bunnies knew where they were safe.

Fleur had always felt safe within the kindness of love. Golda's best message was to cherish life, and those you loved. Fleur's search might include relearning to cherish life.

Chapter 10

Gemma Rae placed the grocery bags on the counter and instructed Rolly to put them away. After she poured herself a cup of coffee, she topped up Fleur's cup. Sitting, she gave a huge sigh. "Thinking I only needed a couple items, I didn't take my cart to tote the bags this time. Never fails—I saw more things that I needed." Her long skirt was done in Mondrian-inspired color patched squares. It purposely looked rumpled. She also wore huaraches.

"That's me, too. Abby has a shopping list and sticks to it with exacting precision."

"You look like someone's stomped you."

"My significant other, Abby, is becoming more unhappy about my quest."

"Woman. I strongly suspected you might be lesbie, but I didn't want to bring up the issue. Not that you look dykey, but I can usually tell. I get messages by watching people. People think I've got some magical power, but no. I say it's just observation, not clairvoyance."

"I wasn't hiding my sexual orientation. Most of the time I don't think it's necessary to announce it. It isn't as if I expect a straight woman to immediately tell me what she and her partner are up to in bed."

"And your partner is giving you fits now?"

"She just doesn't understand," Fleur said.

With a flip of her head, Gemma Rae inquired, "She doesn't understand this *quest,* as you call it? Or she doesn't understand you?"

"I believed she understood me, and so would've automatically understood what I'm doing and why I'm doing it."

Gemma Rae took a sip of her coffee before asking another question. "So the problem is greater than just you going on a trip?"

"Yes. Abby and I have always shared everything. We've been pleased for one another's projects. I mean, she's even working on my major plant research project. Although she isn't happy that it takes away from her business, she's doing it. Plus she's strapped down with doing all the household chores, and she's dealing with Aunt Golda's affairs."

"What's the plant project all about? Are you growing weed?"

Smiling, Fleur answered, "Weeds, but not the kind that make you high. I hope these weeds will one day make people healthier."

Gemma Rae smirked. "The smokin' kind always made me better. So what do these plants do?"

"The study concerns a parent compound called psoralen. In growing and researching multiples of psoralen-containing plants, it's possible to find the timing of the most concentrated and powerful harvest time. Peak performance, I call it. Psoralen occurs in the seeds of *Psoralea corylifolia,* in figs, celery, parsley, and even satinwood. I'm concentrating on *Ammi visnaga.*"

"I've heard of that. It's a tea used for kidney stones. Shit, that goes back to ancient Egypt and India."

"Psoralen along with UV treatments is used to cure psoriasis, eczema, and vitiligo. Also, it's been known to prevent renal crystal deposits. It's been approved for the treatment of lymphoma, so I've been trying to get a grant to continue my research studies. With the grant money, I could afford to purchase more precise technical equipment. Also, being recognized by receiving funding is of paramount importance to a researcher's credibility."

"Shit, just cut out the middleman and send patients over here for some tea. I'll mix 'em up a good dose. Toss in a few additives that will make 'em brand new." She sipped her coffee. "I have a brew for everything. I've got mood enhancers. From erectile dysfunction to having your girlfriend's sex drive heightened—my back shelves are loaded with cures."

Amused, Fleur said, "Well, sex isn't a problem in my relationship."

"Lack of sex is a huge problem in my life. Hell, lately I haven't been up to much in the sack." Gemma Rae roared with laughter. "And I can tell you that it doesn't matter to me who you sleep with. I'm not too sure your mother and I never rolled around a little. Back in those days, we grabbed the nearest to us, so maybe Maggie and I did dabble a time or two. Given unresolved sexual tension blended with frivolity and grass, maybe we did. Horniness amuses nymphets, I guess. As I said before, we didn't have a script on the commune."

"Your mission was freedom and sexual release," Fleur said with a good-natured laugh.

"You bet. We left you a legacy. We were the great *freedom for all* subculture. Everyone talks about drugs and psychedelics. In fact, we used to call Haight-Ashbury district the Haight-Hashbury district. So, yeah, it was about drugs. And *love*. The Summer of Love in 1967 was when your mother and I really rocked out. Flower power."

"Is that where she got my name?"

"Nope. An old Native American custom was to name a kid the first thing a woman saw after giving birth. Your mother heard about it, so thought she would try. After you were born, she said the first thing she saw was the flower Shane had stuck in her hair. When you were being born, the flower dislodged and fell down into her face. When you came squalling out, she opened her eyes and a flower was what she saw."

Smiling, Fleur said, "I'm grateful she didn't first see a flapping umbilical cord."

Gemma Rae agreed. "You might have ended up with a very unorthodox name. We were revolutionaries. We fought middle-class values so everyone could come out. Gays included."

"I've heard that before. If not for the hippies, lesbians and gays would have had a more difficult time."

"I can tell you one thing. The fifties were some pretty damned *rancid* years. We were trapped in a moment of time that was grim. It was restrictive for everyone. We all had to revolt. Sure we passed out acrimonious pamphlets, we shouted vulgarities, but we also read Thoreau and Gandhi. We wanted to battle outdated morality and ethical constraints with more than flower power."

"My father was really a serious demonstrator, right?"

"Both Maggie and Shane. As I said before, Shane was a terrific orator. He cut a figure. His long hair was usually pulled back and tied with a bandana. And his golden-colored mustache would shine bright in the sun."

"Was he arrested often?"

"Often! He wasn't afraid of the cops. He even called them 'storm troopers for the plutocrats.' He was gutsy. The people listening to his speeches were enthralled. One time he got run in… he tells the cop to pucker up while he lowered his pants so the officer could kiss his ass." Gemma Rae's loud chortle continued until she choked and coughed. "Good times."

"What did they arrest him for that time—indecent exposure?"

"Disturbing the peace was his charge of choice, but it might have been for showing ass. He got right up in the cop's face. He said there wasn't any peace to disturb. Hundreds of United States soldiers were being killed every day. What the fuck was the cop talking about? Peace!"

"What did my mother do when he was arrested?"

"Cheer him on. Hit at the cops. Then go bail him out."

"She must have truly loved him."

"Love can go wrong." Gemma Rae fluffed her spinny skirt and pulled at the base of her granny vest. "Has your love for Abby gone wrong?"

"We have differing opinions, but there's more to it. We were having problems in our relationship before. I wanted to split. Aunt Golda loved Abby. She knew Abby loved me. But Abby is too controlling. Maybe now that Aunt Golda is gone, it would be the right time for Abby and me to take a break."

Gemma Rae shrugged. "There's never a good time for a break if you love someone. Golda was damned observant. I can't imagine she didn't realize something was up. Are the problems between you and Abby the kind you break up over?"

"Abby was vehemently opposed to my coming here. Had it been her family, I would have been supportive. She thinks this is a waste of time. Aunt Golda always encouraged me to follow my instincts." As if allowing the thought to marinate, she went silent.

"What did Golda say about your lesbie desires? Or did you tell her?"

"Bernie asked the same thing earlier this morning when I mentioned it to him. I told him Aunt Golda was fine with Abby and me. Her only objection was that I probably wouldn't be a mother. I've always been too busy to entertain the idea of having children. They weren't the first thing on my agenda. Maybe I'm like my mother in that regard."

"It may seem your mother wasn't interested in you, but everyone was so wasted so much of the time. The commune wasn't a good place for kids. Maggie did love you, though. Shane probably did, too. Drugs fuck people up. And when you're on some enhancer, you're way different."

For several introspective moments, Fleur covered her eyes. "You think we really change with circumstances?"

"Sure. Life changes us. It rearranges us. That's what I think. In retrospect, I've damned sure changed."

"So when one of my parents killed the other, and then themself, it was only a bad change?"

"Shane was really goofed out on drugs and booze. He had terrible flashbacks from the war. He could be normal one minute, and the next he'd be raging. Your mother went on head trips to escape memories from her terrible upbringing. Life changed them. And finally, it wasn't in a good way."

"I'd like to have the case reopened to find out exactly how they died. I'd like to know for certain. Forty years ago there weren't as many scientific detection mechanisms available to law enforcement. With current technology, maybe I can find out more about the killings."

"Cops are probably too busy with today's assignments to pull up a really old cold case. You can try, but I bet that's what they'll say."

"I'll get a private detective then. Maybe I can find an investigator to go back through the evidence."

"If you have money to toss away, that's a great idea. But it doesn't, and won't, alter the fact that your parents are dead."

"I don't want it to end there. I want to know who was the victim and who committed suicide. I need to know."

"Everyone's capable of doing things they'd never believe. When I look back at my past, I shudder. I've been on hell's roster a time or two. The next day, it was a love-in. And if I had the choice, I'd go around again for a second chance at the golden ring. I enjoyed the hippie life on the commune."

"What was it like?"

"It was pandemonium. Hell, the place we stayed in on the outskirts of town was a dilapidated old 1930s vintage motel. Paint was nearly chipped off, but it had been a muddied up coral-color on the outside. That paint was dulled down to nearly beige. The windows had been boarded up, but we pulled the damned boards off and in we went. There were about a dozen rooms with crumbling walls and rickety floors. The place was a ramshackle mess, in tumbledown condition. We threw sleeping bags on the floors. There would always be a transistor radio going. Sometimes we'd have musicians doing their thing."

"Amazing. How many people lived there?"

"Dozens. When the rooms were brimming full, there were tents for the spillover. Some kids bunked in their cars, or in the buses. We made do. It was like camping. We'd put a bunch of pots on campfires for eats. Whatever we had handy would become that day's stew." Gemma Rae laughed. "Cheap food, but it filled us up. And they brought a water wagon in. We didn't have water hooked up. We'd take our showers in wooden stalls. The crappers were whatever outhouses the guys would build."

"And what did you do for electricity, lighting?"

"For a while we had limited electricity. One of the guys piggybacked a long cord. Rigged it up nice. But something blew and nearly burned the place down. When the cops boarded it back up, we had to sleep on the streets, but we always went back to the motel. We always returned. Even when it rained, it provided some shelter, even though there were leaks in the roof. That actually helped keep the dust down, but fuck, it was like a wet sty. I didn't like that."

"Why did you leave?"

"The city bulldozed it. After they leveled it, we all went to squat in abandoned houses and tent cities. Anywhere we could find is where we stayed."

"A bunch of people in a shabby place, doing without. I don't get it."

"There was color, there was music, and lotsa dope. Everyone got off on not being materialistic. Hippies became obsolete. I couldn't go on being a flower child after I'd lost the old bloom. And age made me materialistic. I found out I had to get going and produce pottery. I had to find an outlet, so I got this storefront. There's a little plot of land behind where I have my kiln. It's kept me going over the years."

Fleur chuckled. "Golda taught me to make certain I had enough for the basics. She didn't want me to do without. But she wasn't materialistic as much as she was concerned we'd get by. She had insurance from Uncle Walter. She spent some money purchasing a house for us in Denver. The rest was set aside to assist me with my college expenses. Although it took much more for my advanced degree, scholarships helped along the way."

"The old girl never spent the money on herself?"

"No, she really didn't. And any surplus was used for our vacations. Winters, we would plan our summer vacations. It was fun because we sort of traveled twice then—once as we planned it and once actually traveling. Over the years, she took me to many countries. Travel enriched my life."

"When I knew her, she spent her money on those around her. Any nest egg from lessons usually went to helping us hippies. Early on in her career, she'd spent a few years as a concert pianist. Could have had an elite student list and made mega bucks. She insisted on working only with brilliant students, many of them poor, or sometimes with less-talented people who were enthralled with music, like Maggie. After Walter died, Golda came down to the Haight to give lessons practically for free. And almost always free to the kids. She was so good to us all and particularly to your mother. Maggie thought Golda hung the moon."

"My mother truly loved Golda?"

"Like a mom she never had. When Maggie began taking singing lessons, she became dependent on Golda for day-to-day needs—food, basic necessities. And encouragement, naturally. Maggie fancied herself a great singer, in the style of Janis Joplin."

"Golda told me my mother was a marginal singer." Fleur laughed. "I could tell she was being kind. She would say my mother wanted to sing like Joplin, but unfortunately she sang like Scott Joplin."

"Maggie had great aspirations, but she had a *shit* voice. Of course, Janis Joplin never claimed to have a terrific voice, but she did all right. Did Golda teach you music?"

"She taught me piano, and I still play. Unfortunately, I must have inherited my mother's lack of musical talent. I'm what you would call a mediocre pianist, but I did learn the structure of music and I have a love of music because of Golda. Certainly the discipline of learning helped me in my career."

"Golda could tickle those ivories," Gemma Rae said. "She had me in tears one time when she played Chopin. I didn't know I liked classical music, but Chopin got to me."

"She played with so much emotion. Even when she played farcical music, it was with her entire heart."

Gemma Rae peered into her empty cup. "What a heart she had. Well, her spirit is still with us and always will be. Golda has a wonderful essence." She stood. "I'll get us topped up on coffee."

Gemma Rae eased behind the counter. Fleur watched Rolly give a quick, playful shriek when the ex-hippie passed by him. "She just loves goosing me," he stage-whispered to Fleur.

When Gemma Rae returned, she poured coffee from the stainless-steel pot she brought with her. "What a moaner," she teased. "Do you ever goose Abby?"

"No."

"Maybe you should." Gemma Rae playfully wiggled her eyebrows. "I know you're probably both busy, but now and then a little ass grab is good."

Fleur felt her face burn with a blush. "I suppose one of our problems might be that we no longer make it fun."

"Golda enjoyed frivolity," Gemma Rae said.

"Think she would have approved of my being here?"

"I think she would have approved of whatever your decision turned out to be."

Fleur thought of Golda, and how she missed her. "Aunt Golda was my family, and I'm so grateful for her, but there's a force inside me. I want to know what happened to make one of my parents kill the other. So I'm thinking I should try to locate an investigator to help me."

"When you check out the police records, maybe you can find someone who knows a good detective. I've never been on that side of the street. I almost got busted for drugs once, but most of the time when I was drugging, there were so many of us that cops turned a blind eye. The jails weren't large enough to hold a nation of young people."

"Did my mother ever get arrested?"

"No, only your father got hauled in. Shane's temper usually got him tossed in the slammer, but it was never for anything serious. Which was amazing, because as I said before, your father was a real protester. He never missed an antiwar rally. He'd give speeches and usually end up in the cooler. Maggie was protesting, too. I can't imagine how she eluded the pigs, but she did. Shane, on the other hand, could rile the peaceniks up. The badges hated him."

"Maybe someone else killed both my mother and father."

"I don't think so. The door had been locked from the inside. They had to get the superintendent to open it up."

"Okay, what if someone had a key? Maybe it was given to one of their hippie friends?"

"Shane was extremely paranoid over security. And Maggie wouldn't have given anyone a key. You were there with them most nights."

"What about previous tenants? Maybe one of the occupants lost the key or had a duplicate made."

"An intruder with a key? Naw. Who breaks in when two people are fighting? And Shane and Maggie were in the middle of a shouting match. Bernie heard them screaming. It was their voices. Entry by a stranger doesn't make sense. Even if it were an intruder, why lock the place back up? And nothing was taken, if it was a break-in."

"I'm probably just trying to make an excuse for them and what happened."

"Wish I could help with this conspiracy theory, but I can't. It's pretty cut and dried. There was fighting. Voices were identified as Maggie's and Shane's. A gun fired a couple of times. Fast. Boom, boom. According to Bernie, he heard it. He was directly above their apartment. He quickly ran downstairs to Shane and Maggie's door, and it was locked. So he went across the hall to alert the super. Bernie had to wake him in order to get the door opened up. Someone had called the cops because of the disturbance, so cops were coming in. There wouldn't have been time for someone to have exited. They would have had to run down a long hall. But check with Bernie. He can describe it to you."

"It all probably happened exactly as it was reported, but my next stop is to make an attempt to glean any info I can from old police records." Fleur mulled over her thoughts for a moment, then said, "I bet you think I'm crazy, attempting to find anything on this."

"If you're crazy, you come by it honestly. Maggie always used to say she did nutty things because she came from a long line of crazies."

Fleur joined in Gemma Rae's laughter. "I might not have gotten only her good genes. A few crazy ones might have gotten through." Fleur slowly stood and pushed away from the table. She felt a weariness that she found difficult to express. "A few *tired* crazy genes."

"Crazy isn't always bad. It sure as hell got me through lots of years. That, a tumbler of wine, and a little grass, always made me happy," she reminisced. "Maggie and I used to smoke pot in this little wood-and-brass carb pipe. I wonder where it went. I was probably smoking a little wacky tobaccy and lost it."

Amused, Fleur teased, "If you were smoking, wouldn't it be difficult to lose the pipe?"

"Nope. You could lose anything if it was a good lid. Ever toke?"

"Before Abby and I were together, I went to a party with the first woman I dated. There was pot, as well as peer pressure. I tried smoking, but it wasn't successful for me, which was fine. I was in college at the time. I couldn't have afforded a habit and a degree."

"You sound too sensible to be either Maggie's or Shane's kid, but they might have changed had they aged. Some did. "

"And some didn't have the chance to find out if they would change or not."

Gemma Rae twisted her coffee cup around several times. "We'll never know. But you turned out great."

"Thanks. I was always frightened of letting Aunt Golda down. After graduate school, I immediately plunged into my profession. And soon Abby was in my life." With a grin she added, "You don't suppose I'm too old to become a hippie?"

"That ship has sailed. Although there are still drugs around, you missed the big rush by decades."

"Ever regret your wild hippie ways?"

"Yeah. A couple of regrets. I'd like to be able to remember more of the good times." Her voice softened. "And I wouldn't mind being able to forget the bad ones. Your mom was a great kid. I loved her." Her eyes became moist. Her lids pressed out tears. As they rolled down her cheeks, Gemma Rae enunciated carefully, "I don't think she would have killed him. *I don't.* She couldn't even bring herself to kill an ant. And I don't think she would have killed herself. It would have meant leaving you behind."

"But she left me behind when she got high."

"No. She left you with Golda."

Chapter 11

"That's really trying to avoid the rush! Let me see if I have this straight." The police records clerk nearly leaned over the counter. "You want to see the casebook on a forty-year-old murder, slash, suicide? With all due respect, are you joking?"

She was a short, portly woman whom Fleur guessed might be in her mid to late thirties. Lois Trujillo looked at Fleur with an impatient sidelong glance.

"Look, this room is filled with people who want information on cases that happened last week, or yesterday. And you want access to information about what is not only a cold case, but a frozen-solid case."

It had been noon when Fleur approached the police records department. She should have made it her first stop, because they were very busy. She could feel her face flushing, and her eyes smarting with tears.

"I'm sorry, Ms. Trujillo. I only found out about it a couple days ago," Fleur said, examining the woman's name badge. "It's important I find out about this case. The young people I'm inquiring about were my parents. I've been told their deaths were a murder and a suicide. I always believed they died in an auto crash. I flew here from Denver to find the truth. I'm desperate to know about the crime. I realize I'll need to hire a PI, but I'll also need the records on the case." She looked imploringly at the clerk. "Their names are Shane Bradley and Margaret, or maybe Maggie, Heywood."

Lois's demeanor suddenly shifted, and her expression softened. The woman peered into Fleur's face and then patted her hand. "I'm sorry. If it was family, I'd want to know, too."

She pulled out a sheet of blank paper and wrote down a name and number. "My gentleman friend is a forensic investigator with the coroner's department. He works in the lab here. His name is Paul Salvador. He doesn't usually take a case unless the prosecutor won't reopen the case and Paul thinks maybe he can help. He's exactly what you need, a forensic investigator. Paul can maybe check some things for you." She typed the names of Fleur's parents into her computer.

"Thank you."

"Oh, here we go. Howie Schultz was the lead detective. He's nearing retirement. You might want to check with him. I don't know what files would be available, or if they even exist. He hates to reopen a case after a year or two. Four decades is way past his crime sell-by date. But he may be able to help you. Go to the fourth floor and ask for Lt. Schultz."

Fleur profusely thanked Lois Trujillo for her assistance and took the elevator up to the fourth floor, where she found the office of Lt. Howard Schultz.

"My name is Fleur Hamilton. Lois Trujillo told me you might be able to help me with a case," Fleur said as she shook his hand. "It's a very cold case, I realize, but there are things I'd like to know."

When they were both seated, Schultz took a legal tablet from his desk drawer. "And I worked the case?"

"Yes. A murder-suicide. You were the lead detective. Forty years ago. 1970. My parents were Margaret Heywood and Shane Bradley. They were in their early twenties."

His eyes narrowed. "Hippie kids. I remember thinking that they were about my age. It was one of my first murder cases. They were both so young. I kept thinking what a waste their deaths were. Ms. Hamilton, how can I help you?"

"I have so many questions. I'd like to see any official records about the crime."

She sat back in the chair as he picked up his telephone.

"I want everything we have on the Heywood and Bradley case. Circa 1970. We filed it as a homicide and suicide, but the case was never closed because there was no proof of which was the perpetrator. The evaluation forms showed both were killed by near contact shots. And both had gunpowder stippling."

When he'd hung up, Fleur asked, "Do you know for certain it was a murder and suicide? And I'd like to know which was believed to have been the killer."

"As my memory serves me, we leaned in the direction of Bradley being the shooter, since it was his gun. He was the one everyone suspected. But the scene was compromised because they must have struggled with the gun and their blood was commingled, as were their prints. According to the superintendent and one of the renters, the door had been locked from the inside. They were entering as we got there. Windows, also locked from the inside. There was no forced entry, and there was nothing missing. Also, there was a history of the couple fighting. Back then, drugs, sex, and rock and roll added up to violence. And they were smack dab in the middle of it. That's why we concluded it was a murder-suicide."

"My Aunt Golda told me the obvious isn't always as it seems."

"She was right. She kidnapped you right under our eyes. Back in those days, we didn't have time to be quite as thorough. I only met her once. She looked innocent enough to me. Both the renter and the super stated she was either your grandmother or great aunt, I can't recall exactly. But I remember during the interview with Golda Hamilton, the baby—you—started crying. She went into the bedroom to quiet you and brought you out. You clung to her neck and seemed completely happy with her. I had no suspicion you didn't belong with her. Anyway, she said she hadn't heard a thing because she was playing music loudly. She was visibly shaken, but that was understandable, considering that her nephew had just died. I remember thinking the baby wouldn't have a mom and dad. But the other renter, Bernie, Bernie… something or other, kept saying Golda would take care of you."

"She did what she thought best under the circumstances. She raised me with love and kindness. The fact that she kept it from me was probably to shield me from the pain. But now I want to know which of my parents killed the other and anything else I can find out about the circumstances."

"I'll see what I can do to locate what might be left of the evidence. Back then there weren't the sophisticated ways of examining a crime scene, though the outcome might not be any different. The investigation was closed because it had to have been one of them. It's pretty conclusive when the door is locked from the inside."

"Someone else might have had a key."

"I asked about that. The super had a key and claimed no one else had one. There wasn't anywhere to go on the case."

"I'd like to see it opened up again. At least, could I get a private detective to look at the evidence?"

"We aren't crazy about being hassled by amateur sleuths."

"The man I'm thinking of is on your team. Lois Trujillo gave me his name and number." She opened the folded paper. "Paul Salvador. He's an investigator in the coroner's office. He works in the forensic lab."

"Paul. Yes, he's one of our better team members. We don't object to him doing a little moonlighting." Schultz grinned and added, "He knows where the bodies are buried. You know, police need a little gallows humor to keep going."

Fleur smiled. "Yes, humor helps. I feel as though I'm Sisyphus."

"I'll mention the case to a few people around here to see if we can't assist you in rolling that rock up the hill. We may not have any conclusive answers for you, and there might not be any to be found. Paul Salvador is a good man, and he can coordinate with Lois Trujillo for information. Salvador should be on break or about to go on break. I'll phone down to the coroner's office and tell him to expect you. Take the elevator to the basement floor and turn right. And good luck, Ms. Hamilton."

"Thank you, Lieutenant." Fleur hastened to the basement and turned to the right. She spotted a huge block of a man, who directed her to a waiting room.

"I'm Paul Salvador. Howie called. You're trying to find out about a murder?"

His dark eyes and face were serious, yet there was a teddy bear's tenderness in his stance. Incongruous as it might have seemed, given his gruff demeanor, Fleur had a good feeling about him.

"Because it was forty years ago, I'm not sure much can be done. Lt. Schultz said he has no grounds to reopen the case, but he would be cooperative. Finding another suspect or additional information would change his decision not to revisit the case. Chances are probably slim to none, I realize, but I need to know."

"If there's anything, we'll come up with it," Salvador assured her. "I'm relatively certain there'll be crime scene photos and autopsy film. As for the evidence, it'll take some digging. Our vaults are in an old building we use for storage. I'll send an intern to dig out what there might be. Once I get a chance to look at what we've got, I can check the trajectory of the bullets. I'll try to do some computer simulations to figure out who was the shooter and who was the vic. Give you some answers."

"I appreciate your help. This entire thing has been a bombshell dropped into my life."

"The thing about murder with suicide, the police don't think there's a perp on the loose. There's no one in danger, so no big push to investigate. But let me check things out. I'll stay after my shift is over. I'll call you if I find anything."

Fleur wrote her name and cell phone number on a sheet of paper from her journal, and she took down his number. As she went out onto the street, she felt less alone.

Back at the hotel, she opened her computer to check for messages. She'd sent Golda's letter to her linguist friend. The return e-mail sorted out some of the details of Aunt Golda's letter. As Fleur searched for meanings, she realized that, as with what words she'd already translated, the rest was nonsensical. Words were not in sequence.

When she saw that Abby had phoned, she returned the call. "Abby, I didn't get back to you earlier because I was talking with the investigator that had handled the case." Excited, she reported, "And I hired a detective who actually works for the city."

"Why are we spending money on a private eye? How about the police? Can't they give you information?"

"It's their prerogative to revisit the case or not. If there isn't any new evidence, the coroner's verdict stands. It's imperative that I have someone to find new evidence."

"You're going to spend money on this? Remember, next year is going to be a struggle if you don't get the grant money. Which you can expect to lose if you haven't turned in the report on your study."

"We've got savings. I've got savings." Silence was becoming more frequent in conversations between them. Fleur added with an apologetic tone, "And at least I won't need to pay a linguist to translate the letter. My friend did it gratis."

"Did it help?"

"Somewhat. But it still isn't making sense. Aunt Golda and Sophia did have some sort of code. And it doesn't seem like anything except a smattering of words all crumpled together. Nothing I can make sense of. Some phrases appear to be very idiomatic."

"Can you send me photos of the translations you have? Maybe I can work on it."

"You're already busy." Fleur's words were strained. "And I'm tired of hearing how overworked you are. Did you stop by to see Sophia before going home?"

"I'm at my office now. I'll stop by on my way home. If she has the other letters, I'll do the photo thing and send them to you."

"Thank you. Tell her I'm thinking of her, and thank her for the one letter she gave us. That may encourage her to produce more. Do you think she would confide the code for unraveling the letter?"

There was a moment's pause. "That would depend entirely on her state of mind, as well as on her willingness to share their secrets. I'll try to get her talking. Meanwhile, just send me the letter with translations superimposed, and I'll see if I can work anything out."

"Thanks, Abby. I appreciate your help."

"I can't promise I can solve the mystery."

"I was thanking you for everything else." Fleur reworded her thought. "For what you're doing around our house and for everything you do."

"I miss you, Fleur. Because you're determined to stay there, I have some spare time late at night when I can scan the words. I used to be pretty good at unscrambling words. Games, but when I was a kid, I wasn't bad at it."

"I'm sure you were good at it."

"Don't be condescending."

Fleur opened her computer top and pulled up the image of the letter. "I only meant that it was something I hadn't realized about you."

"It sounded like a putdown. Just send me the revised copy."

"I'm doing it now." She heard the phone snap to silence.

Fleur reexamined the fragmented text. There were references to the first days when Sophia and Aunt Golda entered the concentration camp. Over and over, they were called Christ killers. That seemed to be the first of the things that had frightened young Golda. It was another means the German guards had of inflicting fear. A young girl probably would not have recognized the psychology behind it. But when Aunt Golda wrote it in a letter to her good friend, she would have been painfully aware of the Nazis' need to be feared.

The word "atrocious" was found in sentences that also included scratching bedbugs, lice, crying in bed, unavoidable violence, and humiliation. Another word repeated often was "disgusting," which was found in the vicinity of their diet of soup and other food references.

The internment camps were known for using starvation as one way of controlling the masses. Fleur understood that sadistic tactic. The people would become too sick to be combative. There was also the prisoners' fear of actually being murdered.

Aunt Golda had breathed in death from the incinerators. *She knew*, Fleur thought as her eyes filled. *Even in her youth, she knew she was imperiled. As was her entire tribe.*

Fleur wanted to stop looking at the letter. It was as if she was peering into evil more terrible than she could have imagined. But Aunt Golda had been forced to live it. The least Fleur could do was to go in search of the story.

Chapter 12

Fleur stopped for a late lunch at a small neighborhood restaurant. As she sipped mocha coffee and ate an avocado-and-seafood salad, she considered her original decision to fly to California. Although she seemed to be making some progress, she wondered if it was worth it. Abby was right, it wasn't necessary. After pressing the number for Abby's cell, she closed her eyes. This quest was causing more problems between them. Fleur wondered if perhaps there might be a final contentious conversation ahead. They were probably both aware of that danger. Fleur certainly was.

For the last couple of years, she'd felt the potential for one of them walking away. To avoid arguments, Fleur often compromised or surrendered. She felt trounced, defeated. When she'd confided her dissatisfaction to Aunt Golda, Golda had told her "all relationships go through traumatic growing pains."

"Abby, sorry to interrupt you, I just wanted to talk a minute."

"Listen." Abby's words rushed out. "I've been looking up some things. I found Margaret's family by searching for Margaret's birth certificate. Maggie's mother's name was Loretta. Her father was listed as unknown. I checked Loretta's marriage licenses. For a while she used her maiden name of Heywood, then it appears she went through a string of divorces. I had to follow those to find the obit. Loretta died when she was fifty-two. She had three children—Dennis, now fifty-nine; Stephanie, forty-seven; and your mother. There was no Stephanie Heywood in the San Francisco phone directory, so I assumed that she had married or moved. I have a couple of numbers in the area for a Dennis Heywood. The first one I'll give you is the most likely, age-wise."

Fleur took out her journal and began to write down the information as Abby read the numbers. "Thanks, Abby. You're a good detective. I'm sorry about this—"

"If I help, you'll be able to get back here sooner. Maybe you can save your experiments and get your grant. But I still don't think this pursuit of yours is necessary."

Fleur's heart tumbled. Just when she was beginning to believe that Abby understood her, the good will was crushed. "What's important to me," she said, her words purposely spoken softly, "is to find out about my past. It's as if I *need* to discover which of them committed the crime."

"Have you ever considered it might have been a double suicide? Like Romeo and Juliet. One shot themself while the other struggled with them for the gun, then when the first went down, out of shock, love, whatever, the other shot him or herself."

"It's a possibility, but Gemma Rae believes it couldn't have been Maggie."

"Gemma Rae sounds like a real character. I called her earlier. I asked her to please tell you to return my call if she were to see you. I didn't want to try your cell in case you were in the middle of a meeting."

"Gemma Rae is terrific. She's a true relic of the hippie era. And I like Bernie, as well. I'll take their photos with my phone and send them to you." She paused. "Oh, and I talked with the investigator with the coroner's office again. He checked the files and agrees it looks like information might be available to further the case."

"Fleur, this sounds expensive."

"We keep hitting the same impasses we've reached before. I'll deal with the expenses." Fleur disliked bringing up the funds Aunt Golda had left to her. Money had always been shared equally between her and Abby. Spending a large sum was done by mutual agreement. "We have the money."

"I'm trying to be as patient as possible under the circumstances. It isn't helping to have you start up with the fact that I haven't been to charm school and wouldn't have passed a single course if I had, but I'm attempting to help you."

"Thank you for assisting me. I appreciate it. I do." Wanting to change the subject, she asked, "Have you eaten lunch yet?"

There was a laugh before Abby answered, "It's not likely I'd go without a meal. And have you eaten?"

"Late, but I'm having something now."

Abby snickered. "I figured you wouldn't be bitching on a full stomach. Keep eating."

"When I think of Aunt Golda and the camp, how hungry she must have been, I can barely swallow." Fleur spoke slowly. "It just breaks my heart to see the words she wrote." She gazed down at the food resting on her fork tines.

"I know what you mean. It brings the worst home when I see some of the situations she recorded. But she'd want us to keep up our strength. You need to eat." There was a brief silence before she continued. "Speaking of letters, I'll do what I can on the Sophia letters front. But the success of talking with her is always a toss-up."

Fleur picked up her fork and jabbed at a piece of tomato. "I know she's difficult, but the other letters would be a treasure trove. They just would."

"I know, babe. It would be like resurrecting Aunt Golda's past. You do know how much I loved her?"

"Yes. I know we're both frazzled right now. Everything in our life is hitting us at once. Losing her, finding the letters, and the new knowledge that's come into my life are all creating a great deal of pressure. And the research project hanging over my head is monumental." She wanted desperately to add that Abby's attitude was also weighing on her. "Everything."

"It isn't easy. I'm impacted by it all, too. Do you think Aunt Golda was holding our relationship together?"

"We were polite to one another around her."

"Yes," Abby agreed. "Out of respect to her love of tranquility, we did temper some of our rough times." Her chuckle broke the conversation. "And usually we forgot what we were bickering about by the time we got home."

Fleur thought about how long it had been since she'd heard Abby laugh. Aunt Golda encouraged laughter. With Golda around, spats were converted to jokes. "Her demeanor made us more cognizant of being kind to one another. She made everything better. Now we don't have that."

"Do you think we'll survive?" Abby asked.

"Maybe." Fleur said slowly, honestly.

"Hey, I meant to mention this earlier. Make sure you let the detective know there's a cap on what you can spend—"

"I'm not concerned. I've got to take off now. Bye." She rapidly tapped the button to end the conversation. As quickly, she pecked in the telephone number Abby had felt most optimistic about. "Is Dennis Heywood there?" she asked.

"Speaking."

"My name is Fleur Hamilton. I'm searching for relatives of Margaret Heywood. She died in 1970."

There was a long pause, and then he asked cautiously, "Why are you looking?"

"I'm her daughter."

"Look, we aren't wealthy people. No inheritance. No heirlooms. She was killed in a scandal. It had nothing to do with us."

"I'm not looking for money or any relationship. I have questions I would like answers to."

"I'm not getting myself involved in this."

"Your younger sister, Stephanie. Is there a way I can reach her?"

"She married a man named Joe, with the last name of Pierce. That's all I know. We weren't close. She was only seven when Maggie died. Just before that, her father took her and raised her. We didn't have the same fathers. None of us did. I don't even know if Stephanie's alive."

"I'll try to find out. Would you like me to let you know if I find her?"

"Naw. Hell, our family was shit. No good memories. I've spent a lot of years trying to forget everything and everyone. Got it?"

The phone connection ended abruptly.

After arriving back at her hotel room, Fleur opened her small laptop and began searching for either Stephanie or Joseph Pierce. She found a J.M. Pierce living near San Francisco. She dialed the number. When a woman answered, Fleur spoke as calmly as she could. "Is this Stephanie?"

"It is. If you're selling something—"

"I'm looking for relatives of Margaret Heywood."

"Maggie? I'm Maggie's younger sister. But why would you be looking for Maggie? She died decades ago."

"Yes. But before she died, she gave birth. I'm her daughter."

After a gasp, Stephanie said, "You're Flower?"

"Yes. Fleur Hamilton. I'm trying to find out more about my parents. And about what happened to them."

"I wish I could help you, but I was so young when it happened. I certainly remember my big sister. She was so nice to me. Always brought me beads and headbands and always sang to me." A sob broke from the woman's throat. "Are you here in Frisco?"

"Yes. I flew in from Denver. I recently discovered my parents hadn't died in an auto accident as I'd been told. I came here to find out about them. I'd love to meet with you to talk about Maggie." Remembering Dennis's suspicions, she quickly added, "I don't want anything more than information about my mother."

"Of course. There's a restaurant called the Silver Menu. It's between downtown and where I live. Maybe tomorrow at noon would be good for you? I'll bring my daughter to meet you."

"Lovely. I'll be there." She gave Stephanie her cell number and hung up.

It was a moment before the significance of the phone call sank in. She would be meeting bloodline family members. She would be meeting her aunt and her cousin. Seeing them, she could look for any physical similarities. Although Abby couldn't understand, or refused to understand, Fleur knew she was doing far more than dabbling in her past. She was coming to know it. Her mother's family was now tangible.

She'd believed she was part of the Hamilton tribe, even when she hadn't known Walter Hamilton. She felt she was forever a part of Golda, yet she discovered they weren't related by blood. Now, on the journey of finding out more about her great aunt stand-in of forty years, she realized she felt more Jewish than English, or her mother's heritage. It was how she felt inside that defined her.

Chapter 13

After finishing lunch, Fleur decided to walk over to Gemma Rae's to tell her the news. As she strolled, she called Abby in an attempt to smooth over their problems. They'd once prided themselves on maintaining their relationship, now it was turning into some confusing conflict with one another.

In a brief conversation, Abby related that she'd been searching the Bradley families in New York. She found them too numerous and needed a general area to look in and a first name. Fleur promised she would try to find where Shane had lived in New York and also any names she could. Gemma Rae might be able to help run down the Bradley family.

Gemma Rae waved her in. "Good to see you, Fleur. Your Abby called."

"I just spoke with her. She said she'd talked with you. Also said you sounded nice. She had some phone numbers to give me. I located my mother's sister, and I'm having lunch with her tomorrow."

"That's great. Have a seat, and I'll bring you coffee." After she sat, Gemma Rae said, "So you found little Stephanie? That's her name, right? Stephanie. I remember meeting her once. Little speck of a thing, but she resembled Maggie. She had the same large eyes and smile but not the same hair. We'd gone to pick up some of Maggie's mail and things. Her mother wanted her to clear her belongings out of her house. She said if Maggie wanted her trinkets and threads, she'd better get them."

"Abby found out Maggie's mother, Loretta, died when she was fifty-two."

"Amazing the old witch breathed her way to fifty."

"What was Loretta like?"

"Like a damned bitch warmed up and amplified. A hussy on steroids. Undistinguished appearance, mind you. She was small, always spouting off, and thought she was the world's greatest whore. And she must have been, because men sniffed around her on a fulltime basis. She had the gall to call Maggie a tramp for having a kid out of wedlock. Maggie screamed back about how she and Shane took their own vows. Anyway, Maggie promised little Stephanie she would bring you by to see her the next week. By then you were probably six months or so. I don't know whether or not she ever did go by."

"I'll ask Stephanie tomorrow. Since you've met her, would you like to come?"

"I barely met her. She was a little kid and probably wouldn't remember me. She thought the world of Maggie, you could tell. Anyway, thanks for the invite, but maybe some other time. It will be a wonderful get-together for you. What about the brother?"

"Dennis."

"Yes. Abby mentioned his name. The minute she said 'Dennis,' I remembered it. But I couldn't recall whether his last name was the same. Those kids had various dads, I recall. Old Loretta must not have jotted down who it was that she was bonking in her daily reminder book. 'Dennis the Menace,' that's what Maggie called him."

"I did reach him. He didn't want to be involved with anything to do with family. He did tell me Stephanie's married name."

"Good of him. The prick. I met him a couple times. Dennis, that's right. Dennis. You're not missing anything by not knowing him. Maggie couldn't stand him. She said he was the biggest creep who ever broke wind. I thought he was an ape knockoff."

"My mother's family sounds so unloving."

"They were. Maggie felt our hippie friends were much more family than her birth family. I suppose we all shared a camaraderie."

"I always felt as though Golda was my mother and Sophia was my favorite aunt. I don't believe I ever felt anything lacking in my small family."

"There's a theory that you don't miss what you don't know, or something like that. I'm glad Golda was there for you. Good old Golda was one of a kind."

"Knowing her was wonderful, of course. I rarely gave my parents a second thought and probably wouldn't be thinking about knowing them now. The murder is what throws me, maybe haunts me."

"My old lady died, and she haunts me, too." Gemma Rae shook her head. "She was a boring little housewife. She wanted me to be a boring little housewife, too. That wasn't going to happen and didn't."

Fleur chuckled. "My mother would undoubtedly be making similar statements. I have a question about my father. Do you know the exact town in New York Shane was from? Or how we could find out?"

"He mentioned he didn't live far from the Woodstock area when he met Maggie. Maggie and I had gone with a busload of kids to the Woodstock concert. A wild, painted-up VW Kombi bus. The decoration on our bus was a florid, dynamic masterpiece. Big old neon-colored peace symbols painted all over. What a trip."

"They met at the Woodstock Festival?"

"Oh yeah. Shane and Maggie saw each other, and the rest was history. It was probably where you were conceived." She sputtered out a cough mixed with a laugh. "Woodstock. After the festival ended, we came back here to California. Shane came back with us to the commune. He had a boyhood buddy back in New York. His buddy stayed behind for a few months then moved out here. Trinidad or something. He could tell you Shane's hometown."

"Trinidad. Was that the friend's first name or his last name?"

Gemma Rae thought a moment then slapped the table. "It was Trinidad Zucker. That's the name of his friend. It hit me like a flash. Remembering Woodstock made me recall. Yes, his name was Trinidad Zucker. He'd been in Nam with Shane. But he was so straight, he was way out of touch with the hippie movement. Trini Zucker. My brain is processing the name Terry, too. Maybe I'm confused. Trini. How could I have forgotten his name? I slept with the guy once, and sure as hell should have forgotten his performance. Or lack of performance."

"Not a primetime performance, I take it."

With a slow blink, Gemma Rae repeated, "Trini Zucker. He drank a little too much one night, and I'd smoked enough. I was toked out. I must've hogged out on a bomb of grass. Probably laced. We ended up in the same tent together. The next morning, he got in his sports car and zoomed out of there like his ass was on fire. Trini Zucker. He was a fairly big guy but not everywhere. Hell, I called him 'tiny' Zucker." She held up her thumb and forefinger and moved them a couple of inches apart. "Tiny Zucker. I heard he located somewhere in this area."

Fleur giggled at Gemma Rae's antics as she told the story. "I'll try to contact him."

"Don't bother, if you're looking to get laid."

"No. Not even if my situation were different. And after your description, no. But I do want to talk with him. Maybe he could help me find the Bradley family."

"What a sour bunch of stuffy assholes they were."

"Maybe the younger generation mellowed out," Fleur said.

"Maybe. My best guess is they're all just like the parents— fuckin' carbon copies."

"That would mean I could have ended up like them."

Gemma Rae's lips contorted. "Naw, you're too much like your mother."

For the next portion of the afternoon the women chatted. Fleur updated Gemma Rae about the lieutenant, records clerk, and the investigator she'd hired. The conversation enlightened Fleur about more of her parents' past. When the shop closed, Gemma Rae insisted Fleur come upstairs and have a sandwich and salad with her before returning to her hotel room.

As Fleur walked the streets, she studied the westering sun as it eased down toward the horizon. Wondering what her parents thought when they'd walked the byways of San Francisco, Fleur stopped a moment to look around. She suddenly wished Abby was at her side. Looking at where Abby would have been standing, she felt a blankness. The shiver she experienced wasn't from the temperature. The remainder of the stroll left her tired.

Once back at the hotel, she reviewed her progress, pleased at how some of her investigation was coming together. Looking into a dresser mirror as she passed by, she saw the tension in her face. Abby was a major concern. Their relationship was in jeopardy.

Fleur also felt sad that she would be losing the grant. That loss would be an enormous pain in her heart, but she didn't see how the grant would be attainable now. Even though Abby was keeping up with the daily work, there was a report that needed to be written.

She considered her work important, perhaps not earth-shaking, but vital to a continuation of whatever scientific studies could come of her work. *Stair steps,* she thought. Knowledge built each new plateau upon every lower level plateau. She had worked her entire life to add her own small step.

Although exhausted, as she sat on the bed she found a hidden energy that took her to thoughts she hadn't visited. Fleur wondered what Aunt Golda might have thought about her pursuit, whether she would have discouraged Fleur's desire to investigate her lineage. What then? Fleur guessed Aunt Golda would understand. She always had. And she would be supportive.

The trip had already been somewhat successful. Through Gemma Rae and Bernie Maylor, as well as Abby's searches, Fleur was finding out more about her parents. And tomorrow would bring her even nearer to her mother.

Chapter 14

The tawny glow of morning's light brought Fleur a sense of optimism. She would be finding out new information about her parents, and it could even lead to more discoveries about the tragedy. She wondered whether, in addition to having lunch with Stephanie Pierce, she would have time to locate Trinidad Zucker. Before she began her search for Zucker, she called Abby with an update.

"Glad for all your success," Abby said drily. "Sophia has been of no help at all. I went by to see her earlier this morning, and she was wearing this mummified expression. I couldn't even get her to acknowledge my 'good morning.' I just kept talking, and her eyes listed like she was taking her final voyage. I talked with one of the nurses and found out she's being medicated to keep her less agitated. That's what they call it, doping the old girl up to keep her *less agitated.*"

"She never creates a problem. They shouldn't be doing that."

"When I confronted the staff at the desk, they said she wandered. Who the hell wouldn't wander if they lived in that place?"

"Settle down. I'll talk with them when I return."

"I talked with them."

Fleur covered her eyes. Abby's personality was far too confrontational for solving a problem like medication of an elderly patient. "Abby, just back away. I'll deal with it."

"It's dealt with. I dealt with it."

"Let me guess. You screamed at them, and they decided to kick you and Sophia both out of the residence." Fleur knew that Abby's jaw would be clamping tightly. She could envision her lover's anger beginning to rage. "Well, isn't that what happened? Or did they just kick you out?"

"They took me to see Sophia's doctor. I told him that the woman they were doping the shit out of had lived through an occupation, a war, and a concentration camp, and she was not going to be treated like that. I told him I would have every conceivable agency call on him and the residence to question why she was being overmedicated."

"That probably got the job done," Fleur said, her voice dripping with sarcasm.

"Amazing as it may seem, particularly to you, it did. Dr. Rubin ordered her to be taken off all mood-altering medication, stat."

Fleur's eyebrows shot up, as did the corners of her lips. Bemused, she commented, "Obviously, sometimes the heavy hand works."

"Absolutely. By the time I drop by this evening, her mind should be semi-lucid. And I'm going to interrogate Sophia with all the sugar in my voice that I can. I will imitate you. If that doesn't work, I'll try my approach—shout the place down."

"I appreciate you helping."

"I'm doing it for Aunt Golda."

"The plants? My research? Is helping with those also for Aunt Golda?"

"That's for research."

Fleur stared at the wall blankly, taking time to think about her messy life. "Research appreciates your effort."

"Next time you see research, just say it's welcome. You might also say that there is no research going on in our bed. Your side of the bed is empty and cool. Look, I need to scoot. I have a job."

Fleur continued looking at the wall for several moments after Abby had hung up, then she turned her focus to finding Trinidad Zucker. Trini. Her computer search of the San Francisco area yielded only a few Zuckers. One was a T. Zucker. When she called, a gravelly-voiced man answered.

"Terrance Zucker."

"I may have the wrong number. I'm trying to find Trinidad Zucker."

There was an enormously deep laugh from the other end of the phone. "I haven't been called that in decades. Who are you?"

"My name is Fleur Hamilton, but you might know me by Flower Bradley. My father was Shane Bradley."

"The baby," he said. "Shane's baby!"

"Yes. I recently became aware of some of my background, particularly about what happened to my parents."

"God, what a terrible tragedy. Early on, I tried to warn Shane that Maggie was nuts. She must have gotten jealous and went berserk. Blew him away, then herself. I haven't thought about the murder for years. Guess my brain suppressed it."

"I have many questions about Shane, and I hoped you might tell me about him."

"Sure. Shane and I were pals since high school. I was a couple years older. When I joined the Marines, I talked him into doing the same. He was probably attempting to escape from his righteous parents. He ended up getting wounded in Nam. He caught shrapnel in his head and a bullet in his leg. Got a medical release, but if I recall, it was more for mental disability. They diagnosed him with post-traumatic stress. Anyway, we got out of the service at about the same time. And you're the baby? Maggie called you the love child. I think Shane probably called you the accident."

Fleur deliberated a moment. She hoped this wasn't going to all go wrong, as the call to Dennis Heywood had. "I'm trying to find out as much as I can about them. And about what happened, of course. You seem to believe my mother killed him and then herself."

"Of course. Shane loved her. He was pissed about the war, but he wouldn't have killed her. She wasn't the enemy. He had been trained to kill the enemy, not a woman he loved."

"You seem certain."

"Maggie was a loose cannon, Shane was an angry guy. I remember that he met her in New York and then followed along back to California with her. She was his ruination, not Viet Nam. Nam gave him nightmares, but she drove him crazy. The Marines teach you restraint. He never would have hurt her, much less killed her. And he had no reason to want to die, especially after how he'd fought to live. No matter how strung out he might have been on the day he died, surrendering to death wouldn't have been an option."

"Maybe you can help me with finding some of his family. What was the name of the town where he was raised?"

"Our hometown is Bethel, New York. Shane's dad and sister died years ago. His mother, Phoebe, and his twin brother, Samuel, still live in the area. I hate to tell you this, but it won't do you any good to contact them. They were adamant about your mother being a slut and the kid, you, not being Shane's. They called Maggie a round-heeled little whore. When Shane went off with her, his family disowned him. She was no damned good for him."

"I appreciate your assistance, Mr. Zucker. Would you mind if I call you back if I have additional questions?"

"Not at all. There's a chance you are Shane's kid."

She had been making notes in her journal while she listened. "Is there anything you can think of that might help me know him better or discover what might have happened that last day?"

"It would take hours. Maybe I can write a few things down. When you call again, I'll tell you. This has taken me by surprise. You got photos of him?"

"I only have a couple. He was handsome."

"Yes. He was damned good looking in his uniform—one handsome, tough leatherneck. He was a good guy and a hell of a good soldier. I think he'd like to know his kid was wanting to find out about him. If it was me, I'd like it. Look, I'll check in my desk. I may have some photos. I know I have the yearbook. I can make copies for you."

"I'd very much appreciate that. If you'd agree to it, maybe we could have lunch tomorrow. I'm only going to be in San Fran a couple more days before I return to Denver, and I would love to meet you. I can make a list of my questions about things you might know. I could get the photocopies at the same time."

"My office building is in the city. I usually don't go in until after nine. In fact, you just caught me. I'll take the photos in today and have my secretary make copies. How about we meet tomorrow noon at The Plaza? I'd like to see Shane's kid. It'll give me a chance to see if you look like him."

After they disconnected, Fleur made a note of their appointment. She also wrote down the name Samuel Bradley. Even if he wanted nothing to do with her, as Mr. Zucker had said, she would ask if he would send a DNA sample to her so she could test her paternity.

She felt an aching emptiness at the thought of not being wanted by her father's family. And perhaps they were correct. Maybe she wasn't Shane's child.

What troubled her most was that nothing was resolved. Her mother's friends were convinced Shane had pulled the trigger. Her father's best friend was equally convinced Maggie had shot them both. Fleur's science background did not allow for the possibility of error. She would make no determination until there was proof.

Chapter 15

The hour approached for meeting Stephanie for their luncheon. Fleur's spirits were uplifted, for she soon would become acquainted with her aunt and cousin.

As she entered the Silver Menu, she looked for a table that seated a middle-aged woman. The woman she spotted was nicely dressed, as was the college-aged woman at her side. Comparing the older woman to the photos she'd seen of her mother, Fleur discerned that her skin was lighter than Maggie's, and the sisters' overall resemblance was minimal. Only the mouth and eyes were similar. The younger woman seemed pleased to be in attendance. She looked like her mother. Fleur gave the older woman a quick wave.

As she approached the table, Fleur felt a nervous tension. Stephanie Pierce stood and extended her hand, then her arms opened and she pulled Fleur into them. "Little Flower. I'd recognize you from how much your smile looks like Maggie's, the wavy dark hair and Maggie's smile." Tears flooded Stephanie's eyes. "And this is my daughter, Joan. Joan Margaret. I chose her middle name after your mother."

"I'm Fleur. And you're my aunt and my cousin." Fleur's voice cracked, and her eyes began filling. "It's so good of you both to see me."

"There are so many scams around, I admit I was skeptical about being contacted by a relative I'd never met," Stephanie said. "But now that I see you, there certainly is no doubt in my mind that you're Maggie's daughter. I brought some photographs I copied for you, so you'll see for yourself."

When they were all seated, Fleur noted how genuinely happy they seemed to be with her, and she felt a great relief. Thumbing through the photos, she discovered she did look a great deal like her mother. Her eyes were different from her mother's wide, huge green eyes, and her face was slimmer than Maggie's. Her naturally curly hair was less curly than her mother's, but the skin color was precisely the same. As was her smile.

By the time they'd ordered, Stephanie had related the story of when Maggie had brought the baby, Flower, to visit her mother. Little sister Stephanie was overcome with joy at seeing the six-month-old baby. Maggie had proudly introduced her to Fleur as her aunt.

"My buttons were busting," Stephanie said. "You were such an adorable infant. And I was the aunt! Only seven years old at the time, but I knew it was important. I never saw you again." Her eyes flooded with tears, and she quickly wiped them with a napkin.

"When you heard about the tragedy," Fleur asked, "what did your family do?"

"My mother was terrible. She refused to pay for burial, for one thing. Both Maggie and Shane were buried in some potter's field. When I was a young adult, I attempted to find Maggie's gravesite. My husband and I were going to have both Shane and Maggie reburied in a proper cemetery, or at least put up headstones. I couldn't find their burial place. It's lost to us. There are a lot of things I resent my mother for, but that's probably the thing I most despise—there's nowhere I can go to talk with my big sister."

"I'm sure Maggie hears you, wherever she is," Fleur said. "You were going to see that they remained together?"

"Maggie loved Shane."

Fleur reached out to touch Stephanie's trembling hand. "I've just met you, but I can tell you're a decent woman."

"Unkind of me, but I'll say it anyway. I did not take after Loretta."

"I'm glad of that," Fleur said. "I can't understand why Loretta was so antagonistic toward Maggie."

"Maybe she felt some guilt. Maggie actually loved Shane. I recall my mother blustered about Shane being a bum. We'd met him a couple times, heard stories about this quick temper. He was contentious. When they died, my mother cursed, cried, and stayed drunk for a long time. My biological father had been working to get primary custody, and it had come through, so I wasn't with my mother when Maggie died. It wasn't long before Loretta drank herself to death."

"And your father, was he kind to you?"

"Yes. I don't know whether he was really my father, and I doubt if he knew for sure, either, but he took me in. He raised me alongside of my two younger stepbrothers, in a typical suburban home. My stepmother was wonderful. She'd always wanted a daughter. When she got me, she was overjoyed. When Joan was born, she really got spoiled by my parents."

"And are you still close to your stepbrothers?"

"Yes, thankfully we are. My younger siblings never even realized I was a 'step.' I don't think of Dennis as a relative."

"He wasn't happy to hear from me," Fleur confessed. "But he did give me your husband's name."

"Thank goodness he did that much," Stephanie said, shaking her head. "I can't stand the guy. Never could. Joan hasn't even met him. What does she need him for when she's got two perfectly great uncles?"

Joan grinned. "Well, great is carrying it a bit far. They're practical jokers, so if you ever meet them, be forewarned. But they are fun."

"I'm glad you've both been happy," Fleur said. "I wish my mother could have had a happy life."

"Yes," Stephanie agreed. "Although I landed in a great family, they could have been awful to me and I still would have been thrilled to be away from crazy Loretta. Maggie left home at fifteen, and I'm sure I would have as well. Luckily it wasn't necessary."

"I'm glad your childhood turned out happily."

"I'd heard you were taken by Social Services. Foster care. I also heard Maggie's music teacher adopted you."

"The latter was correct. However, she didn't adopt me as much as abscond with me in tow. It was all for a good reason. Golda Hamilton was aware your family was dysfunctional, and the Bradley clan wouldn't even recognize me as being Shane's child. Aunt Golda loved me too much to allow me to be taken into foster care."

"My mother said the music teacher took care of you much of the time when you were a baby," Joan said. "Maggie told my mother how Golda was more of a mother than Loretta had been. Golda also bought food and clothing for you. And yours was a happy life?"

"Enormously happy. Yes."

Fleur thought about the multitude of opportunities Golda had given her, but it was the small snippets that peopled her childhood memories that had made Fleur's life so wonderful. When she and Golda gardened together or played games or whatever, she was always entertained and happy. For a moment, her thoughts took her to Aunt Golda's backyard. Aunt Golda would take hollyhock blooms, invert them, and attach a bud to the top. They looked like brightly dressed dancing girls. It was a childhood delight.

Heartwarming thoughts. "I couldn't have asked for a better life. I was the envy of all my friends. They adored Aunt Golda. She was pure fun. I think they mostly spent time with me because they were so enthralled with Aunt Golda. Many of them came in from out of town for Golda's funeral. So yes, it was a splendid childhood."

"I'm glad. Glad you didn't get placed with Loretta. She was no kind of mother. But my stepmother, I call her my mother, gave me the skills to bring some semblance of order into my own motherhood." Stephanie pointed to Joan. "She's her father's and my pride and joy."

Fleur smiled at the young woman.

Joan shyly returned her smile and said, "How neat to have a cousin I never knew I had. That's great."

"Great is an understatement," Fleur said. "For me, it's extraordinary. I was raised unaware of having any relatives, so this is an amazing feeling."

"I hope we can always stay in touch now," Stephanie said.

"I have a feeling we shall," Fleur replied. "I'm planning to return to California, and your family is welcome to visit me in Colorado. No ocean," she joked, "but there's lots and lots of Rocky Mountains."

During lunch, the chatter was nonstop in an amiable atmosphere that seemed entirely natural. Joan was a college honor student and had a part-time job she liked. She had her own car and offered to take Fleur on a tour of the city. Fleur told the women about her search to find answers about what happened to her parents. Joan offered to help and gave her cell number to her newfound cousin.

Stephanie frowned in thought. "I've always wondered about Maggie's death. It never made sense to me."

"Nor does it to me," Fleur said.

"I heard Shane carried a gun because he'd been in Nam. As it was explained to me, given the drugs and his temper, he shot them both."

"I talked with his war buddy," Fleur said. "He claims Shane would never have killed her. He said it was Maggie on a bad trip."

"No. Maggie had a baby to consider. She could never have done it. Never," Stephanie said. "When she visited, I saw her protectively take you out of Loretta's arms. Our mother was drunk as a skunk. Maggie did allow me to hold you. She made me sit down, so I wouldn't drop you. And she didn't take her eyes from you. No, Maggie wouldn't have destroyed her own life. She loved you in her own way. I always thought if she had lived, she would have settled down."

Fleur reached for her vibrating cell phone. "Sorry, I need to take this. I'm waiting for the investigator I've hired to contact me."

It was Paul Salvador with an update. He asked if she could meet him that afternoon. She quickly agreed.

The parting with her aunt and cousin was heartfelt. Joan insisted she call her if Fleur needed a ride anywhere. Stephanie invited Fleur to come to their home when she took a break from the investigation.

Although their meeting told her little about what might have happened on the day her parents died, it did tell her something of her heritage. Her lineage might not have been all good, but it certainly was not all bad. She'd met the good part.

Aunt Golda had always espoused the tenet that life was to be cherished. She'd say people were loaned life, with the condition that eventually life ends. Fleur would rejoice in having some wonderful relatives. *Also in having had a wonderful great aunt.* She'd had years with an extraordinary woman. No, with two extraordinary women.

Fleur was hopeful the visit with Salvador would reveal additional progress in the investigation.

Chapter 16

Paul Salvador led Fleur to a conference room and took a seat across from her at the large rectangular table. He slid a manila folder over to her. "I warn you, this contains copies I made of the crime scene photos. If you're squeamish, you might not want to look at them. I also pulled a mug shot of Shane Bradley that was taken when he was arrested for disturbing the peace during a protest. They must have used the same photo when they booked him for drug procurement. He was passing out marijuana to a crowd that included a uniformed officer. If you have any reservations about looking at the photos of their bodies, I suggest you stop after page one."

"I was a science major, I studied anatomy and biology along with the botany."

"Postmortem photos might be different from what you've seen, and also, they are your parents."

Fleur slowly folded back the cover of the file and exposed the mug shot of her father. Even with a scowl, he was a young man with rugged good looks. On his temple was a scar, probably from what had been a deep gash. She speculated it was the result of the shrapnel wound. Shane's eyes were angry, but their light coloring softened them. And she saw, as she did each time she now looked at photos of him, her own eyes.

Flipping over the sheet of copy paper, she panned her eyes over a photo of the crime scene. Maggie's body was twisted, as if it had fallen from a high cliff. There was a pool of blood beneath her head. Shane was on his back, and his bloodied face had been shattered. Droplets of blood were splattered everywhere. Between them lay the gun, with smears nearly covering the handle and barrel of the revolver. There had been a fight. And yet, they seemed to be reaching for one another. Their fingers nearly touched, perhaps were touching.

"Anything you can tell from this photo?" she asked.

"The way the bullets entered and exited their heads tells little. In my opinion, he was shot first, but I'll need to review the autopsy reports more thoroughly."

"But most of the people I've talked with don't believe she killed him. I'm not refuting your conclusion. I just think it seems more realistic that he was the killer. But it would be difficult to tell from this photo."

There was a moment of silence. Salvador cleared his throat and said, "I put the crime scene photos in order with the least shocking first. A few pages further will show the autopsy photos. Pretty grisly photos, but they show more about the bullet entry. The shots were fired from only twelve to fourteen inches away from each victim. Shane taking the first bullet is only my opinion at this time. But, as you can see, the struggle that preceded the shootings was brutal."

She flipped the pages to the photo she assumed he was talking about and swallowed hard as she peered down at it. "I see what you mean." Her stomach lurched, and her eyes clamped shut.

"Not a sight for anyone who isn't getting paid to look at it. It's tough enough for me to view these images. They do raise a few questions, though. There's a set of footprints in addition to those of the victims. Maybe the crime scene was compromised. First responders or cops could have tromped over the scene and tainted or destroyed evidence while trying to save the couple. It was a turbulent time back then. There were not many resources, and the cops were always busy. And the case had all the earmarks of a murder and suicide. They weren't expecting a homicide trial, so perhaps they weren't careful."

"You said there were a few questions. What questions?"

"As I mentioned, the extra, unidentified bloody footprints make me wonder. The fact Shane was shot first. The way the blood on the handgun is smeared. There definitely was a fight for the gun. Both victims' prints were on the revolver, but over here," he said and pointed to the edge of the gun's grip, "over here you can see it appears to have been wiped. Could have been that the cop first on the scene might have handled it or even brushed against it. Bradley or Heywood could have rubbed against it in their tussle. But it could also have been something else. And the entry wound suggests that Heywood was shot by someone taller than her, but if there was a scuffle, that might explain it. There are so many variables. I'm checking blood splatter to see if I can discern a pattern. There isn't anything conclusive. Yet."

"You sound as if you expect a conclusion."

"Habit. I like resolution. I'll talk with Lt. Schultz about it, see if he has any input. Schultz is a damned good investigator, as well as a stand-up guy. I think if there were errors made in the investigation, he'll admit to them."

"One other thing, I was wondering. Was the gun stored as evidence, and if so, might there still be viable blood samples?"

"I requested any evidence vault material be searched out. There might be something. If there is, I'll run it for DNA and trace evidence. They didn't take much care in collecting trace evidence back then. Dusting, bagging, and tagging were time consuming, and the cops were convinced this case wouldn't go to court because there wasn't a living perp." Salvador grinned. "I'm a good investigator, so I'm going to assume you're looking for the DNA on Bradley."

"Yes. I've been told his family is convinced he wasn't my father. I'd like closure on that. I'm going to be attempting to contact his family. I'll ask them for DNA samples. He has a twin brother, and his eighty-six-year-old mother is still alive. I'm not counting on either of them being cooperative."

"I'm a curious guy. That's why I've been an investigator all these years. Like I said, I'd like resolution. Even if we've screwed up, I'd like the truth. I'll let you know when I get anything more."

She stood. "May I borrow these copies?"

"I don't know why you'd want the gory things, but I pulled those copies for you. One thing, though. Please do not allow the photos to go public. The crime scene images have only been seen by authorities."

"May I show them to Bernie Maylor? See if they are as he recalls the scene?"

"Yes. Sure. He was there. Poor guy. Just tell him not to discuss them with anyone else."

"I'll mention it. Thanks for the copies. What do I owe for them?"

"Don't worry. The copy charges will be on your bill." He smiled benevolently. "Records department folks are a bunch of cheapskates. That includes my beloved Lois."

As Fleur departed, she glanced at her watch in hopes she would be able to catch Bernie at his bookstore. Fortunately, he was there, and he greeted her as she entered.

"Bernie, I just talked with the investigator. I've got photos of the crime scene. I'm not suggesting you look at them, if that would be uncomfortable for you. They're terribly grisly. Grotesque. But I have a few questions. I'd like to know if it looks as though there is anything about the crime scene that seems different from when it was fresh. Paul Salvador wondered about the way the bodies were, in regards to which of them might have been the shooter. Also, a portion of the gun handle looked as if it had been wiped. But please don't feel an obligation to view them."

Bernie led her to the small table in the corner. Taking the folder from her, he said, "You're forgetting, I was there at the scene. I entered with the superintendent. We found the bodies. So of course, if I can help you, I'll take a look at them."

She took out her journal and pen. "The superintendent," she said. "What kind of man was he?"

Looking deep in thought, Bernie toyed with his spectacles. "He was Hispanic, medium dark skin, and brown hair. Good physique but a little scrawny. Not bad looking. About my age or a little older. Maybe slightly under six-foot tall. His last name was Rodriguez. Let me think... Ed. I always wanted to call him Earl, but it was Ed. Nice. Friendly. A nondescript kind of guy. Got along great with everyone. Well-liked guy."

"And he had a key?"

"Naturally. But he had no motive."

"Was there any way anyone could have left the scene?"

"I lived upstairs, so as soon as I heard the shots fired, I scooted out to the hall and rushed down the stairs. There was no one in the hall. I banged on your parents' door, with no response. I knocked frantically on Rodriguez's door. By the time he answered, it had been maybe a couple minutes."

"Would he have had time to leave their room, lock up, and get back into his apartment while you were going down the stairs?"

"Not unless he was moving with all-out speed. I was younger, however, never a sprinter. It was pretty clear Rodriguez had been sleeping. He was upset because I'd awakened him. He didn't like being bothered when he slept. He mentioned he'd been fixing a faucet and pipe the night before and hadn't slept. He hadn't heard the shots."

"Wouldn't the shots have woken him up?"

"I would have thought so, but they hadn't. I actually heard the fight before the shots. I mean, Shane's and Maggie's voices were loud but muffled. It wasn't unusual for them to fight, so I ignored it. But the shots were loud. Maybe Rodriguez was a heavy sleeper, or he could have been medicated. Golda hadn't heard the shots because she had her record player on. She always had music playing."

"Yes." Fleur's memories took her back to the days of her childhood, where music accompanied her through the day. Aunt Golda would put the radio on, dialing in different music genres every day. Sometimes she would play her collection of records on the well-used record player. She had mostly classical vinyl, but she was eclectic in her musical tastes. She enjoyed Dylan, Baez, The Beatles, and Streisand. If she considered it great music, she made it her own.

Rubbing his brow, Bernie said, "If you're thinking Rodriguez might have been involved, I would say probably not. As I mentioned before, he would have had no motive. He was one of the few people around who didn't have a beef with Shane. And he didn't seem attracted to Maggie. He had a woman he saw regularly. He was a nice guy. He got along great with everyone."

"I'm reaching for straws."

Bernie thumbed through the photos. "I can't really tell. It seems to be much as I remember it. It was such a horrendous scene, maybe I've attempted to blot it out of my memory. However, I'd have to say that it looks the same." He closed the folder. "I'm not much help. What a terrible time. Terrible."

"The footprints in blood, were they all there when you first saw the scene? Or had police traipsed through and made them?"

"I honestly can't remember. When I saw the scene, my first thought was to see if the kids were breathing. I wanted to see if they were alive, so I was watching for signs of life. I'm sorry I'm not a better witness. I wish with all my heart I could help you. I remember mostly wanting to see them twitch or move in any way. Their hands were reaching, so near. I wanted to see the hands move, touch." His eyes clouded as he looked away.

"Thank you for all of your assistance. But mostly," she said and patted his arm, "mostly, thank you for caring about whether they were alive."

Chapter 17

After she arrived back in her hotel room, Fleur sat down to examine her journal. As she jotted down a few notations, she experienced a thought process she often called the X-factor when she was searching for a resolution with her plant-life experiments. There seemed to be something missing.

A pang of loneliness suddenly struck her, and sadness filled her soul. It was as if she'd suppressed the agony that she would never have time to complete her research report, and now it was striking her full force. And she acknowledged that she'd made the decision to stay, no matter how vital her work might be.

Most heartbreaking was the thought that there might have been a chance for her to continue her research. If her hypothesis was proven, the contribution to medical science would be unimaginable. Conflicted, she looked back at her flight case.

If I left tonight, there might be a way I could process the data quickly enough to get the report and grant application submitted on time. She would need to correlate the exact epigenetic changes that were mediated by the production of different splice forms of RNA with her project. The metabolism and transport of plant nutrients had been carefully measured. From phototropism to thermotropism, each documented moment was carefully computed. The mapping and analysis needed to be extracted, but the data was there.

She would not have the time. Her experiment would be concluded. Independent research without the grant would leave her with the same painstaking observations and makeshift trials she'd been grappling with for years.

Throughout the dinner Fleur had ordered from room service, she was filled with sorrow. When she finished eating, she realized she hadn't tasted a thing. She did welcome having a full stomach. Sipping the wine she'd also ordered, she felt alone. When her phone rang, she answered quickly. It was Gemma Rae, inviting her to a late dinner. She declined, saying she'd eaten and also needed to call Abby.

"After I speak with her," Fleur joked, "I'll be ready for a rest."

"Things are still tense?"

"She's got a good heart, but she's probably the most critical human being I've ever encountered. She'll pull apart anything, if she doesn't agree with how it's being handled. I want someone to support me, particularly now."

"*Now* is where we live. The old expression is about life not being a dress rehearsal. I think I first realized that when Maggie died. We were young. And if life can end so quickly… beware. Maybe it spurred my interest in the supernatural. Something is out there in that Great Beyond. I don't think it requires a batch of dos and don'ts from a frocked leader. They'll tuck you away and give you a send-off to that celestial Promised Land for a cash down payment. Altruism for hire. Just saying."

"Aunt Golda was never religious. Although I believe her French Catholic father might have told her about angels. She seemed to believe in them."

"Me, too. I love the thought of chunky little angels zooming around in the sky."

Fleur was pensive a moment before a smile eased across her face. "I remember when I met Abby. We were at a conference on medicinal plants. I was wearing an angel charm bracelet that Aunt Golda had given me. Abby sat beside me. She touched the angel charm and asked me if I believed in angels. I said yes, and I asked her if she did. She said she hadn't been certain before she saw me, but I made her a believer."

"Good line. Whew, a damn effective line. I'd have crawled in the sack with anyone telling me that."

"We got together the next weekend. Now I'm making her believe in devils." Fleur held her arm up and tapped the angel charm that was dangling from her wrist. "Maybe I'll need to change out charms."

"Naw. It'll all blow over. Too bad Golda isn't around to arbitrate. That's what she used to do when Maggie and Shane would have a tiff. She'd tell them to think about the moment they first met and to realize each moment could be their final moment. It always seemed to work with them."

"It helped with our relationship, too." Fleur took another sip of wine before offering an apology. "Sorry I got off on a different topic. I was telling you about Golda's beliefs. Her Jewish mother didn't encourage attending a synagogue. I recall one conversation I had with Aunt Golda when I was a teenager. She said many religions wished to control the minds of their flocks, and if their intentions weren't good and there was brutality in their hearts, it was dangerous. Wars were fomented under the auspices of religion. She believed more in wisdom and knowledge."

"I've seen lots of soul-savers who are really parasites, so I agree with Golda. When one of the frocks talks about reverence for the cloth and infallibility, I scram. But I believe there's something or other that is greater than we are. I'm extraordinarily spiritual, as I'm sure you know."

Laughing, Fleur asked, "You aren't into God fraud?"

"Exactly. But anyone who doesn't believe in anything must be terminally constipated with fear. You show me somebody who doesn't believe in some higher power, spirit, creator... whatever, and I'll show you someone who probably needs to take a good shit."

The women chuckled together, then Fleur said, "I'll give you an example of how Abby's mind works in this realm. One time she asked me which belief set would result in the preferable outcome. You believe there's a Higher Power with all the regulations you follow to the letter. And still you die, and there's no reward. Or, you don't believe, don't follow any commandments, and you die, and there's God shaking a long finger at you."

Tickled at the choices, Gemma Rae mulled her decision. She giggled. "In the first, there's nothing, nothing but wasted time. Maybe wasted good times. The second scenario is more difficult. First, you've got to convert God into a hippie."

Both women laughed until they sputtered for air. Fleur said, "I must tell Abby about your comment. She'll love it." Silent at the concern that surfaced at the thought of calling Abby, Fleur changed the subject. "Before I forget, I'm having lunch with Trini tomorrow. He's bringing photos of Shane. Anyway, I'll give him your best," Fleur quipped.

"He damn well knows my best. But don't spend your time looking for his best."

"No. And the meeting with Stephanie and Joan, her daughter, went great. They are lovely. They treated me like family. Stephanie says I look like my mother. She could tell who I was immediately. Just like you knew me."

"You're Maggie's kid. Of course, I knew."

"Then Salvador called, and I met with him. He had the crime and autopsy photos for me. After we talked, I dropped by Bernie's.

He gave them a quick scan and said the scene in the pictures was exactly as he remembered it when he and the super found the bodies. So there probably hadn't been much tampering or contamination by the investigators."

"Don't ask me to look at the goddamn photos. I want to remember Maggie laughing, with her hair blowing in the wind. Her sweetness, even her off-key singing. No other image for me, thank you."

"You loved my mother, didn't you?"

"I've never had a friendship like hers before or since. She could flip the switch on sunlight. Maggie was a whirlwind of mirth. We made everything fun."

"I used to have that kind of relationship with Abby. Love, yes, but friendship, too. So I know what you're saying."

"Give her a call. I know you miss her. Every topic we've talked about, you get sidetracked and bring up Abby. I can hear the loneliness in your voice."

"Gemma Rae, since the moment Aunt Golda died, I've been lonely."

"Death of a loved one wrings us out, no doubt about it. If you need to talk, just call or come on by."

"I'll be fine. I'll talk with Abby. Or fight with her."

"Hot damn, you need a little spice going on. How about some hot phone sex. Tell her when you get back to Colorado, you're gonna play grab-ass with her."

Laughing, Fleur said, "I'm not sure hot phone sex would lift her spirits. She recently mentioned the catastrophic empty bed ordeal."

"Phone sex. Give it a whirl. Try to shock her with a little fantasy. Make it wide-open wild."

"Gemma Rae," she said in a teasing tone, "can you do vocal impressions? Imitate my voice?"

"I'm not talking some copulatory crap to some crabby lesbian." She sputtered, "Are you kidding me? I'm supposed to talk her down with erotic urges and coition?"

"Abby would probably faint. Maybe a little sensuality would tame her down a bit, but then she'd just moan that I'm not there." Fleur paused. "I think I'll just tell her I'm tired and need sleep. I still have to make a list of questions I want to ask Trini at lunch tomorrow."

"Let me know how your lunch with Mister Comes-Up-Short goes. He's a braggart and a blowhard, but he can't really blow and it ain't really hard." She snickered. "Literally, he was a fucking fraud and a fraud fucking."

"Did you talk like that around Golda?" Fleur asked, remembering how insistent Golda was about not cursing.

"Not a syllable after she corrected me once. She said she could say far worse things and in many more languages, if cursing was interesting to her. I saved my intriguing lingo for Maggie and my private moments."

Fleur tilted her head. "In all the years I knew her, I never heard Aunt Golda utter an expletive. However, I didn't always know the language she was speaking. She could easily have tossed in an f-bomb or two."

"Could have been her mouth was more potty mouth than mine, but I doubt it," Gemma Rae said. "Maggie and I giggled our days away. The same things were always funny to us. I wonder what she would be like now." Sadness filtered through her words. "I bet she'd still be the same as she was. I'm thinking she would still be wild, though probably not as wild as she was."

"You would still be laughing at the same things."

"Yes. Yes, I believe we would. And I'm laughing with her daughter. Same laugh in your eyes as there was in hers." Gemma Rae's voice cracked. "Now then, get a good night's sleep. And I hope your talk with Abby goes okay."

"Me, too." Fleur's eyes closed a moment. "Thanks for calling, Gemma Rae. I'll talk with you tomorrow."

Taking a final sip of wine, Fleur thought about how the good events in her relationship had seemed to evaporate with time.

She and Abby had always worked together without words, as if they already knew the next line one another would say. They knew what to do, what the other wanted or needed. It was as though they were traveling as one spirit. And now they seemed to be going in separate directions, directions that were headed away from one another. With everything that was going on between them, Fleur considered, the walking away from one another had changed into a speeding race.

Chapter 18

"I was just going to call you," Fleur said after answering her phone.

Abby's excited voice rattled on about her visit with Sophia. "I tell you, she was like another person. She was coherent." Abby plunged into her story, as if she were spurring her words to continue. "I talked with her slowly at first. Then she made the little circling motion with her hand, as if she was urging me to finish my question. I dove right in. Asked her where she'd put the letters. At first she couldn't remember, and then she finally spoke. She said she had only two left, and she would only give me one letter at a time. Then she said something about me being on her side, and that she knew I wouldn't tell anyone."

"She's probably still frightened," Fleur said.

"Maybe the facility doesn't allow the residents to hide things because they're afraid of some kind of contraband."

"I think it's more likely she's suspicious because of her experience in the concentration camps, and for the same reason the codes were used. They never stopped being frightened of Nazis."

"Well, she took me into her room and had me reach up on the top of her closet shelf to bring down a hat. It was this crazy old cloth hat that was probably last worn in the fifties."

"A hat?"

"Yes. She turned it inside out and pulled the lining out. Inside was a letter. She handed it to me slowly, as if she might be reconsidering giving it to me."

"But she allowed you to take it?"

"Sure. I told her you and I would take care of her letters. And when I opened it, she watched carefully. I frowned and told her their code had worked so well, that we needed a clue to crack it."

"It would certainly help."

Abby's words rushed out in a flurry. "She said she wasn't permitted to tell. Then her thumb and forefinger zipped her lips."

"Maybe she'll relent. When are you going to be sending me the e-mail photos of the letter?" Fleur could tell her voice had sounded impatient.

Abby's tone changed. "I just walked in the flipping door. The dogs are hungry. I'm trying to get a sack of groceries put away. Give me a minute."

"I'm sorry. Whenever you get time, I'll be waiting."

"It's four pages. Two pieces of paper, and it has writing on both sides. Once again, it looks as if the words are scrambled. The pages are completely filled up. I mean, it's as if Aunt Golda didn't want to waste any space."

"They were without paper or pencil for much of their internment. So it stands to reason after they were released, everything became much more valuable. Even paper seemed a luxury."

There was a moment before Abby replied, "That makes sense. But the clandestine stuff doesn't. The letters were written several years after they'd been liberated. They were both in the United States and safe by that time."

"I'm not sure you could go through all that they went through and ever feel safe again."

"Probably not." Abby sighed heavily. "I wish I could be with you when you go over the letter. I know it can't be easy for you."

"Nothing seems easy right now."

"After you get this letter translated, send it back to me. I've been working with the first letter, trying to work out the system that they used."

"I appreciate your help, Abby. And yes, as soon as I get the translation, I'll e-mail it to you."

"You said nothing seems easy, so I take it there wasn't anything much new today?"

"Some progress is being made." Fleur gave Abby a rundown of all the information she'd garnered throughout the day. "So the contacts are helping," she said with enthusiasm.

"How good can the progress be?" Abby asked. "It doesn't sound like this Salvador has a clue."

Ignoring Abby's discouraging words, Fleur said, "Salvador got the reports released. He got the crime scene and autopsy photos released. And he's waiting on the evidence vault to release the rest of the items. He did say he has some questions regarding the scene and autopsy. Maybe you're right, and his analysis never will be conclusive, but I've got to try to find out."

"No, you absolutely don't. You don't *need* to be there wasting time and money. I do *need* to take care of both houses, the animals, the plant research, my job, and every other damned thing. I'm getting worn out, Fleur. And for the life of me, I don't know why you're doing this."

"I'm compelled to do it."

"Calls are coming in about Golda's estate, about a death certificate, about what to do with this and that." She sighed in exasperation. "I've been going through the papers she had in her little vault. I did find some immigration form letters, along with her passport, but I don't have the answers for these people. It's as though you've left me alone to cope. And I miss Golda, too. We should be consoling one another, not chasing across the country to find something that will probably not yield any additional useful information. You could end up not knowing anything one way or the other."

"I'm going to need another few days, Abby. Things can wait until then. Just let the plants in my lab die. I haven't been there to oversee the daily slide cuttings anyway, much less get accurate readings transcribed, so the research is ruined."

"It's not ruined. I know it probably isn't to your specifications, but I've been doing the cuttings for you, as precisely as I've seen you do them. And I've been keeping the records up to date, exactly like you do it, maybe with even more love than you show the plants. The logs have been kept every single day you've been gone."

Tears filled Fleur's eyes. "You've been doing them exactly like I do them?"

"I didn't want to see all those months of research go out the window. I know how much this means to you. Yes, I've been doing them precisely and completely. When you get back, if you hurry, you can write the final part of the study—that evaluation report."

"Thank you, Abby. I'm grateful for your assistance, but I'll never make it back in time to get it all tied together. You might as well let it all go. I'll try again sometime in the future." It would be one less task on Abby's litany of responsibilities. "Let everything go."

There was a long silence. "Please come back," Abby said.

"I can't. And I won't."

"We're growing apart." Pleading was clear in Abby's voice.

"Maybe we've already grown apart."

"I know we've had problems. But, Fleur, I'm still in love with you."

"I question your love. You're kind to me, but your love is a controlling love. You should be supportive of me, and you're just not."

"I'm trying to be supportive of what's *reasonable*. You're throwing away something that matters to you. We both know it's a very important study. Things need doing around here. You're not here to help with tying up the loose ends that have come with Aunt Golda's death. And you're throwing away our relationship. That's sixteen years. I'm fighting for it."

"Abby, please, give me some time. I'll get this completed as quickly as I can. And whatever negativity I feel, I do love you. Love—that's all any of us can hope for. Sometimes we don't even get love. Stephanie made some attempts to find my parents' graves. She couldn't find them. According to her, my parents were buried in unmarked city graves. My parents' families wouldn't even bury them properly. I don't understand it at all."

"That would explain it," Abby said with a gasp.

"Explain what?"

"In all those papers you wanted me to look through, there were a couple of receipts for plots in a cemetery. And grave markers. It didn't give specifics, but it was in San Francisco. And the receipts looked old. I'll see if I find them again. I'll photograph and e-mail them to you as soon as we get off the phone. Along with the letter."

"I'll bet Golda took care of my parents' plots and the markers. If there are plot numbers, I can give them to Stephanie. I'm sure she would be pleased to know there's a place she could visit."

"Oh, I also wanted to tell you about Fez. Fezzy isn't eating much."

Fleur thought about the elderly Chihuahua that had belonged to Golda and was now her and Abby's little dog. His coat was black, now flecked with gray, and his legs were stringy with age. With a completely white muzzle and many missing teeth, his youth was long gone. Although he loved Fleur and Abby, he was mourning Golda.

Fleur's mouth wobbled. "He never eats much. Did you try getting the pump primed with treats first? It sometimes works."

"Not working this time. I tried. I called the vet. I'm taking Fez in tomorrow morning to get a professional opinion. The little guy isn't himself. He misses Golda, too."

"Please don't make any final decisions without me."

"No. I think we can pull him through. He's been sleeping with me the past nights."

"He loves that. Up in the bed, with you," Fleur said with a laugh. "Maybe he's faking his hunger strike to get the attention."

"Maybe. But I'm not faking that I need you to come back."

"Abby, I'll call in the morning to check on Fezzy. Are the others okay?"

"Yes. And they're all getting along splendidly together."

Fleur's fingers squeezed the phone. "Thanks, for everything," Fleur pondered her next words. She didn't want to be disappointed by Abby's response. "I appreciate your help. Please try to understand why I'm doing this."

Abby didn't issue a retaliatory remark. As she disconnected and hung up, Fleur thought about the three dogs and a cat who were being placed together and were getting along. Animals were so resilient. She wondered why people weren't always as resilient.

Chapter 19

After Fleur received the e-mail containing the attachment with the photos of the second letter, she realized how weary the day had made her. It had been more emotionally draining than she'd let anyone know. Although she had attempted to decipher the words she could recognize, this letter was even more convoluted than the first. She'd e-mailed it to her linguistics friend for a complete translation, but it would take more than translation to understand her great aunt's words.

Aunt Golda's second letter had been sent a few months after the first, but there was an obvious improvement in the women's cryptographic skills. Perhaps they feared having been witnesses to horrific deeds of the Nazis. If they felt imperiled by knowing too much, they would undoubtedly feel frightened. And they'd seen the power of the Third Reich's regime of brutality. They'd personally lived through it and never trusted again.

The smattering of words she'd translated was too limited to give more than a few clues as to where they belonged in the total context of the missive. There were references to music, to vermin, barracks, and purple. Aunt Golda had also written the words "lonely" and "hungry," though the words could never have conveyed the true heartbreak.

Setting her computer aside, Fleur couldn't set aside the thought of her great aunt Golda. She had always felt privileged to be part of Golda's history. She had always felt related to Golda. Now she was aware that Golda wasn't actually a blood relation, and yet she somehow felt nearer to sharing Golda's heritage.

Fleur's restless night ended long before she was ready to get out of bed. Her spirit was sagging. Not only had the night been plagued with thoughts of Nazi horror, but also there had been dreams of parting with Abby.

She chastised herself for having talked with Abby prior to attempting sleep. Henceforth, she vowed, she would call in the afternoon so the impact of Abby's outbursts would have time to lessen. If not for the need to check on Fezzy, she probably wouldn't have placed a call to Abby that morning. That call had thankfully been hurried, but also terse.

After she'd showered, selected clothing, and had breakfast, Fleur attempted to put together an agenda for the day. She was to meet with Terrance "Trinidad" Zucker at noon. She'd prepared a list of question to find out as much information as she could from Trini.

After lunch, she planned to make an attempt to contact both Phoebe Bradley and Shane's twin brother, Samuel. In preparation, Fleur used some of the morning to try and pull up their names in Bethel, New York, in an online telephone directory. Only Samuel had a listing. She jotted it down. He would be sixty-two-years old, and perhaps retired, but if she couldn't reach him, she would try again in the evening.

Her cab delivered her right on time to the Plaza. Seated in a quiet booth, she studied Trinidad Zucker. Trini was polished, well groomed, and wore expensive clothing. She would never have envisioned him entertaining thoughts of joining a commune. Gemma Rae was correct, even his best friend Shane wouldn't have been able to entice him into that lifestyle.

Zucker wasn't hippie material. He was filled with self-importance. Tall, his frame had filled in over the intervening four decades. He was stocky, though fit. His salt- and-pepper hair was precisely trimmed. His bantam-like eyes, what Abby called "mini eyeballs," were covered by tinted glasses. They were bronze-colored when they were open enough to be examined. Much of his handsomeness had worn away, yet a conceit remained. His voice was loud.

Trinidad Zucker had been staring at Fleur from the moment they met, and he greeted her with a patronizing smile and a crushing hug. "So you're Shane's baby?"

"I believe so. However, as you said, his family doesn't believe it," she replied. "I hope to get conclusive evidence before I leave, so that I'll know one way or the other."

"Your eyes and his eyes are exactly the same. And you've got his trim body. Not as tall, but if you were a guy, you'd probably be as tall. Look, I brought the photos." He handed her a large envelope. "I pulled them out of my old war chest. I found a couple of letters I got from Shane when he was in the hospital. The guy could mesmerize an audience of protesters, words poured out of him, but his letters were composed with sparse, single-syllable words."

After they'd ordered lunch, she poured out the photos and letters. They shared conversation as she gazed at images of young Shane, when he was in grade school and high school. There were his Marine photos, where his clean-cut appearance gave him the look of a recruitment advertisement. The many sports snapshots showed his long-limbed body, crew cut, and eyes intent on winning. In a prom photo, Shane the high school boy stood uncomfortably beside a sweet-faced girl with a blond pageboy hairdo and mint green, hoop-skirt formal.

Fleur spread the assortment of images on the tabletop. "These are wonderful. Thank you for bringing them. It's important to me that I get to know him. If he was my father, I'd like to know about his life."

"Like I said, you have his eyes. God, it's like looking right into his eyes. Kind of eerie. I don't doubt you're his. And I have to admit, I was skeptical."

"Was he? Did he have doubt?"

"Not even from the first. When I raised the question, I thought he was going to punch me in the nose. No. He believed Maggie. And from the first, he told everybody he was a dad, even before you were born."

She selected one of the photos nearest her and peered into Shane's face. It was his senior yearbook photo. "He was certainly handsome. The chiseled jaw. Yes, very nice looking."

"Now does that face look like someone who would kill the woman he was in love with?"

"No," she answered. "Not at all."

"That's right. Sweet looking in this photo. Not the strung-out hippie he became."

"And you were my father's best friend?"

"I was. Even though I was a couple years older, we were close. We lived on the same block. We drifted apart toward the end, because I wasn't into his lifestyle. I had a plan for my future. It didn't include wasting my life on drugs and a bunch of nobodies. I now own seven real estate agencies in the area, have a luxury home, and drive luxury vehicles. I've also had three luxury wives. I've done okay. Shane could have done what I did. He could've been saved if the little nutcase—" He bit off the insult. "Excuse me. I've always been bitter about it all. Maggie was his trouble. She could rattle his cage. And she knew exactly how to shake him up. She did it when she wanted attention. He was so crazy in love with her.

Obsessive. He wouldn't budge about getting out of the hippie stuff. What a waste."

"And his parents obviously felt the same."

"They were heartbroken. He came out of the service wounded. Had a bum leg and had been hit in the head. He was never the same. He took meds for the pain. When they tried to wean him off them, he went wild. He got drugs on the street. He wanted the war itself to pay for his injuries, so he went to the fringe groups. He figured he could battle the politics of war, and that might alleviate his pain."

"He became a hippie."

"Right. Naturally his folks were upset. They disowned him. He lost out on his inheritance. The Bradley family had money at one time. Old man Bradley died young. Family money is gone now. When Shane met Maggie at Woodstock, he'd been thrown out of the house and had nowhere else to go. He thought going to California with her would be kicks. I tried to talk him out of it, even told him he could stay over at my place until he found himself. But he said no. He wanted to drink and drug and chase the wild little chick."

"It's difficult to believe his parents weren't forgiving enough to allow him to come home."

"His problem with his parents went back way before he came from the war. He refused to go to college, even though his grades put him on the honor roll. He was a star athlete and a real achiever because his folks pushed him. He was expected to compete and excel. Finally, he'd had enough. I mentioned the Marines, and he joined up just to piss off his folks."

"They weren't proud of him?"

"Hell no. Maggie and him being a hippie was the finale of a long series of disappointments for his parents. After they disowned Shane, they went to their second best, Samuel. That ass-kiss worked them good. After Shane, their daughter, and finally the old man died, Sammy tried to run the business. Hell, he ran it down the drain. There was barely left enough for the old lady to be institutionalized. No, they didn't give a rat's ass about Shane after he turned down a batch of Ivy League scholarships."

"But you cared enough about him to follow him here to California."

"I thought I could talk some sense into him. I stayed because there was opportunity written all over this state. Shane never saw it. I wanted good times for him. Damned jarhead wouldn't listen to me.

The guy was my buddy. He even gave me my nickname—
Trinidad."

"Why Trinidad?"

"Before a battle, or in any time of danger, I would always say
I'd rather be in Trinidad, so he started calling me Trinidad. Then
Trini. It was all a big joke. But the nickname meant something
special to me."

"Did you hang out with him when you arrived here?"

"When I first got here, we'd go out. He'd get wasted and tell
me how he was always waking up sweating and reliving the war. He
could hear the bombs exploding, see the bodies. He'd scream. I
thought he needed to go to get help at the VA. He thought he needed
to be getting comfort with his little slut." He grimaced. "Sorry, I
keep forgetting. Anyway, I tried to maintain our friendship."

"He was living on the commune then?"

"Right. I took him back there after an evening of barhopping,
and I ended up too tired to drive home. I'd had a few too many
brews. So I spent one night out there with him. I couldn't
understand how he could live that way. The war not only made him
angry and unhappy, it made him not care about his personal
appearance. Nothing mattered except the girl." His haughty
expression reemerged. "No offense, but I don't see what he saw in
her. I don't."

"Maybe he liked her voice," Fleur said dryly.

He chuckled. "It was her sex appeal that attracted him,
probably not the voice. Gawd! She had this fluty voice she thought
was like her idol's, Janis Joplin. When she was a kid, she saw a
movie called *Breakfast at Tiffany's*. She was always singing the
theme song, 'Moon River.' I recall that Shane's favorite song was
by the Animals. 'House of the Rising Sun.' He would hum the song
all night, but she never sang it that I know of. If there was some
commonality keeping them together, I'd wager it was red-hot sex."

"Maybe they fueled one another's addictions."

"I'm not so sure which came first. They were both addicted.
And they didn't want to get clean. It was the culture they'd chosen
to be part of. They scoffed at guys like me. Thought I was missing
out on freedom. I had some damned heated arguments with Shane,
but I couldn't get through to him. He had his own agenda."

"People say his temper was bad."

"He'd been badly wounded. That's when he changed. Hell, yes,
he was pissed off. Your temper would be bad if you'd been wading
in the mud and filth every day. Nam was filled with bugs and

snakes. A couple of years of being in-country would have been bad enough, but the constant death and the blood all around us made it seem like decades. Sometimes it was like it was raining blood. Smoke and explosions were common. Our nerves were always tensed up, never knowing where the enemy, Charlie, was. They were everywhere. Charlie even sent kids with bombs strapped to them. Shane witnessed a little kid die that way. The blast took out a couple Marines, too. Shane cried for an hour. I asked him if he was crying for the soldiers or the little gook. Pissed him off. He said kids weren't gooks."

"That's understandable." Fleur winced. The sour taste in her mouth was like tasting battery acid. "I can see the sympathy you had for collateral damage."

Fueled by his tirade, Zucker didn't notice her putdown. "Charlie was all over the place, killing our guys by the truckload. Death pissed Shane off. Kids dying, starving. Jesus. He hated war. The entire damned war pissed him off. It wasn't long after that he got shot up. We all came out of Nam damaged. Tarnished. Some destroyed. People have no idea how lousy it was over there."

"I appreciate your service. I'm sure Nam was terrible. It must have also been a nightmare for the innocent women and children, the civilians."

As if in a trance, he stared down at the empty glass in front of him, then he called the waiter and ordered his fourth bourbon and water. "It was a terrible place. A terrible war. So why would he come back here to live in the filth and stupidity of those damned hippies? Why would he choose the despair of drugs? I don't get it."

"I don't know about his motivation, but I'd wager he believed in what he was doing." Fleur's eyes cast downward, and she took a quick sip of wine. "I'd like to believe he was a good person."

"He was a damn good man. One thing I'd like you to take away from this meeting is that Shane was a good man before the war, before Maggie. He was a brave soldier. And I can tell you, on my life, he didn't murder your mother. He didn't take his own life. I'd seen him fight for his life. He might have thrown life away for a couple years, but he never would have killed himself. He wouldn't have. It was his flipped-out chick. She wasn't at all stable, not in the least."

"I've spoken with friends of Maggie's who would swear that she was innocent of the murder, too—a man named Bernie and a woman named Gemma Rae."

"I never met a Bernie." He paused. "The name Gemma Rae vaguely rings a bell."

I'll give her your warmest regards, Fleur thought as she smiled. Their lunch had concluded, and she thanked Trinidad Zucker for his time and for the photos of Shane. She promised to let him know when and if the paternity question was resolved. Then with goodbyes, they parted.

Chapter 20

Fleur took a cab directly to the hotel. She'd seen the return e-mail from her linguist friend, and it had an attachment. Undoubtedly the translations. She wanted to spend time gleaning what she could from the completed translation.

As expected, her friend commented on the difficulty of word swaps in the cryptogram. It made the idiomatic phrases impossible to decipher, and she doubted if it could ever be fully reconstructed. She had ended her e-mail with wishes for good luck in the effort.

Fleur structured some words that could be gathered together. She put together vermin, revulsion, and watching live rat. She also put together food and purple powder and then considered the possibility that skin disease would be nearer purple powder.

After doing a search of Holocaust archival documents, she realized that purple powder was the medication given for every ailment. Fleur continued reading a few of the oral history testimonies.

Armed with some understanding, she again attempted to sift through the patterns in Aunt Golda's letter. She felt a numbness throughout her body at the horrendous events that the woman who raised her had endured. And she had lived through them. Perhaps fear, and Golda's desire to express her thoughts only to another woman who knew their full import, had provided a reason for continuing to hide her story from others.

Fleur felt the need to talk with Abby. Nearly clicking off before Abby finally answered, Fleur announced that she'd just sent the e-mail with a translation of the letters.

Abby's words seemed calm. "Hon, I've been looking through both letters, and I see a pattern in the words. I think the second letter will help, as the more examples I can look at, the better. My brother and I used to try to crack codes. It was far from the cryptography that's needed here, but I may be able to get a handle on it. I'm also dropping by to see Sophia. I'm holding out hope that she'll give me a hint."

"I appreciate your assistance." Fleur felt her voice warming.

"I'm getting caught up in it," Abby admitted. "Not the part about who killed whom in your parents' case, but in this history about Aunt Golda."

Fleur's eyes closed. "How can you not be interested in something so vitally important to me?"

"Damn it, have you once asked if the company vehicles have been repaired? Or if I'm scheduled out so far with my business that we'll be snow-covered before I finish? You called this morning to see how Fez is doing and didn't even ask how I'm doing, so don't start in about me not being interested in your ancient history."

"Point taken." Fleur swallowed some of her anger. "I'm stressed right now and shouldn't take it out on you. I'm just glad you're interested in all things Aunt Golda."

"I loved Aunt Golda," she said curtly. "And one of my vehicles is in the shop, one has been fixed, and I don't know how the hell I'm going to get through next week's workload."

Fleur shut the lid of her computer. "I'm sorry."

"Me, too," Abby responded without enthusiasm.

Fleur attempted to smooth over the moment with a topic change. "I'm going to take a walk over to Gemma Rae's, so I can give her a report on what I found out about my father from Trinidad."

"I'm going back to work."

Fleur heard the snap of the line going dead.

As she made the few blocks' walk to Gemma Rae's, Fleur considered what she'd tell her mother's best friend. She decided she would report only that she had been given photos of Shane and told of Trini's confident claim that Shane wasn't culpable in the deaths. She wouldn't mention that Trinidad had forgotten his one-nighter with the potter. Gemma Rae was not the type of person to believe that a night with her would not be memorable.

"Glad you stopped in," Gemma Rae said. "I was going through my crates of crap. Found some old memorabilia—a couple of letters and some things Maggie gave me. Also, Abby called earlier. Said to tell you your little dog is improving, and you shouldn't worry. She said the little thing was acting like he could eat a grain elevator empty."

Fleur laughed. "That's one worry off my chest. Abby is wonderful with the four-on-the-floors."

"I don't know her, but I like what I know from the couple of times I've talked with her."

The women took seats, and Rolly brought coffee. "Thanks, Rolly," Fleur said. "You make the best cappuccino in the world."

He smiled shyly, and Gemma Rae giggled. "Hell, you are the wrong train on the wrong track if you're trying out your cougar skills."

"As if she couldn't recognize my flounce," the young barista said with a chirping laugh. "I'd be glad to take you round to the clubs," he offered.

"Thanks, but it's been a decade since I've been in a bar. And I wouldn't go without Abby."

"See," Gemma Rae said. "You do love her after all."

"Yes. Yes." Her second response was more heartfelt. "I don't understand her, but I do love her."

"She requires a tweak or two," Gemma Rae joked. "Maybe you're getting her attention."

"That might be the case."

After coffee, Fleur followed Gemma Rae to the small backyard that held the freestanding kiln. Not far away was a tiny garage. Gemma Rae pulled open the door and moved past the shelves holding supplies, equipment, and pottery in various stages of processing. The center space held a clay-splattered pottery wheel.

At the back was a table that ran the length of the rear of the garage. She lifted a small overnight case down from one of the shelves. As she opened it, Fleur could see various knickknacks and trinkets inside. Gemma pulled out a packet of letters and notes. The rubber band surrounding it had disintegrated into a strip of powdery, broken rubber.

"I found her letters. I'd like you to have them," Gemma Rae said. "Maggie wrote the letters to me when she left the commune to live in the apartment. We didn't have phones out at the commune, but we did have a postal box. She'd write when she was lonely or sad or happy. Sometimes she wrote how she was lonesome for me, and that she wanted me to come to the apartment and pick her up. We took you out on the town a couple of times."

"Was I a yelping baby?"

"Nope. You were tranquil. Oh, yes, and in one letter she said she wanted you to become a rock singer. As I said, your disposition was probably way too tranquil. But I think she'd have been pleased to have birthed a botanist. Not that she probably knew what the fuck a botanist was."

"Being a botanist, I feel as though I can do some good." Fleur's heart felt constricted, and she caught her breath. "Maybe I could have."

"You aren't dead, so you can still do something."

"Of course." There was dejection in her answer. "Yes, I'll try."

"Hell, yes. Maggie never gave up on a battle in her life. Anyway, I thought you might like to have her letters."

Fleur's mind flashed to the crime scene photos. There had been a terrible struggle, and one way or another, Maggie had obviously not given up. "Thank you. I would love to have them." She pressed them to her heart. "I'll read them tonight. Are you certain you want to give them to me?"

"I have no one to leave them to, and I know you'll take care of them. Here, she made these for me." Gemma Rae handed Fleur some bead necklaces. "They're worthless trinkets and beads, but I've kept them all these years. Maggie made love beads. She was a creative kind of person. Music, beads, and she was funny. You'll see her zest for living in her writing."

"I'll cherish her letters, as well as her bead creations."

As they passed by the rows of pottery, Gemma Rae stopped. "This little vase, she threw this. Not too bad, actually." She lifted the piece of glazed pottery and inspected it. It was round, and sized as if to fit into the palms of one's hands. The colors were autumnal rusts and muted greens. "Unfortunately, her talent for pottery was only slightly better than her vocal range. But I think she'd have wanted you to have it." She handed the vase to Fleur.

Fleur hugged Gemma Rae. Both had tears in their eyes. "How can I thank you? This means so much to me." Fleur felt the woman's warmth against her. "I'll treasure these gifts."

"Maggie was a treasure. A mixed-up kid, but there was goodness in her heart."

Fleur recognized that on this day she had heard about two mixed-up kids. The descriptions of Shane and Maggie were from two different perspectives. Each recital was a clue from their past, from the friends' memories through which Maggie and Shane lived on. None of the bits and pieces answered Fleur's overriding question, but each tidbit of information was one more strand in a skein of versions, impressions, opinions, and truths.

Chapter 21

The following morning, Fleur woke with a start. Her iPhone was ringing. She reached across the bed to answer it, plucking the phone from beneath the pile of letters and notes that Maggie Heywood had written. Fleur had spent the shank of the evening reading them. In a wild, looping penmanship, Maggie had expressed her everyday life and her dreams.

"Fleur Hamilton," she answered.

"This is Howie Schultz. I wondered if you could come to my office this morning so we can talk about this case. It's becoming a real trash pile of entanglement. The more we know, the more we know we don't have a clue. I thought I should bring you up-to-date on what we have so far."

"What time do you have free?"

"Let's make it ten. I've got a desk filled with papers that need sorting."

"I'll be there at ten." Fleur looked at the clock. Half past eight. Normally she never slept that late, but reading her mother's letters had kept her awake.

She quickly showered and dressed and set out for the precinct. As she walked, she thought about Maggie's letters. They were mainly written to update Gemma Rae on her baby, on what was happening with Shane, and on her music.

In one letter, Maggie expressed how thrilled she was about her upcoming twentieth birthday. She'd expressed such joy because it would be the first birthday party her infant daughter could attend. Her music teacher, she noted, was making the cake.

Fleur pensively reflected on Aunt Golda's cakes. They were as sweet and jovial as Aunt Golda herself. On Fleur's last birthday, Golda had insisted on making the cake. With Abby's help, Golda had constructed a radiant pink cake, decorated with icing violets, roses, and daisies.

As she continued her walk to the precinct, Fleur's thoughts returned to her mother's letters. Melancholy loomed as she considered how dependent her mother's moods were on her relationship with Shane. When he was happy, her letters brimmed with cheer. When he was moody, or angry, her letters were sad.

Maggie expressed how it frightened her when he woke in the middle of the night, screaming at war flashbacks. However, she also mentioned his softness, warmth, and vulnerability and how his love made her feel. Vulnerability, she wrote, was something Shane rarely shared. His macho appearance was of strength and invincibility, but there was a tenderness inside him. Maggie believed they were right for each other. He'd written her a poem.

A poem now lost in the files of eternity, Fleur thought.

Seeing that she would be early for her meeting with Lt. Schultz, she sat for a moment and rested on a bench. She decided to try to call Samuel Bradley. She immediately realized her presumptive father's twin was unhappy that she had called.

He brusquely insisted his mother must not be bothered. Phoebe's heart was weak, and hearing from a *pretender* granddaughter would probably kill her.

"Look, Miss Whoever-You-Are, my family has no intention of accepting you or anyone else as Shane's daughter. Even if it were proven, you aren't welcome," his husky voice boomed.

"Mr. Bradley, I haven't any intention of become part of your family, I promise you."

"The family wants nothing to do with you, or Shane."

"He was your brother."

"Shane's actions killed our father, and our sister, too. Both went to premature deaths. Thankfully, although we are identical twins, I'm not and never have been the way he was."

"I believe that," Fleur said with sarcasm.

"He ruined the family. But I've attempted to bring honor back to the family name," Samuel said. "And don't try any of that DNA crap. Nobody will submit to a test. You aren't coming into family money."

"I have no intention of taking your money."

"Well, you aren't getting any," he said. "Mother's money has been spent on senior care over the years. Eighty-thousand dollars a year for her staying in the retirement and rehab homes has left nothing of the original family money."

Fleur assured him the call was not about money. She removed the phone from her ear when she heard the click that indicated

Samuel had disconnected. Fleur immediately called Abby. Abby's report reassured her. Abby had located recent photographs of Samuel Bradley on the Internet from when he'd run in a local school board election a year ago. Abby said she'd e-mail the photo. If Shane and Samuel were identical twins, it would be the nearest Fleur would come to seeing what her presumptive father would look like in his early sixties.

Glancing at her watch, Fleur saw she was right on time for her meeting. Entering Lt. Schultz's office, she noticed a weathered manila folder on his desk. When they were seated, Schultz began with an apology. "Ms. Hamilton, I'd be remiss if I didn't begin by saying I'm personally sorry this case was apparently bungled. It wasn't given the attention it should have had. In my defense, forty years ago, we were somewhat lackadaisical in our approach to investigating. An apparent suicide and murder didn't rank very high in importance, as the public was not in any danger. With all the social unrest and turmoil, we needed to chase down the bad guys."

"I fully understand, Lieutenant. There wouldn't have been a criminal on the loose, nor would there have been a trial to prepare for."

"Admittedly, things should've been saved, and they weren't. We no longer have bodies to check under fingernails for DNA. Back then, there wasn't DNA testing. Even so, we should've taken clippings. But we did find both the firearm and a few swatches of bloody clothing in the evidence vaults. I sent them to our lab to see if there is anything there that might help illuminate the case. Sometimes DNA disintegrates. More often, we're lucky and can capture it. Salvador said you were interested in your parents' DNA. We'd like to also do a test on you."

"A test?"

"Yes. The murder weapon will undoubtedly have both your mother's and father's blood on it. If there's DNA, it will certify your parentage. So, after our talk, head down and Salvador will swab your mouth. The least we can do is give you closure in regards to whether or not Shane is your father."

"I'd appreciate that. I still wonder whether someone else had a key to their apartment. I've got the name of the supervisor. Although everyone seemed to have liked him, and apparently he had no motive, maybe someone else—a prior renter—had a key."

Schultz shuffled through the report book. "Edward Rodriguez. He signed his name, but the middle initial is nearly obliterated with his poor writing. Could be an *O, P, D, Q,* or even a *C.* He was thirty-six at the time. We didn't question him carefully, because he wasn't a suspect. We didn't check him out, because it wasn't procedure to check scene witnesses when suicide-murder was evident. Window locked from the inside. Door locked from the inside. Screams heard from the inside were identified as Heywood's and Bradley's voices. And the renter, Maylor, claimed he woke Rodriguez. But I'll check out Rodriguez to see if it leads anywhere. And you're right, someone may have had a key made. I won't hold out much hope, but we can attempt to get a list of prior renters. Highly improbable a list still exists."

"Thank you, sir," Fleur said as she stood. "I know this is an old case, and you aren't required to give it any attention, so I'm most grateful for your help."

"We'll do everything we can. Might be that all we can do is determine your parentage, but sometimes that's enough. I searched for years for my own father. He'd bailed on my mother, my two brothers, and me."

"Did you find him?"

"No." His smile seemed to have forced itself onto his creased face. "And I'm a cop. He must have been a flipping escape artist. I strongly suspect he went back to Europe. In which case, becoming a cop wouldn't have helped my search anyway. I never could have found him. But I looked. I'm still looking, even after it doesn't matter."

"When I was a teenager," Fleur said, "I thought about how young my parents were when the auto crash occurred. They wouldn't have had much time to do anything good or bad."

He issued a three-quarters grin. "Back in the sixties, those kids did plenty, and some of it was far from good. No doubt about it—civil unrest and war seemed to have turned the world upside down."

She returned his smile. "Yes."

Her ride down in the elevator to meet Paul Salvador was quick. She saw him across the hall in one of his examination rooms. He carried two large envelopes into a conference room where they took seats. "Sorry I haven't had time to change into my civvies. I'm taking a quick break now, so forgive my appearance."

"I'm just happy you were able to meet with me."

He opened one envelope and carefully lifted out a stiff wad of clothing. Blood-stained swatches had been cut from the clothes. He explained that the blood from the clothing was being processed for DNA. In the other envelope was a plastic bag that contained a pistol. He carefully removed the plastic bag by its sleeve. Salvador's update informed Fleur that after a thorough examination of the gun, partial prints had been lifted, and blood samples had been collected.

Fleur was then given the traditional swab and told that the test would be completed within the next couple of days. "There is," Salvador explained, "a huge backlog of priority cases, but your sample will be processed as soon as possible."

Salvador's loose-fitting scrubs were dotted with multicolored sprays, and his hands were still red from the tight rubber gloves he'd worn. The scent of powder and chemicals was pungent.

"How is it going to affect you if you find out Shane Bradley isn't your father?" he asked.

Shaking her head, Fleur answered, "It isn't as important as knowing. I want the answer. If he isn't my father, another question has been answered. I've been without answers, as well as without questions, for four decades. Since I never knew Shane, I don't know that it would even have an impact on me. For the past few days, I've assumed he is my father, but assumptions are easily disproved. Our hearts tell us what we want to believe."

"Looking at the photos of him, you sure seem to have similar eyes. My gut tells me that if he wasn't your father, he was a close relative of your father."

"*Similar eyes* is exactly what his best friend said. But then, I was raised believing Aunt Golda's husband's eyes were precisely like mine."

With overt kindness, Salvador said, "I'll let you know when the results of the DNA tests come back. Also what I can find out about the prints. They didn't always take victim's prints. Imagine. Different procedures back then. But I've got driver's license prints coming. And Shane's prints from his arrests and military service are being sent over. As I said before, I'm curious by nature. I'd like to determine what's what. And who's who." He smiled.

"Lt. Schultz verified the name of the superintendent—Edward Rodriguez."

"I beat you to the punch. Schultz said the middle initial is anything in the alphabet between *B* and *X*. Which means it could be *A*," he said with a laugh. "I can't find a thing on him. Without a middle name, it's tough. Lots of leads, but none have panned out. Lois has been chasing him down for us, too. She's had nada luck. Might be, and probably is, a dead end or not relevant, but we'll keep trying."

"You appear to be terrific at bulldogging a case. I'm sure if anyone can help unravel what actually happened, you can. If you don't mind my asking, why did you go into forensic investigation?"

"So I wouldn't have to deal with busted up people left in the aftermath of a crime. My dad was a homicide detective. He'd tell me about kids left behind when one parent had offed the other. The kids were forever scarred by it. So, maybe not knowing about your parents for all these years was a blessing."

Fleur took a deep breath, nodded, and walked away.

In the door panel's reflection, she saw Paul Salvador's gaze following her. She recognized his look of sympathy. It was the same look she had seen when she was a child and told schoolmates that her parents had died when she was a baby. As a child, that had been the stock answer she'd been taught. Aunt Golda had provided her with an easy, acceptable reason for her parents' death.

Until now, she reflected, she'd never dissected that look. She only recalled wondering why it occurred. There was nowhere she'd rather have been than in the home where she'd been raised. And no one with whom she would rather have been than Aunt Golda.

But now, she wondered how she might have turned out had her parents raised her.

All of the new knowledge had changed the coordinates of her life. Abby just didn't understand.

Chapter 22

Back on the sidewalk, she found she wanted to review and analyze the data. She switched her phone to silent, so she could contemplate the information she had gathered.

There was Sophia, back in Denver, and sometimes not of rational mind. When she returned home, Fleur vowed to glean as much information as she could from the elderly woman. She'd already found much of the truth during her trip to San Francisco, but she wanted to ask Sophia about Golda, the facets of her "great aunt" that she didn't know.

Although Sophia had consistently maintained there was a third letter, it was difficult to count on that until it was found. Fleur knew Sophia might or might not have memories of how to decode the cryptic, postwar letters. Sophia might have forgotten or might not relinquish the key.

As for her findings about her parents, Fleur considered the investigation would be providing some answers, but many questions might still remain. She took stock. She'd talked with both her parents' best friends, presuming Shane was her father. She'd scoured his two abbreviated letters to find out more about him. They were both written before she was born. In fact, they'd been written prior to Shane meeting Maggie. Those letters were sad, frightened, and lonely. She'd devoured the letters her mother had written. Her mother's sadness was only apparent when Shane was despondent.

There'd been important discoveries about her background. Maggie's mother had died long ago, and the father was unknown, and probably also dead. She'd located and met with her mother's sister and niece, her own aunt and cousin. Her mother's brother had no interest in knowing her.

She deliberated on the other side of the family, or possible family. There was Shane's elderly mother and twin brother and his children. His brother wanted no part of any reunion. Fleur would respect his wishes. She'd been told not to bother the mother or to ever contact him again. That was acceptable to her. She resented the family for having been so hateful to both Shane and Maggie. And they'd been particularly cruel to Maggie.

She evaluated the information carefully. It could have been her mother, high on drugs, tripping badly, who killed Shane and herself. It could have been Shane's temper, with the drugs, alcohol, and anger propelling him into a rage. He killed Maggie, and then himself. It could have been a double suicide. One killed themself, and then the other, in sorrow and shock, killed themself. Or there could have been someone else there, someone who had used a key.

The authorities were searching for the former apartment superintendent. He had been on site immediately after the deaths of Maggie and Shane. They would also check for records on who might have had a key from having rented before. Records that both Schultz and Salvador doubted still existed.

Fleur thought she had done nearly everything she could, for the moment. For the next couple of days, she'd wait for information. She was resigned to being subjected to Abby's request, in a demanding tone, for her to return home. She'd continue to refuse. She'd find out as much as she could about the wild young couple who'd had everything to live for. They had one another, and they also had a child, yet they had not lived.

In one of her father's letters, she had read how he only wanted to be healed of his wounds and be rid of the nightmares. In one of her mother's letters, she read that Maggie wanted her daughter to be able to dance in the morning, sing in the afternoon, and love in the night.

This was something Fleur also wanted for herself. She wanted the current instability of her heart to be calmed. She wanted to find comfort from the pain of losing Aunt Golda. There seemed few answers to lift Fleur's sadness. Aunt Golda had often said that everyone fell out of the earth's rhythm once in a while. Thoughts of riding earth's loop across the solar system only increased Fleur's desolation, for she was feeling very much out of the rhythm of earth.

She cautioned herself not to do too much binge thinking. She wanted her once-tranquil heart returned to her.

Back in her hotel room, she checked for calls and messages. Abby had left a call telling her it was urgent that she speak with Fleur.

"Abby," she said with a quick breath, "is Fez ill?"

"No problem with Fez. Sorry I scared you, adorable. I've been studying these letters, and I think I might have broken the code. In both the correspondences, there's this strange jump from sentence to sentence and word to word. What I'm thinking is that before each letter, the women had a brief phone conversation. They decided on two sets of codes. Say, one for sentence placement and a second for word placement."

"Words and sentences rearranged by number?"

"Exactly." Abby's voice broke off, and there was the sound of papers being shuffled. "Two, four, one, and three. Then the second numerical code is for word placement—three, one, four, and two. That's what the codes seem to be for the first letter. I'm working on the codes for the second letter now. They might have kept the same codes, but it looks as though the numbers are shifted around."

"It was probably similar to one they used in the camp." Fleur powered up her computer. She grabbed her journal and quickly scribbled down the numbers Abby had given her. When the first letter appeared on the screen, she lifted out the various sentences, beginning with the second, going to the fifth. She quickly put the words numerically. "That's it, Abby! How in the world did you crack the code?"

"I honestly wandered into it. I know they have code-breaker programs. I'll order one and have it installed on your computer. It will only take a couple minutes to decode the first letter. Meanwhile, I'll be working on getting the second rearranged."

"Do you have time?"

"Fleur, I'm getting caught up in this thing. We can actually read Aunt Golda's words and know her even better. A part of her that was so important, it's in these cryptic messages. Now they are one more voice relating the terror she lived through. That's important."

"I…" Fleur choked back tears. "I want you to know how much I appreciate your assistance on the codes."

"I told you, I'm doing it for Aunt Golda. She was always there for me."

"For me, too."

Silence reminded Fleur of the enormous impasse that existed between them. Her face warmed before her words were again swallowed away.

Abby's voice strengthened. "I'll get on ordering the decoding program, and I'll work on attempting to find out the second letter's codes. Also, I need to see if I can shake the branches of Sophia's memory and get the third letter."

"I was thinking about that earlier. It may have been lost, or maybe it never existed."

"Lots of things may have been lost or never existed."

They both knew exactly what the words meant. And why Abby had echoed them.

Chapter 23

Fleur was pleasantly surprised by the mid-afternoon call from Stephanie Pierce.

"Fleur... my niece. Those words sound so lovely to me," Stephanie said in a warm tone. "Words I certainly never thought I'd be saying. I called to ask if you might be available tomorrow. Joan mentioned that she isn't working and she would love to take you to lunch and maybe show you around the city. I'd go, but my schedule is full with a time-consuming to-do list. My busiest time of year. Since Joan has the day off, she volunteered to pick you up and escort you around."

"Are you sure?"

"She really wants to get to know you."

"I'd enjoy it," Fleur said.

"Joan is a responsible driver and has taken many people on excursions through the city."

"I want you to know something up front. I'm a lesbian. Abby and I are 'married,' as much as we can be. If that's a problem, please feel free to take the invitation back. I'll understand if you have reservations about me being with your daughter."

Stephanie's laugh chimed. "I sort of figured it out when you mentioned Abby was your companion. Also, you've lived together for sixteen years. And in answer to your unspoken question, we're not of the homophobic persuasion. You needn't be kissing cousins," she teased. "Seriously, I'm aware it isn't contagious. My daughter isn't at all alarmed by a gay cousin. I think we already have a couple of them. And," she said with total conviction, "it never occurred to me Maggie's daughter would be anywhere near the conventional norm. Maggie certainly freely exhibited her own differences."

"Thanks," Fleur said softly. "Then I'd love to go."

"Joan said to ask if eleven would be good. She'll pick you up at your hotel. You could have lunch together, maybe jaunt around

Maggie's old haunts in the Haight area. Joan is great at finding those out-of-the-way places in San Fran."

"I'd like seeing the area where my parents lived." She held back from saying she wasn't certain she wanted to see the building where they died. Redirecting that thought, she concluded that it was also the place she'd lived as an infant, and where Aunt Golda had taught her the first joys of life. It was where her mother had sung songs to her. And where her father had held her.

"Eleven it is."

When they hung up, Fleur resumed her wait for the code-deciphering program Abby was sending. When the software had been received and loaded, Fleur followed the instructions Abby had e-mailed. With the method selected, the words were decrypted and rearranged, with the translations appearing in English so that Fleur could read the text.

Reconstructed, Golda's missive related all that Fleur had guessed about. The horror of the concentration camp was clear even in the splattering of words.

> *There they believed us to be stupid. We knew the marching music was played to drown out the sounds of the executions. Mother was part of the ensemble, and she hated the repertoire that included the camp anthem. She would grumble about such ugliness in music. Before the war, Mother would never have thought it possible that murderers could turn music into their own madness. Tears dripped from every note that she played.*

Fleur continued reading through the blur of her tears.

> *My mother and I mused about how hearts could be converted to hating. Even in animals. Recall, Sophia, my dear friend, how the viciousness of the dogs frightened us. They became as heartless as the guards. I could not comprehend how this could be so.*

Fleur considered the many pets that her aunt had rescued. Throughout her life, Golda insisted on treating pets with the same kindness with which she treated people. Aunt Golda encouraged her to allow animals to follow her home. Golda was a rescuer. Always, there was room to care for lost or neglected pets. More amazing, her aunt had never been frightened of an animal or a human being. Fleur wondered how that could be possible. Continuing to read the letter, Fleur tried to imagine her aunt as she wrote it.

We heard the scraps of information telling of the furnaces in a death factory. It was difficult to imagine such harsh and sadistic games by heartless executioners. It seemed that the entire nation wanted to liquidate an entire race of people. Their hearts had been turned to hate. And now our hearts turn.

Hatred itself couldn't understand the heart of a woman who, once liberated, remained kind. But Fleur knew her aunt well enough to see anger within the long-ago written words. Anguish and anger were indeed represented. How could it not be?

She sent the entire reconstructed text back to Abby, with a note of thanks.

With nothing else demanding her attention, Fleur took time to reflect on how grateful she was that Golda had survived to raise her. While counting her blessings, she also included Stephanie's acceptance of her lifestyle. She was glad that she'd announced her sexuality up front.

Although her sexual orientation wasn't something she usually mentioned, it was also something she would never deny. It had been one of the reasons she'd left teaching. A decade and a half ago in Denver, there was the fear of being outed. Even now, it was a secret many educators chose to keep. Those who targeted gays and lesbians found ways to ridicule and torment them, or worse. Working at the lab turned out to be her calling, and as a bonus, there wasn't a constant fear of being exposed by bigots.

As she made notes in her journal, Fleur felt a pang of homesickness. She missed her work. Tenderly caring for her species experiment in her small upstairs lab was heaven. She missed Abby, missed the "livestock," as Abby referred to the pets, and she missed Golda. Fleur admitted to herself that she hadn't been prepared for losing Golda.

Her present loneliness required company. The need pulled at her like a magnet, and Fleur ended up walking to Gemma Rae's, where she was greeted by Rolly Li.

"Gemma Rae will be right back. Oh, and Abby called earlier."

"Thanks, Rolly. I had my phone turned down, but I've spoken to her since then."

"How about a cappuccino?"

"Great." Rolly effortlessly whipped up the drink. "Are you getting tired of me hanging out here?"

"Not at all. So, you got everything all figured out with your love interest?"

"No," she replied with a slight smile. "Love interest is a rather weak description of a sixteen-year affair of the heart."

With a lift of his eyebrow, he said, "Affair of the heart is a little outdated, too. Whatever you call your relationship, is it going any better for you two?"

Fleur bit her lip a moment. "We may not be able to repair our relationship."

Seeming to sense her sadness, and as if out of words, he changed topics. "Gemma Rae says you're a botanist."

"Yes. I work with a medical research laboratory. I'm also working independently on a private study. At least I was before I came here."

"My mama can grow plants from the ceilings. Green thumb. That woman can grow a box of nails green."

"Abby has a knack with plants." Thoughts of Abby filled Fleur's mind. She was also tender and patient with plant life. Fleur always teased that she could resurrect any landscape greenery from the brink of death.

"Landscaping would be a cool profession," Rolly said.

"And what do you want to do with your life?"

"I'm in college now, studying to be an engineer, even though I love being a barista. Hanging out here is great. Gemma Rae has helped me out when I need time off, and she's also helped with the costs of my education. She's a great gal."

"I'm sure you'll make an excellent engineer."

"Anyone who can fix Gemma Rae's antiquated cappuccino machine when it's on the fritz should be ready for MIT. I settled for the local college. I don't like to think about leaving Gemma Rae on her own. When she loads her kiln, she's a danger to humanity. Why don't you move here?"

"I'm glad you're here to watch after Gemma Rae. My roots are firmly in Colorado. I love my area of the world, but it would be great to vacation here."

"What if Abby wanted to move here?"

"With all her family living in Colorado, it isn't likely." Fleur frowned. "Did she say she wanted to move here?"

"No. I didn't talk with her long, but she said California is nice. She seems nice."

"Abby's got a good personality with those she likes, but she only likes certain people. She must like you. I'm not so sure she likes me. She makes me feel inadequate. Anything that isn't in complete agreement with her is deemed wrong."

"To me it sounded like she's lonesome for you."

"She's manipulative. It's her ploy to get me back there."

"She talked more about your Aunt Golda than she did about you. I told her that Gemma Rae has told me so many stories about Golda, I feel like I knew her. Abby said she was like a mother to both of you, and that she misses her."

"We both miss Aunt Golda." Fleur considered how much more she would miss her once she returned home. Being away dulled the reality. Golda had been aging, and they all understood that her time would come to an end. Also, there was the fact that her teenaged body had withstood two years in a concentration camp. Fleur always believed it was Golda's mind that had brought her through the difficult years. She had depended on inner strength to save her. In later years, her spirit saw her through physical ailments. Fleur's great aunt, or the woman pretending to be her great aunt, had seemed to be an indomitable force.

And then, a week ago, Golda had called them very early in the morning. Abby and Fleur rushed to Golda's side. Deteriorating quickly, the old woman was unable to lift her head from the pillow. When Golda lapsed into unconsciousness, Fleur was too distressed to react. It was Abby who called 911 and began trying to help Golda, while Fleur stood immobile beside the bedroom door jamb. Her mind was numb as she realized she might have to come to terms with not having Golda in her world.

Fleur traveled in the ambulance, while Abby followed behind in her vehicle. While the ambulance took Golda and Fleur to the hospital, Fleur could do nothing except whisper her love into her great aunt's ear. She also thanked Golda for her love. When Aunt Golda's lips moved, Fleur leaned in close, so as not to miss a syllable. Golda's eyes flickered. Her voice was weak, nearly just breath alone. She said she was saved by Flower. She'd called her Flower. Then mumbled the words, "Best a cold meal."

They were separated for a few minutes while medics worked on Golda. After that, Golda was taken to a side room where Fleur was allowed to sit with her. By that time, Abby had arrived at the hospital. Together they watched Golda's breath slowly ease away.

Time and her own frail body had done what the Nazis had not been able to do. Her talent as a pianist had kept her alive when she was a young girl. Her spirit had forced her to go on after the loss of the man she'd loved and married. Finally, she was succumbing to time's elapsing moments. Like a piano concerto diminishing to a stop, Aunt Golda's breathing ceased.

Fleur glanced up into Rolly's face. "I'd forgotten she called me Flower before she died." Tears filled her eyes, as she repeated, "We both miss Golda."

"Easy to miss the people we love." Rolly moved away to take care of a customer.

Fleur felt her throat contracting, and she wanted to sob. She took a quick sip of her cappuccino.

Chapter 24

Grateful for Gemma Rae's return, Fleur told her about the DNA test and the investigatory updates, as well as how thrilled she was to get the call from Stephanie.

"It will do you good to go on a little field trip. It isn't far, and since Joan is taking you by Haight-Ashbury, I'll give you the address where Golda and your parents lived."

Fleur handed Gemma Rae the journal and a pen. Quickly, in large, squiggly, backward leaning letters, Gemma Rae wrote the address, along with directions.

"It's not the same as it was, but you can get the idea. The Haight's changed, but so have I," she said with a deep, throaty laugh. "Goddess knows my thunder thighs have doubled in size."

Fleur grinned. "I'm finding sags that weren't even part of my body two decades ago. Golda used to say it was best to age healthily and happily, but *aging* was the most important thing."

"Golda was inventive when it came to optimism and when it came to fun. Maggie told me Golda had fun with music, and her students felt the fun. She always made her students feel as though they were having a party. It was never just practice and learning."

"I was recently thinking about her and her ideas about teaching. Golda's soul was the embodiment of plants and flowers. I remembered how she would make little dancing girls out of the hollyhocks. You know—where you turn the flower upside down and fasten a bud on as the head? She'd make me an entire dance floor filled with dancing girls, and I would name them, play with them, and pretend they were alive. Flowers became my favorite toys. Actually, anything growing in the backyard became a plaything."

"Golda was a born teacher. She had to grimace a time or two when Maggie began caterwauling." Gemma Rae fluffed her hair and lifted her shoulder, then looked back over her shoulder with an exaggerated head bob. "She'd get all flirty and sexy and then howl.

Golda's sweet eyes would close a moment. She had those sensitive, chocolate-colored eyes that searched deep inside you. Then, with a deadpan face, she would instruct Maggie to bring it down a notch."

Fleur's eyes crinkled with amusement. "What did my mother do?"

"Hell, she beamed like Golda was giving her the best critique in the world."

"Golda was never unkind. I can't imagine going through a concentration camp and still coming out with love."

"Maybe she learned to act docile in the camp." A flash of anger crossed Gemma Rae's face. "Maybe she wanted to bash some skulls, but she learned to control those urges. How can we search the human soul? Especially if the soul has been nearly destroyed."

Fleur felt a chill. "Maybe her love of beauty helped her. Music, art, the loveliness of life might have saved her from the horrors. She knew the fragility of life."

Gemma Rae's eyes were cast downward. "Seeing so much death, so early—it must have been crippling."

"At a very young age, she taught me there's a cycle of life. Even the hollyhocks helped teach me. I'd put the little flower dancers safely near a tree. The next day, the little flowers would be shriveling. She said that was the reason we must enjoy each day. She would make me another party of dancers." Her eyes shut a moment. "Until the frost set in. Then she would say we had another task to do until next spring. Our new mission became counting, examining, and determining snowflake types."

Gemma Rae patted her hand. "You miss her terribly, don't you?"

"Yes. I wonder if the pain of loss ever truly diminishes."

Gemma Rae reached across the table to touch the necklace she had given Fleur, the one Maggie had made. "I'm glad you're wearing your necklace." She looked into Fleur's face. "They say in time the pain will lessen. I say sometimes there isn't enough time to make it better. But we go on because that's what our loved one would want us to do."

Fleur sighed a nearly silent sigh. "Now I'm also missing my parents. Missing not so much *them*, but the *knowing* of them."

"What happens if Shane isn't your biological father? Not that I expect him not to be. Would your search for your father continue?"

"No. I only want to know what happened forty years ago, how this tragedy happened. There's no reason to go beyond that."

"Will you contact Shane's twin brother with the result of the DNA test?"

"No. Samuel Bradley told me he didn't want to have any reminders of his twin. He claimed Shane had, in essence, killed his family. And maybe both Shane's and Maggie's families helped kill my parents as well. However, none of it truly matters. I'm certain Samuel expects me to beg him for a DNA sample. I am not chasing him down for familial spit."

"Maybe he thinks you'll fly to New York and follow him around picking up his cigarette butts to get his DNA."

"No way. I hope the DNA from the crime scene hasn't deteriorated and can be analyzed, but either way, I won't be contacting Samuel or any other Bradley. If there is a definitive result from the DNA testing, I'll tell you, Bernie, and Stephanie the results."

"And Abby?"

"Of course. I'll tell her first. Not that it will matter to her."

"Fleur, I've talked with her, and I believe she's truly concerned about you. If I were you, I'd give her the benefit of the doubt."

Fleur smiled. "She's infuriating, but I certainly don't think she's a bad person. Not at all. She's worked hard to retrieve Golda's letters from her friend, and she actually cracked the code. If you'd like a copy of the letter that's been decoded and translated, I can give you one. It's almost exclusively about the concentration camp."

"Not even. Too grim. But it is lovely that Abby worked with you on it."

"As I said, she did much more than work on it. And I appreciate that. It's this trip she isn't happy about. But no matter what, I've got to know what happened to my parents."

"Maybe Abby's love doesn't allow her to understand."

"We should back one another. Be there. In years past, we were always supportive of each other."

"Even if you believed something might be harmful to her life, you'd be supportive of her doing it?"

"As I told you, with Aunt Golda's intervention, our arguments were always smoothed over. And I can't answer about how I would respond if I thought Abby wanted to do something that would threaten her life."

"What did Golda say when you and Abby squabbled?"

"There weren't many squabbles. Our disagreements were mini-debates. To be honest, I'm not certain what the problems even were. When there were discussions, Aunt Golda would never side with either of us. She would say things like: Each moment counts. Love is the important part of life. Don't bicker about minor problems, only things that can't be resolved. But it seems those less-important things began to accumulate, and I think we harbored resentment because we just buried them." Fleur rested her head on her hand. "Right now, Abby's upset about my being off work and also about my losing the grant to continue my research."

"I have a feeling Abby's upset about more than that."

"Probably. But those are some of her complaints."

"You told me that Golda used to say she had learned firsthand how everything can be quickly taken from you, that her family had lost everything they had. Because of that, she tried not to become attached to things, but it was impossible not to stay attached to people."

"Aunt Golda wasn't materialistic, in any way, shape, or form. Events, doing things, were always more important than appearances or belongings. Although our small house was always straightened up and clean, once in a while, Aunt Golda would spot dust on a curio cabinet. She would say, 'Don't mind the dust, we're off to Paris next week.' She would always make me laugh."

"That's a hell of a good excuse for dust. I always say, 'don't mind the dust. I think of it as my life's patina.' Raised by Maggie, or by Golda, you were bound to end up with a sense of humor. Yes, you were destined to have a little comic relief in your life. And you would also have learned a disdain for materialism from Maggie."

"Do you think Maggie and your radical hippie philosophies rubbed off on Aunt Golda?"

"No. Golda's words, and those of people of a similar ilk, were the bedrock of the hippie movement. We were against war. We weren't materialistic. We wanted our planet to be saved."

With a playful smirk, Fleur teased, "Really? Because I heard you trashed Woodstock."

Chapter 25

Fleur woke feeling somewhat more at ease and rested than she had the past mornings away from her home. She'd talked with Abby last night and found out that Abby had stopped by to visit Sophia again. Although she'd questioned the older woman, there were no new revelations. Sophia diligently stuck to her story of there being a third letter.

Fleur considered how the conversation had ended in another feud. "Abby, thanks for visiting Sophia," she had said.

Abby had retorted, with a twinge of irritation, "You do realize that Sophia has been part of my life for sixteen years. I'd be visiting her, regardless. The old girl is special."

"I know that. I was thanking you! How's the code-breaking going?"

"I'm going to need more time to unravel the numerical twists of this one. I'd hoped it would be similar to the first letter, but it isn't."

"Well, Abby, I know you're trying."

"You have no idea how flipping busy I am. Added duties and all. So the time working on this code is really cutting into everything else. And there's your experimental study." Her words were harsh."

"Why don't you let my work go? I won't be home in time to save the study." Fleur was convinced all was lost.

Annoyed, Abby spat back, "You want me to just let the samples of plant life die? After all we've sacrificed for this opportunity, you want to abandon the report!" Abby's temper flared. "And now you're wasting time on a needless, stupid trip."

Fleur quickly found a reason for disconnecting, resolutely vowing not to allow the conversation to impact her sleep. Thankfully, she had slept. But when the phone rang in the morning, she knew she didn't wish to repeat last evening's conversation. She answered Abby's call tersely.

"I can't go through another conflict right now," Fleur said. "I'm way too tense."

"I'm calling to tell you I shouldn't have snapped at you last night, Fleur. I'm under a lot of pressure right now, but we've got to work through it. What I really called to tell you was that I think I've got the numbers on the code. Anyway, what I've unscrambled is making sense. Unfortunately."

"Why unfortunately?"

"Because it's sadder than anything in letter one."

Fleur leaned up to grab her journal from the nightstand. "Let's take the numbers of the sentence transitions, then the words."

"Okay. Sentences come together beginning with four, two, one, three, and five. Words seem to jump five, two, four, six, one, and three. In one place, it seems as if there are a couple of skips in the encoding. I'm not sure why. But if you put it through the program, it may work out."

"I'll do that now." Fleur opened her computer and rapidly entered the data. "Abby, I can't believe you've been able to do all this. I had no idea. You've never picked up a puzzle of any kind."

"And because you don't see me doing crossword puzzles and games, you think I can't handle codes?"

"I'm sorry if you've interpreted my comment like that. See, I can't say anything to you anymore. I was attempting to compliment you." Fleur's voice had faded to a dull monotone. "I wanted to tell you it was impressive."

"So I took it wrong?"

"No. I'm not getting into this with you. We're going to stop now. I appreciate your skill at cryptography, that's all I'm saying. I'm working on the letter, and as soon as I get some resolution on it, I'll e-mail a copy to you."

"I'll look in on Sophia."

Fleur heard the somberness in Abby's voice. "I'll let you know if I find out anything else from here."

The click of the phone reminded Fleur of the days they not only shared sweet words before hanging up, but they longed for the conversation to continue. Early in this talk with Abby, Fleur felt encouraged that things between them could be okay, but when the phone speaker went dead, it was as if it heralded the finality of their relationship.

When her phone rang immediately, Fleur guessed it might be Abby calling back. The phone call, however, was from Lois Trujillo. After an exchange of greetings, Lois gave Fleur an update.

"I'm sorry to have to report that there is absolutely no trace of a paper trail on any seventy-five-year-old Edward, Ed, Eddie, Teddy, or Eduardo Rodriguez, or any similarly named person with that approximate birth date, not even so much as a traffic stop. And I didn't find anyone fitting our parameters residing in San Francisco or its suburbs at that time. The building superintendent was apparently using an alias, or it is also possible Rodriguez moved to another area or died an early death.

"I also checked with the state income tax department. There was no record of him paying taxes, but with the job he had, he might have received a rent-free apartment in lieu of a paycheck. His handyman work was probably compensated by cash under the table."

"I can't thank you enough for all of your efforts," Fleur said when the report was concluded.

"Don't worry, I'll continue searching."

As the call ended, Fleur wondered whether the man whom Bernie had known as Ed Rodriguez had vanished off the face of the earth.

Most of her energy that morning was delegated to Internet searches. When the information from the second letter had been successfully entered, the deciphering text software systematically reprogrammed the words.

Golda's words were numb with fear:

> *Mother's health was declining. The barrack was without air, and the smoke awful. Mother said everything was restricted—our space, our freedom, and our dreams. She held me tightly and promised we would not perish. One day, she would tell me, we would be liberated and returned to our family.*
>
> *I often asked Mother how men could be so evil, and she replied that we were seeing such suffering because there was an evil devil with power. We had been incarcerated by the devil, a devil who had the power to spawn more devils to further the work of terror. It was our misfortune to have been caught by a lurking devil.*
>
> *In the hands of God, life was precious and held in a kind way, my mother would say. We should have great awe to be held within the hands that elevate the human spirit, but when clutched in the devil's clasp, the soul was wrung toward death.*

Tears blurring her vision, Fleur looked away from the computer screen a moment. After blinking several times, she continued to read.

> *Mother said we would need to fight to live. Justice had to be seen to by the living.*
> *Food had become scarcer. We feared starvation, but we would rather be starved than be murdered.*
> *Remember, Sophia, you must keep my letters of remembrances. We should never forget. So keep them.*

Fleur closed the lid of her computer and went to get ready for Joan Pierce to pick her up. She looked forward to spending the afternoon exploring the places her parents had spent their last days on earth. She braced herself for seeing the apartment building where her parents had lived and died. It was also the place where Aunt Golda had lived and helped to raise the infant Flower.

Joan arrived to pick up Fleur exactly on time. She spoke rapidly and moved speedily. Her tawny-brown hair was pulled back into a ponytail at the base of her neck. Her eyes were green and in sunlight appeared golden. The features on her rounded face were symmetrically balanced and attractive. She carried a bit of weight but still appeared athletic. She was clad in shorts and a fancy T-shirt. Her face, arms, and legs were well tanned.

"Sorry about the family sedan," Joan said as she gestured Fleur into the passenger seat. "Mother insisted. She says my car is a rust bucket. I would have liked to bring my boyfriend's car. It has a lot more oomph under the hood." She pulled smoothly away from the curb.

Amused, Fleur thought back to when she was twenty. Oomph was a good thing.

After they stopped at a local restaurant and enjoyed a sumptuous lunch, Joan drove to the Haight-Ashbury area. They easily located the apartment building where Maggie, Shane, Aunt Golda, and infant Fleur had resided four decades earlier.

It actually wasn't far from where Gemma Rae's shop was located and would have been a fairly easy walk from Fleur's hotel. Fleur decided she would return the next day and do some questioning of any elderly people still living there who might possibly remember the murder. She hadn't figured on Joan pulling into a parking space near the front of the building.

"Let's explore," the young woman said gleefully.

"Explore?"

"Sure. You know, go look inside the building."

As they approached the front door, Fleur saw there was an entry system requiring them to be buzzed inside. "Joan, we don't know anyone here." She feared if they entered, they might be kicked off the premises. She was also worried about the potential emotional impact. Her parents had died inside this building. "And we can't get in if we don't know who to ring."

"True enough." The impetuous young woman pushed each of the buttons. "Bet five bucks someone will spring the lock."

Fleur laughed when the door released. "I owe you five."

Joan swung the door open, and they entered. "Where to?"

"Gemma Rae said the lower level is the garden floor. The first floor would be a few steps up, and the second floor would be above that." They went up the stairs and walked toward the center of the first floor. "Okay, it should be these two. In the middle would have been Aunt Golda's. On the other side, one apartment away would have been Bernie's apartment."

"I wonder," Joan mumbled, "if anyone might still live here who was here when the crime occurred. My guess is we'll need to check at the houses around the building. People usually don't remain as long in apartment buildings as in homes."

"You're a pretty good investigator," Fleur said.

"I'm sticking with my safe little business major." She turned to Fleur. "Do you think the current super would still be in the same apartment? Down to the garden level, right?" Joan made a rush for the stairs. "Let's check."

"It would be the garden level, directly below Bernie's apartment."

By the time Fleur caught up with Joan, she was already knocking on the door. When a woman opened the door, Joan asked, "Is this the superintendent's apartment?"

"No. They changed the super's place to down at the end of the hall, last door on the left."

"Thanks," Joan said as the door closed. She hesitated a moment. "Okay, maybe it's a good thing we got the wrong apartment. We're likely to get tossed out after we check in with the super. Let's go back up and scope this place out. We'll make our first stop the apartment that was your Aunt Golda's. ."

The apartment where her aunt had lived seemed like a historical temple of sorts. It was such an integral part of Fleur's past. She touched the door reverently.

Joan knocked loudly. When the door fanned opened, Joan explained, "My cousin's great aunt once lived here. We were passing by, and for old time's sake, stopped by."

Her friendly, benign demeanor didn't alarm the elderly man. "You can come in and have a look, if you like." He gestured them inside and showed them around the apartment.

After the mini-tour, Fleur stopped inside the front door. "We really appreciate you letting us look around. Do you mind if I ask you a question?"

"Go right ahead, young lady."

"Do you by any chance know, or have you ever heard of a building superintendent named Ed Rodriguez?"

"I'm sorry, Miss. I wish I could help, but I'm unfamiliar with any Rodriguez associated with this building. Perhaps our current superintendent might have knowledge of him."

The women went directly back down to the garden level. As Fleur passed by the middle apartment that had belonged to her parents, her breathing became labored. She glanced down at the doorknob. Her parents had turned that knob the last time they entered their apartment, and then they had died.

"Are you okay?" Joan asked.

"Yes. When I passed the apartment back there, I realized it had belonged to my parents."

"This must be where the super lives." Joan again knocked loudly on the door.

The man who opened the door appeared to be in his mid-fifties, and a heavy scent of garlic and spices wafted from him.

With quick calculation, Fleur realized this man was probably too young to have known Rodriguez. She asked him anyway.

"I heard the name," the man said. "He was super a ways back. I been here for nearly twenty-five years now. Musta been nearly a decade or more before I came that he was here. Only way I know is 'cause there was a big killing happened when he was here. You lookin' for him 'cause of the murder?"

"Yes."

"I can't tell you nothing about it. My mother lives with me. She keeps up with the gossip. Hey, Ma," he yelled. An elderly woman pushed her walker across the room. "These ladies wanna know something about the super who was here back when those folks were killed."

"I'm Fleur Hamilton," Fleur said, "and this is Joan. We were wondering where the former super, Ed Rodriguez, might be now."

Her eyes drifted into remembrance. "I remember the murder business and him. Why, he's the brother of one of the women in my church. That's the only reason I know anything about it—she told me. I never had nothing to do with him. The woman from church said her brother had been in jail most of the time."

Fleur recoiled. "Jail? Are you certain?" She felt chilled. She'd been told the search being conducted by the police had come up empty-handed. That search had included state institutions.

"Yeah. He was a rotten one. Charming, but come to find out, he was a bad 'un."

"I don't understand. Are you sure we're talking about the same man. Ed Rodriguez, who managed the apartments here forty years ago? He would be about seventy-five-years old."

"That's the one. But he only went by the name Ed. Edward. It was his middle name. According to his sister, his name is Davy. Well, David, but she calls him Davy."

"Middle initial could have been a *D*. If so, he switched his first and middle names," Fleur said, her thoughts jumbled. "He must have had a record when he got the job here, so he used a fresh name."

"From what his sister says"—the old woman's laugh turned into a cough—"he was plenty fresh alright."

"Thank you for your time."

When they stepped onto the pavement, Fleur pulled out her phone. As if a powerful fist had been thrust into her solar plexus, her body buckled for a moment. When she had regained her equilibrium, she quickly called both Lt. Schultz and Paul Salvador and told them of their discovery that Rodriguez had possibly switched his middle name for his first name.

Schultz acknowledged it was sometimes done, but it was more usual for names to be faked in far more elaborate ways. Aliases derived from eluding tactics such as altering the spelling of the first or last name were common. In this case, perhaps the first name was vital. If they had found out Rodriguez's first name early on, they might have also uncovered his criminal background. Ed Rodriguez's information had been checked, and there was no middle name or initial on record, not even on his birth certificate. And on the police report, the middle initial was illegible. *Now* the hunt would begin anew.

After Fleur disconnected, she turned to Joan. "They're on it. Nice work, Joan." Fleur deliberated. "He went by his middle name. When I was a baby, I wasn't even given a middle name."

"Sure you were," Joan said. "Mom told me about it. Your middle name was ReineRae. Mom said Maggie told her she was going to surprise her music teacher and her best friend by combining their middle names to make your middle name. Flower ReineRae. Yes, and she said Maggie planned to tell them about it on your first birthday."

"My mother died before I turned one." With a somber frown, Fleur said, "Golda never knew I was named after her. Golda Reine Hamilton. And Gemma Rae *will* be told."

"Mom said that was the story she remembered. She's told me several times, so I know I got it right. ReineRae. When I was small, I thought it was the niftiest name I'd ever heard. 'Even on days when it is raining, there is a ray of sun.' That's how I remembered it. I certainly thought you knew."

"No. I wish I had. I learned two important names today. ReineRae and David." Fleur paused for several moments. "It was because of you, Joan. I don't honestly think I would have had the nerve to knock on those doors if I'd been alone."

"You're Maggie's child. I know you would have eventually worked up your courage." With the lift of an eyebrow, Joan added, "I guess I exhibit her brazen ways because I'm her namesake."

"Not too brazen, I hope," Fleur said with a smile.

"Maybe my brazenness is tempered by my parents' conservatism. But let's say I know my way around brazen."

Fleur gave Joan's shoulder a squeeze. "Thank you."

"I haven't done anything."

"You have. You got us inside the apartment. The discovery that David Edward Rodriguez was a criminal is of vital importance. It could provide a motive. After all, it seems as if he was a serial criminal."

"For sure," Joan replied.

"And thanks for being you. You're my favorite cousin."

"Aw, shucks. I'm your only known cousin. But I've got lots of them, and you're my favorite also. I never thought I'd ever meet my namesake aunt's daughter."

Chapter 26

After being safely delivered back at her hotel, Fleur decided to visit both Bernie and Gemma Rae. They were part of the story, and she wanted to keep them informed about the important developments. This latest Rodriguez information was certainly of great importance.

When Fleur arrived at Bernie's shop, he was just finishing up with his poetry group gathering. When he welcomed her, she announced that she was heading to see Gemma Rae and would like to talk to both of them together to tell them what had been discovered.

When they arrived at Gemma Rae's, Fleur asked if they could adjourn to a private place. After each of them had ordered coffees, Gemma Rae led them up to her tiny kitchen.

"So how did your day go?" Gemma Rae asked. "Talking *in private* sounds suspiciously like either you've gotten the results of the DNA testing or there's something new about the case."

"The case," Fleur said. "I'm not certain whether it means anything, but from the sound of the lieutenant's voice when I told him, it could mean a great deal."

She related what had transpired during her visits at the apartment, smiling at the stunned faces when she told Gemma Rae and Bernie that Rodriguez had spent the major part of the last forty years in jail.

"Although there isn't yet any corroboration that the current superintendent's mother has her facts correct, she seemed completely believable to me and knowledgeable in her allegations.

"The lieutenant promised a new search would be made of archival prison records. He will also send detectives to speak with the elderly woman at the apartment, as well as the woman's church friend, who is possibly the sister of David Edward Rodriguez. When I spoke with Lt. Schultz, he seemed alarmed, and his voice held an urgency. He said if Rodriguez was a career criminal, he would be legally considered a new person of interest, and the case could officially be reopened."

"Shit!" Gemma Rae sat back. Her normally rosy complexion had paled to white. "Aw fuck! It could be that all these years we've been wrong. Maybe neither Shane nor Maggie did it."

"If the investigative report," Bernie said, "comes back confirming that Rodriguez is a hardened criminal, it would be an easy stretch to believe he was guilty of murder forty years ago. If he has, in fact, been incarcerated for so many years, it probably wasn't for shoplifting."

"I can't wrap my head around this." Gemma Rae closed her eyes. "And the sister is correct, the guy was sort of an undercover womanizer, but he watched himself around the apartment building. I always felt he suppressed his desires, but lots of men do. I've always had insight when it comes to seeing into people. He didn't wag his genitals at us, but I sensed he would have if he could have. Still, he didn't pester us. He also knew that with Shane having a hair-trigger temper *and* a gun, he'd better not make a pass at Maggie. And he probably knew most of the female hippies weren't interested and would only blow him off." Gemma Rae clarified, "Figuratively speaking."

Fleur sighed deeply. "Based on what everyone had said about him, Rodriguez didn't sound dangerous."

"True. He gave no indication that he was. No, none at all," Bernie said with regret. "I think of myself as a pretty reliable judge of character. He seemed almost too harmless. Maybe that's part of what makes criminals appear trustworthy enough that a person will take a ride with them, or go into their apartment, or whatever. If this was a dangerous guy, I was totally taken in."

"We all were," Gemma Rae said. "That blows my mind."

"And I would have sworn he was absolutely credible if he was acting as if he had just woken up. His eyes were red, as if he'd been sleeping. He even fumbled with the key to Maggie's apartment. But now, with this information, I wonder if it might have been a case of the nerves and a good acting job."

Gemma Rae cocked her head in recall. "He was a slight man. Average height and slim, almost skinny. Most of us could have taken him in a fight."

"Wiry people often have amazing strength," Fleur said. "Abby is lean and sinewy, and she can manage the weight of huge landscaping trees. And around the house and garden, she was always lifting things for Aunt Golda."

"You'll let us know right away when you hear something?" Bernie asked.

"As soon as I know anything, you'll know. Because we don't know what Rodriguez has been convicted of in the past, we still haven't any conclusive evidence that he had anything to do with my parents' death," Fleur said with a furrowed brow. "But my speculation about him being involved has increased."

"And mine," Gemma Rae said. "Examining that day more closely, I can see where he would possibly have had the time to do the killings then act out a scene for Bernie and the police. He could have skated on a double murder."

"He had time," Bernie agreed. "Although back then I wouldn't have imagined so, it is possible that I miscalculated. I had to put my shoes on before I went down to Shane's apartment, and it took time to travel the stairs. I see now where he well might have done it. And it seems as if he was the only one with the means of getting in and out of your parents' apartment and back into his own."

"It sounds plausible to me," Fleur said. "If he were a habitual criminal, he could have known how to make the timeframe work."

Bernie cupped his chin. "All he really would've needed to do is lock their door behind himself and scoot across the hall into his room. I arrived and pounded on Shane and Maggie's door. After that, I tried to rouse Rodriguez. He didn't open the door for a couple of minutes. I thought he was waking up and getting to the door, but it also would have given him time to get cleaned up, as well as time to appear disheveled when he came to the door."

Gemma Rae fixed sandwiches, and the three of them explored their theories until twilight. Each was speculative and introspective. Things had definitely changed.

When Bernie walked Fleur back to her hotel, she noticed that he was more fidgety than normal, and his morose quiet made her suspect he was experiencing an overwhelming turbulence within.

"I apologize for my silence," he said at last. "I feel as though I'm in the center of a great morality play. My own testimony helped aid and abet a possible killer. Although I did nothing deliberately, I inadvertently deflected attention away from Rodriguez. The timeline was a big part of what ruled him out as a suspect."

"You told the truth, so you can't think you were responsible for any of it. If Rodriguez is responsible, it was *his* crime, not anyone else's. And if you hadn't contacted me, this wouldn't be coming to light now. You were moral and heroic."

"Contacting you, as well as providing my take on the crime, was wrong. Both were stupid mistakes. Yes, I stupidly contacted you. And forty years ago, I stupidly helped exclude Rodriguez as a killer."

"I don't believe either of those things, Bernie. I'm glad you called. If Rodriguez killed my parents, you calling me to express your condolences about Aunt Golda might lead to the resolution of an old murder. You've been wonderful about all of this, and you've helped me enormously."

"All these years," he repeated several times, "and it may not have been as we believed. In Kipling's *The Secret of the Machine*, he says, 'We are not built to comprehend a lie.' However, my reading should have prepared me for recognizing something as a lie."

"I'm beginning to believe there isn't much visible truth in anything. The most we can hope for is the justice of truth. Which may never be known. One thing is clear—half of those who knew my parents believed Maggie was the killer, the other half believed just as firmly that Shane was the one who did the shooting. If nothing else, maybe this investigation will bring resolution. I wonder if it matters."

"I've lived three decades more than you. Please believe me, the truth always matters."

Fleur gave Bernie a hug and watched his slope-shouldered frame slowly hobble away. Pensive, she moved up the walkway and entered the hotel. Overwhelmed by the intangible sense of being uncertain about something important, she didn't want to be alone. She would call Abby. She would pretend they were as close as they'd once been.

Memory summoned fleeting glimpses of their one-time happiness, when smiles had moved across the room, warming as if being caught each by the other. For a dozen years, their romance had felt newly created and continually exciting. Every event was a celebration. Each touch, each kiss, each moment of orgasmic pleasure captivated them.

When the elevator door opened on her floor, Fleur was still debating with herself about phoning Abby. Finally, she sat on the bed and pressed Abby's number.

Abby rapidly said she was concerned about Fez and immediately dove into the report on her visit with Sophia. Absolutely nothing was revealed about the third letter. "In fact, the second was so damned sad, I'm uncertain I even want to see the third. The way Aunt Golda wrote, reflecting a childhood with pain none of us can ever understand, broke my heart."

"I had the same feeling," Fleur said. "As I was reading, I wondered who had written the letter. Maybe some of it was due to the translation, but the words didn't seem to have been written by the aunt I loved."

"I love her even more now." Abby's voice became softer. "I admired her before, but now I've been able to know her in another way. That's why I'm working so hard on the letter project. When humanity is shut out of evil hearts, everyone can learn from this girl's life."

"Yes." There was a tremor in Fleur's voice. "Yes."

"What adventure did you get up to today?" Abby asked.

"Are you being snide, or are you interested?"

"Now who's being snide? You sounded excited, so I asked you a question."

"Apologies. I *am* excited." Fleur quickly related what she and Joan had discovered.

"Holy—" There was a pause before Abby, surprise clear in her voice, said, "You mean to tell me there's a chance your parents' deaths weren't murder and suicide?"

"That might be a reach. But until I know what's going on with the building super, Rodriguez, it is a possibility."

"This whole deal is incredible. How are you with it all?"

Fleur glanced at her journal notes. "I'm not certain Shane is my father. I'm not positive my parents were killed by this guy… I'm feeling unnerved by it. Ultimately it will depend on how the rest of the inquiry goes."

"Wish I could be with you. If you need me, I could hop on a red-eye and be in San Francisco in the morning."

"You can't leave. The animals, the house, and your work require you to stay put. Besides, this may be nonsense. The woman at the apartment building might have it wrong. Thanks for the offer—I truly appreciate it—but I'm fine. Just your offer of support means the world to me. Abby, you've been a darned curmudgeon, and I couldn't imagine you ever being supportive again. You know what a curmudgeon is, don't you?"

"I actually do know what a curmudgeon is. Imagine *that*." There was irritated dejection in Abby's sarcasm. "Fleur, the last times we've talked, you've sounded as though you've given up on us. I've heard it in your voice. No matter how difficult things are now, I don't want to lose you."

"We've been experiencing my trip from different perspectives. You haven't felt it was important. I did. So I've been reexamining other areas of importance. Yes, I think we need to talk but not now. I've got to sort out my own feelings about me before I can understand my feelings about you."

"From the day I met you, I have loved you. I've never felt anything less than utter and complete love for you. I'm sorry if I can't prove my love to you. Maybe you're right, maybe you need someone who can better express themselves to you."

"Can we talk about it later?"

"I don't have much else to say. I've told you I love you."

"Abby, if you love me, give me time. Time to figure us both out."

"You've always seemed to know yourself, Fleur."

"The key word is *seemed*. And until I actually understand myself, I can't hope to understand you. And if I haven't a complete sense of you, and of myself, I can't hope to know *us*."

Chapter 27

Waking early gave Fleur a chance to reinstate her regimented walking routine. Being a botanist at the research clinic, and in her own minilab, was completely sedentary, so for many years she had integrated exercise into her morning program. Sometimes she ran and, recently, more often walked. Abby joined her whenever she was able. Although Abby's work provided regular exercise, she said she enjoyed the conversations they had as they went along.

Wearing her denims, a floral T-shirt, and walking shoes, Fleur walked the couple of miles to where her parents and great aunt had lived. She found the apartment building easily and stood watching it for many moments. This was a place where her mother and presumed father had lived. And died. Now she wanted to get the feel of them.

Certainly they must have walked hand in hand in the early morning, experiencing this sun and this place. Perhaps they'd felt the joy and freedom of young lovers. It was cozy. Her parents would have felt the aged simplicity of the area. These were dollhouse homes, built long ago and recently cosmetically enhanced with bright paints.

She leaned back against a tree and watched the sunlight brighten over the horizon. She wondered what their thoughts might have been on such autumn days. Even back then, Aunt Golda would have gone shopping and looked at the flora and fauna with the same wonder she displayed in her own backyard. She would have noticed everything and appreciated every single sound, sight, touch, and smell of the neighborhood.

Allowing her daydreams free rein, Fleur could see Aunt Golda pushing a stroller with baby Fleur inside. She also would've had the same look of pride when she gazed at Fleur each day. Aunt Golda loved her and the glory of life around her.

Tears gathered then trickled. Before she had juggled her way out of the daydream, a stream was flowing down her cheeks. Had her parents lived, she might not have known Aunt Golda. They might have moved, roaming as many hippies did. She might not have known the extraordinary soul of the woman who had loved her enough to raise her.

When her phone rang, it was a moment before she was able to speak. "Fleur Hamilton."

"This is Lt. Schultz. We have some new information. At this time we are verifying our findings. I wonder if you could come down to headquarters sometime after lunch. Say one or two?"

"I'll be there at one." Her heart was pounding, and her mind seemed to be spinning with the anticipation of hearing whatever news he had. "At one," she repeated.

She stopped by a corner grocery store to purchase an energy bar and some orange juice. She would walk back to the hotel, get ready for the meeting, and grab a quick lunch. The time seemed to pass slowly as she sat in a small coffee shop, attempting to eat a sandwich. Each few minutes' increment crawled past in slow motion as she walked to Lt. Schultz's office.

Her nerves were tightly strung when she finally arrived for the meeting.

"Ms. Hamilton." The lieutenant escorted her to a conference room. Paul Salvador was already there, along with a man she hadn't met. "Please be seated. You know Detective Salvador, and this is Mike Alton."

Mouth dry, she swallowed hard. "You've discovered something?"

"Yes. Yes, we did." Schultz's shoulders drooped, and his eyes shifted to a file. He picked it up and opened it. "We found the David Edward Rodriguez we've been searching for. And he *has* led the life of crime the witness you found alluded to."

"Is he alive?"

"He is. First, I'd like to tell you some facts about his life. He's seventy-six-years old now. He has spent thirty-seven of the last forty years in prison. In the seventies and eighties, he did a nineteen-year stretch for raping and murdering four women. He made a deal to exchange his guilty plea for having the death penalty taken off the table. Two years after his release, he was convicted of killing two more women. This time his sentence was life without parole."

"So it's possible he might have murdered my parents prior to those murders?"

"Probable." Paul Salvador jumped in. "I spent a couple hours at the prison this morning, and he wouldn't confess to it, but he didn't deny it. Reading his body language and expressions, it's my opinion that he hinted about his guilt. He has an agenda of his own."

Schultz buried his face in his hands for a brief moment. "We missed him. My gut churns when I try to come to terms with our failure. My investigative team blew it, and more women paid with their lives for our mistake." Tears shimmered in his eyes.

Fleur patted his arm. He cleared his throat and regained his staunch demeanor. "A minimum of six women lost their lives, possibly more, because Rodriguez went under our radar. Even now, instead of just confessing, he's trying to work a deal. He wants an early compassionate release."

Salvador added, "The guy is dying. He's been trying to get sprung for the past several months. Now, according to the doctor, he's only got days left. And he wants out. He alluded to a possible trade of information for his release."

"Can I talk with him?" Fleur asked.

Schultz quickly stood. "Look, we're going to do whatever we can, however we can, to get you some answers. If nailing down the truth means we spring the guy for a few days, so be it. That would be *your* decision. We would like a confession before he's given his freedom. You want to visit him, you can. I'd guess we can have it scheduled for tomorrow morning. I'll have Detective Salvador take you there. Maybe Rodriguez will say something to you. You can promise to petition for his release in exchange for a confession from him. Also, as I said, it's to be your decision whether or not he should be granted a humanitarian release."

"Thank you. I do want to see him."

"Okay. Meanwhile, I've got charges drawn up. Mike, here, is from the prosecutor's office. We're charging Rodriguez with the deaths of your parents. He'll never live long enough to get to court, so it won't result in any punishment for him as far as your parents are concerned, but at least we will be able to officially change the coroner's verdict of murder and suicide. If he confesses to you, we'll have a speedy trial in absentia. We'll have a camera set up on Rodriguez to get audio and video of his confession."

"I'm curious. Do you know if he was working under a false name because he'd been in prison before?" Fleur asked.

"He had been inside on a violent felony conviction."

"And was he released early?"

"He was." The lieutenant's voice broke. "If he hadn't been released for good behavior, he would've been in prison at the time your parents were murdered. Even when we catch them, they get sprung." His eyes shifted, and he turned his head away. "And usually early."

"And *early* killed my parents."

"Anything we can do," Schultz said, "won't be enough, but we'll get you up there to see him. Or anything else you'd like that's within our power."

As Fleur walked away from the conference room, she heard Salvador's heavy sigh. He followed behind her. "It's an hour drive. We'll set up the visit for eleven. Can you be ready at ten?"

"Yes. I'll be ready."

"I'll pick you up. Also, I have something else for you."

She turned to him. "Yes?"

He pulled an envelope out of his coat pocket. Handing it to her, he said, "DNA. You are the daughter of Margaret Heywood and Shane Bradley. It's an undisputable biological match. I know it's late in the game, but if you want the documents for a name change, Lois will push them through for you."

"Eventually I'll need to get my legitimate name sorted out, but for now, there's no need. All I plan on doing is having the 'Bradley' recorded and legally changing my name to Fleur Hamilton. I was Maggie and Shane's infant, but I was Golda Hamilton's child."

"I understand."

"I appreciate your help. What do I owe you for the tests, for everything?"

"There's not a charge. The DNA test is on the house. It's now a double homicide investigation. Tomorrow, maybe you can get a confession, and that will close the case."

"I may not get the confession."

"You will. I can tell. You have a calming way about you. You should have been a prosecutor. Lull the jury."

"I assure you, *lull* will not be the first thing that comes to mind regarding Rodriguez."

"Don't promise him anything unless you're all right with him being released. He's in bad shape. He hinted that he'd deal, because he doesn't want to die in prison. But he's already in the custody of the devil."

Fleur glanced up into Detective Salvador's eyes. "My preference would be for him to stay in the custody of The People until his body's released into the devil's custody."

They nodded their good-byes, and Fleur walked out into the late-afternoon sun. Her spirit needed the brightness. *Most people,* she mused, *think about evil, and many experience it, and still it tends to evaporate or find its way to a back chamber of the mind.* Through her great aunt, Fleur understood the malevolence of war, now she was personally faced with the depravity of evil. *Many are content,* she ruminated, *to be surrounded by heinous, villainous acts, as long as the hostility doesn't touch them.* Aunt Golda often said that hatred must be eradicated. She had lived the struggle of good and evil.

Fleur stopped walking and looked around. She was suddenly weak at the thought of never seeing her beloved aunt again. Then something filled her body with warmth. She believed her aunt would still always be walking alongside her. It occurred to her that this was the first time she'd walked toward her future as both Flower Bradley and Fleur Hamilton.

Chapter 28

The time since Fleur had arrived in San Francisco had been filled to exhaustion. She was drained after a long day, and she envisioned tomorrow was going to be far worse. She'd talked with Abby about the new developments, and Abby had been unusually quiet. She was distant, and Fleur sensed her preoccupation, but she was also glad for the brevity of their exchange. She wanted a good night's sleep so she would be ready for her visit to the prison.

What sleep she did get was fitful and shallow. As she awoke, she had a sense that this day would be one of the worst she would ever know—though not as painful as when she'd lost her Aunt Golda. She was going to be facing the man she believed to be her parents' murderer. Until he admitted to the crime, she wouldn't know for certain whether he had killed two young people over four decades before. The clock read five o'clock. Fleur got up, showered, and dressed.

When the telephone rang, realizing it was six a.m. in Denver's Mountain Time, Fleur answered quickly. "Abby, is everything okay? You aren't at work?"

"I dropped by to see Sophia. She was eating an early breakfast of toast and tea and in her hand was the letter. The third letter. She handed it to me and told me that was the end of the words. Fleur, I've got the final letter! Can you get in touch with your friend about a quick return on a translation? I know your friend is in New York, and it's eight there. I can send the letter directly to her, then she can send us each a copy. While she's translating it, I'll stick around my office so I can try to decipher its key. After I find the code, I'll send it to you for the decrypting."

"That's moving it pretty quickly. Why the rush?"

"For whatever reason, I want you to have Aunt Golda's last letter before you meet with Rodriguez. Will you wait for me to finish it?"

"Yes, absolutely. How's Fez?"

"I'm not sure, but I think he'll be okay. I'll give you a full report later. Contact your friend. I'll be waiting. Fleur, I'll forever be waiting for you."

Fleur contacted her friend, and she agreed that she would translate the letter as soon as she received it. And the minute she finished, copies would be going to Fleur and Abby.

Although she'd called Gemma Rae and Bernie last evening with news of the Rodriguez report and the DNA test, Fleur wanted them to be kept informed about anything concerning Rodriguez. They had known and loved her parents. She called each of them and asked if they could meet her in the hotel coffee shop before Paul was slated to pick her up. Gemma Rae and Bernie agreed to the confab.

Fleur told them she would tentatively meet them at nine-thirty, because she was awaiting the translation of Sophia's third letter and the key to decoding its hidden message.

Continuing to watch the clock, Fleur realized that her friend sending the translation and Abby discovering the proper cryptogram solutions and downloading the software conversion would probably not be doable within the timeframe they had to work with. But within half an hour, the translation was complete. After another hour, Abby called with the numerical combination. Luckily it had been similar to the code for the second letter. Loading the information into the decryption program seemed quicker this time, and when downloading, the solution also appeared more rapidly.

Thankfully, at two minutes until nine, Fleur received the completed conversion. She glanced at the four pages of the letter, looked skyward, and silently thanked Aunt Golda. She called Gemma Rae and Bernie and confirmed that nine-thirty would be a perfect time for them to meet for coffee. First, she would read the decoded messages in her great aunt's letter.

As she read, an anger as none other she'd ever experienced burned her to the core. Some of the sentences were fragmented. Fleur guessed it was because of the emotional strain. She had probably never discussed it with anyone before. Golda told of the secrets kept in an abused, frightened child's heart. Scratching through sentences, dissecting words, Fleur forced herself to read on.

My friend, Sophia, you saw when I was dragged away and taken to the commandant's quarters. Everyone thinks that I was carried to the hospital—the butchery. But I was taken to the terrible man. He brutalized me and took my innocence from me. But this was not the worst of it. My mother knew. Even though I didn't tell her, she knew. It was then that Mother's mind began to crumble. She had knowledge of what had happened to her child.

Visualizing the kind, young girl being harmed, Fleur blinked her eyes as tears flooded them. Her tears were for the child Golda and also for her mother, who was being driven to madness.

Mother was always fastidious, yet now she was seeing dirt beneath her nails.

She would no longer play the piano for the enemy. When she refused to play, the Nazis threatened to take her away. She whispered to me, "How can a musician play with filthy hands?" They took her away. I never saw her again.

I kept this secret from you, my dear friend, because I wanted to spare you. That is when I began playing music for the enemy. But it was with hurting smiles. As conditions deteriorated in the camp and the war dragged on, I worried nothing could save us.

Fleur continued reading, her mind overwhelmed by each new revelation. She wanted the words to stop—then wondered how they ever could.

Men and women were in a fugue state, unable to even twitch—as they once had—when sirens filled the airways. Their bones showed through sallow, sunken skin, and their weak bodies shuffled toward death. Only miracles of the heart helped them to stand, to await freedom.

The final section of Golda's missive explained that messages could rarely get smuggled out by prisoners, but when they did, the typical note was two words: TAKE REVENGE.

Golda wanted to take revenge, when revenge was warranted, and revenge was a meal best served cold. She had not asked for the terror, had not designed the hatred. It had all been visited on them.

Fleur's eyes closed before the final sentence. She knew that despite the horrors the letter had disclosed, it would end the same way all Golda's letters ended: *With peace, justice, and love, Golda.*

Now Fleur knew why Golda had inserted the word *justice*. And she comprehended the dying words of her aunt. Golda had murmured the words *cold meal*.

Fleur dried her eyes and shut down her computer. It was time to meet Gemma Rae and Bernie.

The hotel coffee shop was crowded. Gemma Rae waved Fleur over to the table she had secured. Coffee had been poured. "Sorry I'm a few minutes late," Fleur said.

"You're exactly on time. Bernie will be here in precisely two minutes," Gemma said. "He's never early and never late."

"Thanks for coming here to the hotel. It gave me a little more time to comb out and dry my wet hair. Also, it allowed me the time to read Aunt Golda's final letter." Fleur managed a troubled half-smile.

When Bernie appeared, he asked in a comical tone, "Isn't it usually the ladies who are late?"

"You're on time, but barely," Gemma Rae bantered. "And the coffee isn't as good as I make, but it's passable."

Fleur sat rigid for a moment then leaned toward them. "I wanted to ask whether either or both of you would want to ride along with me to the prison. To be there, since you knew my parents."

"Not me. I'd rather not be there," Gemma Rae said solemnly. "Hell, no. I'm a peacenik, but I might freak out and murder the fucking weasel. I hope Shane's spirit forgives me for blaming him all these years."

"If we hadn't blamed him, we would have had to blame Maggie," Bernie said. "And I'm sorry, Fleur, but I would rather not go either. I wouldn't want to be near such evil."

"I understand you don't want to be subjected to being in his presence. I just wanted make certain. If I had a choice, I'd also opt out of giving him any attention, but I've got to attempt to get his confession. So I'll know. So the case can be shut. Mostly so my parents' names can be cleared of the suspicion of murder or suicide. And their names can be added to the list of those Rodriguez murdered. The lieutenant says he would be charged with their murders, and he is confident that if Rodriguez lives long enough, he will be convicted."

Bernie gently said, "If you would like me to go with you to make you feel better, of course—"

"No. I'm fine. The detective will be with me. It's something I need to do."

"To think, for all these years, Rodriguez has gotten away with it," Gemma Rae said with rancor. "And now the fucker wants to die on his own terms. He should be publicly hanged." She paused. "I hope my spirit guide is understanding about how emotional I am over this."

Fleur smiled. "I'm sure you're fine with the spirit world, Gemma Rae. And I'll stop by on the way back from the prison to let you know what happened."

"You tell him how hated he is. You tell him he murdered a special human being. Two special human beings," Gemma Rae said.

"I'll tell him." Fleur looked toward the lobby and saw Paul Salvador at the entrance. "My ride is here." She leaned down to give both Bernie and Gemma Rae a hug. "If nothing else, Rodriguez will die knowing he didn't get away with murdering my parents. The world will know that both of them are innocent."

"Maggie and Shane would like that," Gemma Rae said, nodding. "Damn straight they would. I see you're wearing the love beads Maggie made."

"Yes." Fleur caressed the beads circling her neck. The jewelry Maggie had made didn't match Fleur's outfit, but it definitely suited her emotions. Her love of those innocent human beings was uppermost in her mind.

Chapter 29

When Paul Salvador directed Fleur to his car, he seemed to understand her introspection. The trip to the prison was quiet. Paul related facts about the prison, and he also added the few additional details about David Edward Rodriguez he'd garnered after their visit the day before. Rodriguez was confined to bed or a wheelchair. They would bring him to the visiting area, and Fleur would be on the other side of the glass from him.

"When I saw him, he looked frail. He's on oxygen. Death's pallor gives him a pathetic look. But once he began talking," Salvador said with intensity, "he was as evil as anyone I've ever met. He'll try his charm out on you. He'll work for sympathy. Don't play your cards too soon. Make him ask for clemency, ask for his final days to be spent out of prison. Don't agree to petition for his release out of pity. Get his confession, and then do what is in your heart—for you… and for his victims."

"I'll do my best."

"I'll be standing beside you, and you'll be seated directly across from him. He'll attempt to play you, get you to agree to spring him. I told him yesterday it would be up to the next of kin, the baby he'd left orphaned. Because this is a new case, with a new set of rules, everything changes. New charges mean we have the upper hand. Are you any good at debate?"

"Not in the least," Fleur said. "I've only won one argument in sixteen years with my mate. I came here without her approval."

"Well, this Rodriguez is a stone-cold manipulator. I caution you not to see a dying old man. I want you to visualize a man shooting a couple of kids to death, a man raping and killing at least half a dozen terrorized women. Six. And those were only the convictions. There were many others. We know that. Knowing and proving are different. Evidence in your parents' murder was missed or contaminated over time. No witnesses. Only the killer's confession will provide the unequivocal proof."

Salvador parked the car, and they went inside together. It was arguably the most unnerving time Fleur would have to endure. Though she had never experienced claustrophobia, she was certain that was the cause of the pressure she was feeling in her chest. When she tried to catch her breath, she noticed there was an awful, unrecognizable stench in the air.

In the visiting area, she was guided to the row of chairs separated by a glass wall from a large holding room. The prisoners' room was lighted, as if it were under a microscope. They took the third visiting cubicle. Fleur sat, with Salvador standing at her side. Behind her was a technician with a camera on a tripod. Microphones had also been installed.

Fleur watched the door in the holding room open, and the monster who was suspected of killing her parents was wheeled across the tile floor. He had also killed a number of human beings. Tortured, raped, and murdered, each of those women had died at his hands. Those rough, twisted, palsied hands now clutched at his lap blanket. His wrinkled, jaundiced face was pinched, as though years of hatred had carved each line.

His body sat low, as if he were hiding inside the wheelchair. He coughed several times and said in a scratchy voice, "You gonna help me?"

Bristling because he was thinking of himself first, Fleur said, "Are you going to help me?"

"I don't wanna die here." His phlegm-filled voice choked. "I need to be free when I die."

"*I* need to know if you killed my parents."

"If I tell ya, then you gonna see I get outta here?"

"You tell me, then and only then, I'll consider it."

"Death is a free ride out now." He fumbled with his oxygen tubes. "Well? You gonna get me out?"

"I told you, I'll consider it. *If* you tell me about the day my parents died."

They sat glaring at one another. Finally, reluctantly, he spoke, breaking the stalemate. "The only thing I want is to die outta here. I'm seventy-six-years old. I'm sick. I'm dying. The big C caught me. My final request. Please have mercy." She stood and began to turn away from the window. He called to her, "Listen, lady. You're my only chance. Help me. Please."

She returned to the stiff, molded-plastic chair and eased down into it. "Tell me about that day."

Tears spilled from his eyes. "Let me live free just one day."

"I want to know about my parents."

There was silence for nearly a minute. Neither of them blinked as they glared into one another's eyes.

When he realized she wasn't going to break, his tone changed from wheedling to disdain. "They was smug, punk hippies. The girl wouldn't give me the time of day. I think she knew she was a doll. Didn't care if she gave men like me woodies. Barely said 'hi' to me. Looked down her nose at me. She deserved it. And he strutted around like he owned the goddamn place."

His voice rose as his anger grew. "The bitch and the soldier. She thought she was a rock star. He figured he was tough. He'd been to Nam. He thought he was a hero. Hell, them guys got spit on when they came back. Hero! Hero, my ass." His spittle-flecked diatribe skidded to a stop. In desperation, he gave a loud foghorn moan. "I want out."

"Tell me. I won't agree to anything until after you've told me exactly what happened."

His gunnysack body seemed to sink even lower. "Okay, okay. It was the easiest crime I ever committed. I heard them fighting, then he leaves. Slams the door. It was my moment of opportunity. I wasn't gonna lose it. I knocked on the door, and she opened it. Surprised her. She figured soldier boy was comin' back. This hippie cunt didn't want to give me a little."

Fleur flinched. She swallowed her hatred before asking, "And you decided to rape her."

"She said she'd cry rape. I tell her she's a drugged up little slut, and I'm gonna have her. Nobody would believe her if she said I attacked her. She fights me. I like that anyway, so I fight her right back." His cold, rheumy eyes squinted. He stopped a minute to cough before he could continue. "I'm getting turned on, and he comes back in. He'd forgot his goddamn gun. Left it on the table. As he goes for it, I go for it. I get there first. He gets in between me and the girl, then lunges at me, yellin' not to hurt her. I shoot him up under the jaw. His hand is grabbin' for the gun, so he gets the pepper spray coverin' his hand and arm. He crumbles. Knew it would kill him."

"You knew it would kill him," Fleur repeated.

"It was a first. The only *man* I ever killed." There was another moment's pause as Rodriguez remembered. "She was all hysterical. Screamin' her head off, trying to get to his side. I fire, hitting her in the head. They're laying down there on the floor, both with powder residue all over 'em. And the bodies are almost together like. Hands almost touching."

Fleur felt Detective Salvador's hand pressing her shoulder, and she looked up at him. His reassuring nod prompted her to carry on.

"Go on," she said.

"There was a towel. I wiped the gun handle, then smeared blood on their hands. I rolled the gun around in their hands. Fingerprints. Then I let the gun fall down between 'em. Funny, it still looked like they were touching. Barely, maybe. It was a coincidence."

"And?" She inhaled deeply. "After the coincidence?"

"Blood is sprayed all over. Hell of a mess. I wipe my hands, then use the towel to lock their door up without getting it bloody and leaving fingerprints. I moved fast. Fast, back then." He slapped the arms of the wheelchair that held him captive.

"And your acting job began."

"Yeah. I didn't even need an alibi. Them punks fought all the time. But I was ready anyways. I'd say I was sleepin'. I run back across the hall. My door hadn't been locked, but I use the towel to make sure there's no blood on it. I lock up, I get my bloody T-shirt off, wash my hands and arms. Ditch it and the towel under my pile of laundry. Put on a clean undershirt. Take off my work pants so it would look like I was sleepin' and just crawled outta bed. In case anybody comes."

"And then?"

"Then I hear the guy from upstairs coming down, screaming about the shots. I mess my hair and make like I been sleeping. Pressed my hands up to my face. Rubbed my eyes hard. Taking my time gettin' to the door, so's he'll think I'm groggy. Also to make sure them kids had bled out. The upstairs renter keeps saying how he heard the shots. Gunfire. I play ignorant. The bookstore guy. That's the guy. He heard the shots. The lady piano teacher had music playing. Never heard the shots."

"But he heard it, and you said you hadn't heard it?"

"Correct. Yeah, the dumb-ass cops never even asked why I hadn't heard it. But I had my alibi. I would'a told 'em I'd taken sleeping pills. The pills alibi popped into my head." His eyes sparked with the remembrance of the long ago crime. "Had it down pat."

"Bernie Maylor, the renter, made you rush?"

"Yeah, that's right. But hell, I drug my feet like I just woke up. Fumbled with the key. Like I said, I wanted time to make sure them kids were wasted. Well, somebody called the cops because of the fighting. The girl screamin' made 'em call, I guess. I hadn't figured on the cops comin' right away. As I'm opening their door for the bookstore guy, the cops show up. I never even went inside. The cops started right in saying it was a murder and suicide. The kid had gun residue on him, and the girl did, too. Cops didn't know who killed who. Dumb-ass cops. I got away with it, slick as shit."

"Until now."

"I don't know what you're pissed off about." His breathing was choppy.

Fleur was incredulous. "What?"

"If you was that baby, you was kept mostly by the music lady. So I saved you from bein' hurt by them worthless-as-shit hippies. I did you a favor. I backed up the bookstore guy by sayin' she was your aunt. Now I told you how it happened, you gonna do me a favor and let me outta here?"

She glared. "The world will be a far better place when you're gone."

"You gotta get me free. Please?"

"I'm considering it. But there's the matter of a woman doing without her best friend and a man doing without his best friend. It's about parents, brothers, sisters, sons, and daughters, all doing without loved ones. The pain you've inflicted has harmed so many. A man who risked his life and came back from war a broken human being, wounded and in pain. In Nam he put his life on the line for you, for your useless life. And you killed him. A young woman, who only wanted to sing and to be happy for the first time in her life. Her childhood never brought her happiness. And you killed her. You murdered two innocent people. You saw them as a couple of throwaway kids, and you murdered their dreams, destroyed their future. What a pathetic lowlife you are."

"I tell you, I'm sorry. I need a humanitarian release. You can request it. I got me the Lord. I got Jesus in my life. I tell you, I'm sorry."

"Are you? Are you really?"

"Yeah. I'm sorry I killed 'em. Please?" His groveling was accompanied by tears.

"I want you to know what I consider the most egregious, ugly thing that you did to my parents after you took their lives. You allowed someone who fought for your liberty to be branded as the killer of the woman he loved. For forty years, his legacy was that he had died as a killer, who then committed suicide. You allowed the woman who loved him to be tarred with the same brush by the people who defended him. Either my father was an insane, angry man, or my mother was a crazy bitch. That was what you called her—bitch. You set up the lie that made one of them a murderer. And they were in love. He didn't run from you. He threw himself in front of her and begged you not to hurt her. She didn't attempt to run away. Her last act was to reach for him as she saw him fall."

Rodriguez's face contorted into a mask of terror. Fleur looked up at Salvador.

Detective Salvador said, "Ms. Hamilton, what would you like Corrections to do with this man?"

"Please," Rodriguez begged. "I told you what you wanted. You said if I told you, you'd consider gettin' me out."

"I have made my decision for all of them, for all their unrealized dreams, all those evaporated dreams that fell into the empty vacuum of time. For all of your victims and for the promise they had. And most especially, for me. This is my decision. Stay. Die here. Die incarcerated for your crimes."

"Bitch!" he said, seething, "You bitch." The mottled blue of his veins stood out on his clenched hands.

"That's what you called my mother. Remember the old adage? Like mother, like daughter." She stood and leaned nearer to the glass. "I must have gotten the bitch gene from her side of the family. Your victims were primarily women, but your final skirmish with a woman, you lose. Stay. That's your final payment for all those lives. Stay. Die where you belong, in prison. Die as a captured, cornered, snared loser. A prisoner. You're exactly where you should be. You will take your final breath in captivity."

His anguished expression twisted with pain; his imploring eyes stared through the welling tears. His arguments were as depleted as his breath. He gave a long, gasping, bloodcurdling squeal that sounded like the yowl of a dying animal. Yet no animal could ever equal David Edward Rodriguez's chilling cruelty.

Fleur walked away and didn't look back. One thought stormed through her mind: *The mantra of a true bitch must be to never look back.* She vowed to remember that credo so that she might heal.

When they reached the car, Paul Salvador eased her into the passenger seat with a soft smile of understanding. He patted her arm and said, "When I touched your shoulder, it was because he'd said that Shane's and Maggie's hands were nearly touching. That clinched it. Only the police, you, and Bernie Maylor knew that particular murder scene fact. He killed your parents. We've got a taped confession. It is incriminating and completely actionable. Great work. Your parents would have been proud of you."

"My parents believed in hippie peace, antiwar, and planetary forgiveness. I denied a man his dying wish."

"People change as they age. My old man was a juvenile delinquent—spent most of his youth in juvie—then he joined the police force. Maybe your dad would have left his hippie peace signs and antiwar demonstrations behind like my dad set aside his delinquent days. Either way, Shane Bradley would have been proud of you."

"They say the only way to heal is to forgive."

"I think forgiveness is overrated. A good dose of revenge has never left my wounds open. Prisons and death penalties protect us all. Tomorrow there will be someone else acting heinously, and enforcers will *need* to exact justice's equivalent of revenge. Do you understand what I'm telling you?"

"That's a justification for denying forgiveness?"

"I believe it is. However, my personal justification has always been simple. I put myself in the shoes of the victim. From the victim's vantage point, I imagine the fear, the pain, and the blank nothingness that comes with death. I visualize a monster taking my life or the life of a loved one. I envision heartache. Justice isn't a matter of *equitable* reparation. People can't be replaced." His eyelids flickered, as if they wanted to shut. "For me, forgiveness is little more than disregarding misplaced compassion. I've never understood someone who says they forgive but won't forget. Like with the Holocaust. I can't see how a person can fail to forget, yet forgive."

"Aunt Golda spent two years in a concentration camp."

"And did she forgive?"

"She never said. I didn't have any reason to ask. She went on with her life, regardless." The words *take revenge* were seeping deeper and deeper into the recesses of Fleur's mind.

Salvador said, "I'm sorry I didn't get to know her. I think I would have liked her."

"I can't imagine anyone wouldn't have." Fleur covered her face for a moment as she thought about Golda. "You were right about my father being shot first. Early on, you said the footprints and smudges were suspicious."

"I think we would have eventually seen that the evidence was questionable. Most resolutions that come after forty years come from pure conjecture."

Fleur touched her beads. "After years of chasing microscopic clues, and theory, I realize how difficult satisfactory resolution is." She considered the scientific experiment she'd worked so hard to carry out to its conclusion. "At any rate, thank you for helping on the case."

"Nearly all cases have their twists and turns," he said. "This case was solved by a fortunate confluence." He laughed abruptly. "Think your Aunt Golda sent you the solution?"

"She probably had something to do with sending some darn fine people into my life when I needed them the most."

Fleur sobbed for a few minutes, then she sat in silence and watched the patches of landscape off to the side of the road.

It was still early enough in the day to catch a plane back to Denver. She needed to go home. Home was where she wanted to be.

Chapter 30

Bernie and Gemma Rae offered to drive Fleur to the airport, and they arrived promptly at the hotel to pick her up. Gemma Rae's car was not a loud, rainbow-painted VW bus; it was a decade-old Chevrolet sedan. And Gemma Rae drove purposefully, cautiously. It made Fleur smile, for it was not with the total abandon she would have expected. The aged hippie had certainly changed, though she had retained the wardrobe.

Gemma Rae's wild, streaming hair was held down by a multicolored headband. She wore a fuchsia blouse, a long, hand-painted amethyst-, peach-, and mauve-splashed skirt, and jeweled sandals. When the sun hit each color, she dazzled as if she were a stained-glass window.

Bernie was wearing a charcoal-colored suit, with a primly buttoned pearl-gray vest, a red beret, and was carrying a carved cane. He was content to be a passenger, watching the flow of traffic. There was, however, a flicker of fear behind his spectacles as Gemma Rae tried to merge into the heavy traffic.

At the airport terminal, the three friends sat waiting for Fleur's flight. Fleur carefully packed her laptop into her shoulder bag. Her carryon was filled and heavier than when she had left on her odyssey. She had picked up a gift for Sophia and had purchased a couple of gardening books for Abby and a poetry book for herself at Maylor's Books. She had also purchased some of Gemma Rae's smaller pieces of pottery. The books and pots would serve to keep her close to the two people who helped change her life forever.

"Have you decided whether you're going to stay with Abby or split?" Gemma Rae asked.

"I'll probably stay. She was absolutely behind me and my decision about Rodriguez. She apologized for doubting me and for giving me *Abby attitude*. Working things out will require us both making compromises."

"I'd like to meet her," Gemma Rae said. "She sounds delightful on the phone."

"I'd like to meet her, too," Bernie said.

Fleur wondered whether it might actually be possible to get reacquainted with Abby, as if they were meeting for the first time. She tapped the angel on her charm bracelet. "I hope one day soon you'll be able to meet one another. Maybe you can both come out to Denver and visit us."

Gemma Rae lifted an eyebrow. "You're coming back to visit, aren't you?"

"Yes. On our next vacation. I talked with Stephanie and Joan, and they insisted I return. Actually, I had a five-dollar bet with Joan that I lost. She wouldn't take the money when I offered it. She said that way I would have to return to pay off my debt. Being indebted makes it a certainty I'll be returning soon."

"What was their response to finding out the truth about Maggie's death?" Bernie asked.

"Stephanie seemed greatly relieved. The older sister she idolized was not a killer nor was the man her sister loved."

"Was she in agreement with your decision not to ask for Rodriguez's release?"

"Totally supportive. She initially said she would gladly trip the execution lever herself, but after a couple of moments, she changed her mind. She decided he was better off having every last minute to suffer the loss of his freedom. He'll die where he belongs—in a penal institution."

"Can you dig it? So many years have passed," Gemma Rae said with a distance in her eyes. "We were all a bunch of wide-eyed young people. Life was an experiment. Death wasn't even on our radar screen back then."

Bernie added, "Rodriguez terminated lives, young people with promise. The world will be well rid of him, as you told the detective. I agree, throw away the key. Leave the sunshine and freedom for those with agendas of kindness."

"I also," Fleur said, "gave Stephanie the location of the burial plots that Golda purchased for my parents. If she finds them, I'll have her call you. You might want to visit their gravesites."

"We'd like to," Bernie said. "Very much."

"I could take roses." Gemma Rae attempted to be unemotional, but her eyes blinked back tears. "Yes. She loved peace roses. I'll take a bunch."

"There's something else. I wanted to verify it with Stephanie before I told you. Joan told me my middle name is ReineRae. My mother combined the middle names of the two women she loved most. Maggie had intended to announce it to Golda Reine and you on my first birthday. Unfortunately, Aunt Golda never was aware of the tribute, but I'm glad I got to tell you."

Gemma Rae's eyes filled. "How do you feel about having a hippie namesake?"

"I'm honored and proud to have two of the best namesakes I could ever imagine."

Gemma Rae swiped at an escaping tear. "I'm proud, too."

"It is a mouthful to say, though," Fleur said with a chuckle.

"Trust me," Bernie said, "you'd have to have known Maggie to realize she was somewhat unorthodox about her focus on the rhythm in names. ReineRae probably sounded about right for Maggie to call her infant. Flower ReineRae is not without melody. She referred to me as Bashful Bernie."

Gemma Rae laughed. "I'd forgotten. And her name for Baby Flower was often Buttercup. Yes." She nodded to Fleur. "Now I recall. Little Buttercup, she would call you. And I was Jabbering Gemma Rae."

When the trio stopped laughing, Gemma Rae said, "At least we now understand the importance of a middle name. The middle name 'Edward' and first name 'David' certainly made a difference in finding the truth of this case."

"About keeping Rodriguez in prison… Are the two of you in agreement with my decision?"

"Completely," they said in unison.

"Your support means a great deal to me."

"I knew Maggie so well," Gemma Rae said. "I know she would have done the same thing. I see your mother in you."

"And I've come to know my mother through you. Oh, by the way, I called Trinidad to thank him again for the photos and to tell him he was right. Shane Bradley would not have killed his lover. His best friend did not kill Maggie."

"Good old Trini," Gemma Rae sputtered as she said his name. She held up her little finger and waved it a few times. "Tiny Trini."

"I also told him I'm in touch with you. He sends his love," Fleur jested.

"His love! Well that's worth…" She waggled her little finger again.

Gemma Rae's cackle continued until it was time for Fleur to walk to the concourse where she would board the plane. The three of them hugged goodbye. A few steps later, when Fleur turned back, she saw Gemma Rae's hand waving, then a peace sign. She heard Gemma Rae yelling for her to "peace out, and hang loose. And don't forget to try a little grab-ass on Abby. It always cheers up Rolly."

Fleur smiled as she returned the peace sign, then she walked toward the Jetway.

As she sat on the plane, Fleur experienced a rush of loneliness. Closing her eyes, she visualized Abby's smile, felt the tenderness of her touch. The same touch Abby used to caress flowers that she'd grown.

Fleur took out her phone. "Abby. I'm on a plane. It's about to take off on my return flight. I'm coming home."

"Home to Denver? Or home to me?"

"Both," Fleur replied. "I know things will be tough. Aunt Golda's death, getting through the sale of her house… It isn't going to be easy to get our lives back together. But if we respect one another, it's possible."

"We'll make it possible. All the small stuff we've been bickering over, nothing really matters. I admit I'm too controlling, but I can change. I can, and I will. Give me a chance. It's not that you mean the world to me, you *are* the world to me, Fleur. After sixteen years, you still make me tremble with love."

"That's how I feel about you, too. I'm prepared to give us a chance. This isn't going to be easy. The grant will be gone, and I'll only have half the salary I was making at the research clinic. It will be a difficult year. We might have a struggle getting back to living comfortably."

"About the study—"

"It was due in two days ago, so it's lost for sure. This study grant is one with a great deal of competition. There wouldn't be any kind of extension. I've lost the grant."

"Well, maybe not. I figured if it was already lost, I couldn't hurt it, so I went ahead with it. I continued logging the experiments, and I wrote the final report. I did my best to make sense of it all. You already told me the premise of it, so I completed the report as scientifically as I could. At least it's been submitted. And it was in on time."

Fleur had to collect her emotions before she could speak. "Thank you, Abby. I don't know what to say."

"Chances are, it won't work out. I can do the meticulous detail work, but I'm not certain how good I was with the explanation of the results. The literary arts aren't my strong suit. The report, summation was really a regurgitation of what you've told me over the months, along with the notes I found. My rotten verbal expression might not impress the committee, but I tried."

"It doesn't matter if we get the grant or not. What matters is that you made the effort on my behalf. You worked with me, for me. That took love." Her heart trembled as she realized how much they cherished one another. She blinked back the tears that were welling.

"The decision on the grant is to be made late this afternoon. Amazingly, the committee promised to have their decision announced only twenty-four hours after the deadline."

"That's because each of the submissions was e-mailed to the committee. And mine," she said and backtracked, "*ours* was probably the last submitted. They probably had the decision made before the actual deadline."

"Maybe not. Maybe they gave special attention to yours. We can hope. You'll know by the time your plane lands. The determination will have been made and announced by five this afternoon, Eastern Time. If you sign in on the site when you land, you'll know. You'll be here by dinner time?"

"Probably a little later. I want to stop by Aunt Golda's gravesite on the way in and then check to see if Sophia is doing alright. I want her to know what I've found out, that everything's okay. She's been staunchly supportive of her friend Golda all these years. I want her to know that I understand."

"And you're still calling her 'Aunt Golda,' so you still consider her your aunt."

"She is much more than just my aunt. I understand her love now, her protectiveness of me. Abby, for almost a week, sorrow has weighed on me. I believed my parents could have been tragic people who were involved in a murder and a suicide. And I found out that when they were both dead, none of their family wanted me. If Aunt Golda had told me that, if that had been my burden to bear over the past decades, my life might also have been tragic. She didn't want my life to be touched with tragedy. She grappled with bad memories her entire life. It wasn't what she wanted for me."

When the conversation ended, Fleur slumped in relief. Things would work out, as they nearly always did. She would see that they did.

By the time the airplane landed at Denver International Airport, it was mid-afternoon. Before going to the terminal parking area where she'd left her vehicle, Fleur stopped and took a seat in the waiting area. She punched in the web address of the institute and typed in her grant number.

A sudden irrepressible smile appeared on her lips. All the work, all the time, and her theory had been rewarded. She had been awarded a full grant. The final sprint to the goal line had been completed through an act of love by the woman she wanted in her life for the rest of her life.

Before signing out, she pulled up the research summation Abby had completed. It was perfect. Brilliant. Fleur was jolted. She had expected Abby's scientific evaluation to be lacking.

As if an icy breeze swept through her mind with a fresh viewpoint, she understood what had been happening. While raising her, Aunt Golda had never done anything to lower the young girl's self-esteem. She had raised Fleur to appreciate her own value and the value of her thinking process. Abby had been raised in a loving household, but with so many children, she needed to vie for attention and praise. Although the landscape artist excelled in her field, maybe she always felt as if she had to fight her way to the front of the pack.

Confident in her own expertise at critical analyses in the sciences, Fleur had been condescending to Abby. And, she realized that even at this moment of epiphany, her amazement that Abby was mentally her equal was another putdown. Abby had referred to "putdowns" when they argued. Fleur had to admit she was proud she excelled in the scientific world, and somehow she had assumed Abby was without the mental acumen to complete an advanced degree because she hadn't finished her graduate studies.

In this encapsulating report on the plant research study, with great verbal intensity, exactitude, and eloquence, Abby had expanded the basic premises Fleur had outlined. It wasn't only as good as Fleur could've done, it was exemplary in language skills as well as interpretation. Abby was a woman who could sort word patterns and break codes. And in that one moment of realization, Fleur understood that her lover could have done anything in life she wished to do.

Abby *elected* to be in the sunshine, with the flora and the sense of freedom her landscape business provided her. Abby had scrimmaged with her own soul and found she wanted no part of the academic hierarchy.

But because of Fleur's superior attitude, Abby overcorrected by being controlling. Abby hadn't been controlling when they met; the trait had developed over the years. And it had intensified.

Fleur was numb as she thought about how easily one human soul hurts another, even when love was the main ingredient in their relationship. The spirit of every person was vulnerable and tender. Neither she nor Abby had intended to cause the other pain, yet they had. She wanted to start the healing. If she were to become less judgmental, self-absorbed, and haughty—both in her heart and her words—she was sure that tensions between them would ease. She'd begin immediately by pruning the negative offshoots of her own nature. She would reinstate compassion in her life.

For several moments she sat motionless, reflecting where she had gone wrong. Her mind reeled back to her very early school days. She had learned that flowers fell into classifications—such as "perfect flowers" and "imperfect flowers."

Everyone else in the class selected perfect flowers—the ones with both male and female reproductive organs—as the objects of their studies. Fleur had been the only one who'd insisted on writing a term paper on imperfect flowers—those that contained only one sex organ. She had, even at that young age, determined that nomenclature and pretense held no importance to her. She disliked snobbery and elitism. She wondered when the hierarchy of academia had changed her.

Abby was perfect. And perfect for her. Why had she not recognized and appreciated that unique and wonderful perfection?

Fleur smiled with her awakening. That epiphany demonstrated how she must have been practicing the bitch's credo all along. For the remainder of her life, she would work at being selective about her credo.

Chapter 31

Fleur wanted to get to the cemetery before dark, and she made the drive before twilight settled in. She stood silently looking at the rectangular plot of ground with its new coverlet of sod. She had no doubt Abby had taken the care to integrate the squares of grass. She wouldn't have wanted it to appear freshly laid. Part of Abby's genius in landscape design was her attention to detail. She liked having the trees, shrubbery, grasses, and flowers appear as if they were natural to where they stood, no matter how recently they might have been planted.

At the head of the grave, where the tombstone would soon be, there were several bunches of flowers. Abby had obviously stopped by every day while Fleur was in San Francisco. Abby's signature sunflower had been incorporated into each cluster of flowers. Fleur snapped one of the tiny petals from a miniature sunflower.

She recalled one particular day when Aunt Golda and Abby were discussing their favorite flowers. Aunt Golda had refused to select only one flower. Abby had told Golda she was therefore going to issue an edict announcing the sunflower as the favorite flower of both of them. Aunt Golda chuckled, denying she could possibly have a favorite; there were too many flowers to choose from. Abby began listing flowers, watching carefully to see whether she could deduce Golda's favorite from the older woman's expression. It became a playful game that lasted for years.

Fleur touched the petal to her lips, tears streaming as she fought for breath. She wept until her body stopped shaking and the tears had dried on her face. Small convulsions of grief continued to wrack her.

With darkness nearing, Fleur whispered, "I love you more than you knew. Thank you, Aunt Golda." Standing at the gravesite, it was natural that her thoughts strayed to another saying Aunt Golda had often cited. When someone would haul out the old cliché about "the truth shall set you free," Aunt Golda would say, "Truth sets

179

you free in its own time, as well as your own time. And with its own interpretation." Now Fleur understood what her great aunt had meant. This had been the time for truth.

She silently thanked Aunt Golda again. "Your letters will be placed in the Holocaust Memorial Museum. They will serve as a cold meal's dessert. There they will matter, just as your life mattered to so many, especially to me."

Walking back to her car, Fleur contemplated what life had taught her. Perhaps, she ruminated, it began with how many bromides are said but not heard. Her loneliness had been assuaged not only by what had been said in her past, but what had *been*. Memory was more than the gentle blur that sometimes focused. No singular odyssey solved all queries. There was the soul to consider. Apparently the soul only listened in on the shouts of time that were directed to it.

She drove to the assisted-living unit where she went to find Sophia. She told the old woman what had transpired in the several days that had changed her life. "I understand why you shielded me from finding out the secret of my past. I know it was because of your friendship with Aunt Golda."

Sophia violently disputed her conclusion. "No. You know nothing. Golda said you were not to know, so you were *not* to know."

"You were her best friend. A true friend."

"I was alive because of her, and her alone."

"What?"

"She saved my life. When we were young, she played piano. The Germans were cleansing the camp. She saved my life, I tell you." Sophia broke down crying.

Fleur put her arms around the frail shoulders. "Please, don't upset yourself. It's all okay."

"Golda's mother was the pianist in the camp. This camp, the Red Cross and men, important looking men, would come through it. Anything good in it was all for show, and there had to be music. But when Golda's mother was taken away because she was sick and could no longer play, Golda told the guards she would play the piano, and I must be her page turner. And so she auditioned. She was a brilliant pianist, even at a young age. I knew nothing about music, but she told me she would blink twice when I was to turn the page. We both were allowed to stay. That kept us alive for many months. Until the Allied Forces came."

Fleur clutched Sophia tightly, as if she was frightened to let go. When the old woman's sobs stopped, Fleur stepped back and brushed the tears from Sophia's cheeks. "Thank you for telling me."

"She saved me. Remember, I told you. Even after the flowers were trampled, they lived. They saved us both."

"Yes. And both of you saved me. Thank you, Sophia."

"Good people save one another with love." Sophia covered her eyes. "And bad people have lost because of their own fear, pain, greed, and hatred. Do you understand?" Her head tipped, and her eyes flashed open. "Truly understand what I say?"

"Yes. Now I do." Fleur gave her a hug. "Abby and I will come visit you tomorrow."

"I know. Abby told me when she was here today. She hasn't missed a day. Abby and I cry because Golda has gone. As we cry, you cry." She sniffed several times as she swabbed her eyes with a tissue.

"Sophia, the letters are safe, saved for posterity. The story of the violated souls, the children, will be told and retold. Aunt Golda's letters to you will be placed in protected archives. Thank you from all of us, for saving them."

"Because they were careful, just like our flowers."

"Yes. They were careful, and because they were in your care, they were saved." Fleur stood. "We'll see you tomorrow afternoon," she promised.

Sophia disappeared back into her world of yesterday. Fleur hoped it was the yesterday when Sophia was chasing butterflies in her small village. Or maybe she was reliving her wedding day, happily exchanging vows. Or perhaps she and Golda were nurturing a clump of careful flowers.

Pulling into her driveway, Fleur noticed the lights were off in the house. She guessed Abby was probably resting while watching a TV program. She quietly opened the backdoor. When she reached the doorway between the kitchen and entertainment room, she spied her partner. Their larger dogs were asleep on either side of Abby. Rolled into the circle of her lap was the cat, Sugarplum, and on Abby's shoulder, Fezzy was stretched like a fur stole around her neck. The Chihuahua had wrapped himself comfortably to sleep warmly. Abby was leaning back, drifting off to sleep.

Until that moment, Fleur hadn't realized how much she truly valued Abby. She quietly set her carryon case down and slid the traveler's handbag onto the cabinet. It felt good to be home. She was no longer in a world where there was doubt; she was back where she was safe from the unknown.

Aside from her love for Abby, Fleur reflected on the other truest known facts. Aunt Golda's favorite flowers were the careful ones. Love allowed people to save one another. And Fate had a way of making things work out as they were meant to. Her heart was again beating in time with Abby's. She vowed to keep her heart in tune with the woman she loved. And for Gemma Rae, she would goose her lover's backside at the first opportunity.

Fleur stood for many moments, gazing at Abby and letting the memories flood through her. When the rush of her past had reached the present, she knew her future would be wondrous. Aunt Golda had always encouraged her to make the world finer. Fleur's scientific research to make life better was to be continued. And her love for the two remarkable women who had shaped her life would survive.

The historic truth was that Fleur Hamilton had grown up without any inkling she was a lovechild. However, she had always felt as if she was exactly that—someone's lovechild.

She whispered softly, "Buttercup."

Author Kieran York

About the Author

Kieran York has authored both Sapphic fiction and poetry. Her lesbian mystery series *Timber City Masks* and *Crystal Mountain Veils,* featuring Royce Madison, were written and published in the mid – 1990s. She also wrote a collection of lesbian short fiction entitled *Sugar With Spice* – published in 1989.

In 2012, York's book, *Appointment with a Smile,* was published and was a 2013 Lambda Literary Society Award Finalist in the romance category. Her next novel, *Careful Flowers,* was released in 2013, followed by two releases in 2014 – *Earthen Trinkets* and *Night Without Time,* published by Scarlet Clover Publishers. Forthcoming is *Touring Kelly's Poem* and *Loitering on the Frontier*

York was also a contributor in *Sappho's Corner Poetry Series – Wet Violet, Volume 2; Roses Read, Volume 3;* and *Delectable Daisies, Volume 4.*

In 2014, her volume of poetry, *Blushing Aspen,* was published as the Sappho's Corner Solo Poets book of poetry, and won The Rainbow Award Honorable Mention for poetry.

Previously, during the seventies and eighties, Kieran worked as a reporter and reviewer for both newspapers and magazines, and was a newspaper publisher for three years. She also wrote and performed songs with a woman's band. She has been guest lecturer and panel member at various events, including Rocky Mountain Book Exhibition, Colorado Musicians Series, Sisters in Crime Mystery Writers, and Mystery Writers of America, Inc. She is a member of Lambda Literary Society, and Golden Crown Literary Society.

She has written for *Journal of Mystery Readers International.* In addition, she has given numerous campus and coffeehouse poetry readings, as well as taught poetry and creative writing workshops.

She graduated from a Kansas university and attended Mexico's University of the Americas her junior year. She has done graduate work at the University of Colorado.

Kieran lives in the Rocky Mountain foothills of Colorado with her schnauzer, Clover. She enjoys gardening, music, literature, and art. She considers her valuables to include Clover and other family and friends, her library, her antique typewriter collection, her guitar, and her garden.

Additional information is available on her websites: www.scarletcloverpublishers.com and she has a blog – Embellish Your Smile at http://kieranyork.com.

FORTHCOMING IN 2015......

Touring Kelly's Poems

Touring Kelly's Poem takes place in 1963. A small-town Kansas student travels to Mexico City to search. 'Search' is the keyword for her year of finding herself within the constant grip of adventure. It is two books in one – a very large read.

Kelly Benjamin is turning twenty when a skiing accident redirects her life. With humor, and with the pathos known to youth, Kelly wants one thing most – to be a poet. Her new roommates are: a 'proper' fellow student, a wild European prostitute, and a lesbian archeology student. That should have been enough excitement for her.

Then she met the beguiling Doctora. Now that was enough excitement for anyone.

Loitering on the Frontier

Things were different in the gay and lesbian world of the mid-sixties. Olivia Kirby had just moved to Denver, Colorado. She entered the shabby lesbian bar, where she witnessed the commission of a crime. From then on, she was endangered – she was hunted. Terrified, she hid out - and hoped.
Hatred and bigotry are always dangerous. On the way to saving herself – she fell in love.
Human beings reside within the heart of time. We are born inside a slot of actuality. Our soul lights up at the time and place where we become our own.
If love is the art of shelter, maybe we can all become more cognizant of taking care of one another – sheltering one another.

OTHER PUBLISHED TITLES BY KIERAN YORK

Fiction:

Sugar With Spice
Publisher: Banned Books (November 1989)

Timber City Masks
Publisher: Third Side Press, 1st Edition (May 1993)
Publisher: Scarlet Clover Publishers, 2nd Edition, (November 2014)

Crystal Mountain Veils
Publisher: Third Side Press, 1st Edition (April 1995)
Publisher: Scarlet Clover Publishers, 2nd Edition, (January 2015)

Appointment with a Smile
Publisher: Blue Feather Books, 1st Edition (March 2012)
Publisher: Scarlet Clover Publishers, 2nd Edition (January 2015)

Careful Flowers
Publisher: Blue Feather Books, 1st Edition (October 2013)
Publisher: Scarlet Clover Publishers, 2nd Edition (January 2015)

Earthen Trinkets
Publisher: Scarlet Clover Publishers, (September 2014)

Night Without Time
Publisher: Scarlet Clover Publishers, (November 2014)

Touring Kelly's Poem
Publisher: Scarlet Clover Publishers, (forthcoming 2015)

Loitering on the Frontier
Publisher: Scarlet Clover Publishers, (forthcoming 2015)

Poetry:
Blushing Aspen
Publisher: UltraVioletLove Publishing, (May 2014)